TITLES BY ALANA QUINTANA ALBERTSON

Ramón and Julieta

Kiss Me, Mi Amor

My Fair Señor

PRAISE FOR

Alana Quintana Albertson

"*Ramón and Julieta* is a passionate and joyful romance about honoring family legacies, celebrating your heritage, the importance of community, and the power of love. A beautiful novel!"

—*New York Times* bestselling author Chanel Cleeton

"This novel's got a little Shakespeare and a lot of tacos, with a very steamy haters-to-lovers relationship at its core."

—NPR on *Ramón and Julieta*

"Excellent tropes wrapped up in an irresistible package: a fake relationship *between* two enemies. . . . Try not to swoon as you watch Enrique and Carolina fall for each other in real time; I dare you."

—Paste on *Kiss Me, Mi Amor*

"Albertson's refreshing, nuanced tale captivates, exploring issues of racial identity, immigrant culture, and breaking free from abusive dynamics—and offering tasty descriptions of tacos along the way. . . . Readers will be enchanted."

—*Publishers Weekly* on *Kiss Me, Mi Amor*

"As this love story shaped by the complexities of Latinx communities unfolds, Albertson insightfully dramatizes the contrasts between Julieta and Ramón as he becomes increasingly conflicted about his identity as a Mexican American and his business plans for the neighborhood and its impact on the culture."

—*Booklist* on *Ramón and Julieta*

My Fair Señor

Love & Tacos

Alana Quintana Albertson

BERKLEY ROMANCE
New York

BERKLEY ROMANCE
Published by Berkley
An imprint of Penguin Random House LLC
1745 Broadway, New York, NY 10019
penguinrandomhouse.com

Book design by Kristin del Rosario
Title page art: Sugar skulls pattern © xenia_ok / Shutterstock

Library of Congress Cataloging-in-Publication Data

Names: Quintana Albertson, Alana, author | Quintana Albertson, Alana. Love & tacos
Title: My fair señor / Alana Quintana Albertson.
Description: First edition. | New York : Berkley Romance, 2025. | Series: Love & tacos
Identifiers: LCCN 2025010268 (print) | LCCN 2025010269 (ebook) | ISBN 9780593336267 (trade paperback) | ISBN 9780593336281 (ebook)
Subjects: LCGFT: Romance fiction | Novels
Classification: LCC PS3617.U589655 M94 2025 (print) | LCC PS3617.U589655 (ebook) | DDC 813/.6—dc23/eng/20250310
LC record available at https://lccn.loc.gov/2025010268
LC ebook record available at https://lccn.loc.gov/2025010269

First Edition: November 2025

Printed in the United States of America
1st Printing

The authorized representative in the EU for product safety and compliance is Penguin Random House Ireland, Morrison Chambers, 32 Nassau Street, Dublin D02 YH68, Ireland, https://eu-contact.penguin.ie.

This book is dedicated to my brother,
Joseph Chulick III. And our beloved hometown
in Marin County.

My Fair Señor

Chapter One

Jaime Montez sat on his oceanfront deck in La Jolla, California, watching the birds perched on the rocks in the distance.

A blonde girl in yoga clothes posed for pictures that her probable boyfriend was taking. Jaime had definitely been in that guy's shoes when he had dated Instagram "models." But he couldn't complain because they had returned the favor for his own accounts.

Next to the girl, a few tourists wearing oversized San Diego sweatshirts sat on a bench overlooking the sunset. And a couple most definitely living the van life was parked right in front of his garage. His cliffside mansion was sleek and sophisticated—clean lines that blended natural and modern design, creating a perfect blend of indoor and outdoor elements. With views of Crystal Pier, Coronado, and Point Loma, the hot tub on his deck was the perfect place to watch the sunsets. Palm trees swayed, reminding him that the Santa Ana winds were brewing and would make an exhilarating day for surfing.

Yup. Another day in beautiful, sunny San Diego.

His home was eerily quiet since his brother Enrique was at some charity event with his girlfriend, Carolina, and his other brother Ramón was tasting wedding cakes with his fiancée, Julieta. Ramón had moved to Coronado with Julieta but still spent time at the brothers' home when he surfed in La Jolla. Jaime couldn't believe that soon his eldest brother would be a married man.

So, it was just Jaime, the cool sea-salt breeze, and a bottle of tequila that was sent to him from yet another thirsty brand hoping to hire him as an influencer. He poured himself a shot and sipped it slowly. Though the liquid was smooth with just a hint of spice, Jaime couldn't help but feel that something was off about this liquor. He preferred this type of spirit mixed in a margarita with a Tajín-rimmed glass. The taste alone burned his throat, but maybe that was a good thing. He honestly didn't truly know enough about tequila to judge. He prepared another shot but didn't drink it yet.

He perused the press kit the company had sent him, which was filled with glossy product pictures, detailed background on the brand, and a fact sheet about the process of making the liquor. The proposal for the campaign was simple—a free bottle of tequila and a two-thousand-dollar payment for one Instagram post, two IG stories, and three TikToks for his twenty-two million followers to view. They even included a list of content suggestions such as pairing this liquor with "traditional" foods. No doubt they would love for his future sister-in-law, celebrated chef Julieta Campos, to cook them. But the joke was on them—Julieta would never pander. This brand, like the last thirty he had heard from, probably wanted him chomping on a taco, sporting a handlebar mustache, and wearing a serape so the ad could be as pandering and stereotypically Mexican as possible. It was all so gross.

Whose brand was this anyway?

He flipped through the materials, and a picture caught his eye.

A famous movie star and his bar-owner buddy—equally infamous for his supermodel wife—sat side by side on motorcycles driving through a field of agave plants. Both men were ageless, cool, and, most noticeably, not Mexican.

Not that one could discern someone's ethnicity from a picture—Jaime wasn't stupid enough to think that. He knew blond Mexicans, red-headed Mexicans, and pale-skinned Mexicans. But these men were beyond famous and if they were of Hispanic origin, they most definitely would've claimed it—especially since it could them help with their tequila sales.

And their publicist had sent this campaign, so Jaime, a Mexican-American influencer, could lend his stamp of approval.

What idiots. He wouldn't be their pawn and give them his Latino thumbs-up.

Was that all he was to these people? Some beautiful brown face to use to hawk their non-authentic goods?

Jaime threw the bottle at his clear plexiglass wall, shards from the container shattering everywhere. He hated to admit it, but the momentary bout of rage soothed him, in some fucked-up way. After taking a deep breath, a technique ingrained in him from his brother Enrique's regular meditation sessions, his nerves eased. He grabbed a broom and a dustpan from the closet, and a bunch of paper towels and some floor disinfectant from under the sink. He swept the glass safely away and then sopped up the liquid and sprayed the floor—he wasn't such an asshole that he would leave this mess for his maid to clean up.

Why did all these non-Hispanic influencers have tequila lines? He wasn't all woke like Julieta, but her words rang in his head.

Fuck those pendejos.

Jaime would drink to that.

He downed the shot that remained in the glass.

The second round of the liquor was decent but he would not promote it.

Even so, that small taste of tequila awoke something in him. A crazy thought he had pondered over the years. It had never been the right time before. He hadn't had the confidence in his ability to run his own company when he was younger.

But now, he had no doubt that he could be a success.

His mind raced, and the idea took hold.

What if *he* became involved in the mezcal business?

Why not? What was he doing with his life, besides partying like it was 1999 nightly and hooking up with some hot chicas? Fine—make that many, many hot chicas.

Nothing, that was what.

Well, it wasn't nothing. But it was nothing he was particularly proud of. He was a top-paid influencer, man he hated that word, but it was what it was. He also occasionally did some modeling gigs for different brands. For years, he had run the social media accounts for Taco King, his father's company, but after his eldest brother Ramón took over, Jaime had slowly transitioned out of the daily posting grind and focused more on brand deals and his own influencer career. One of his shirtless pictures for a hot sauce company had gone viral. The attention had been fun for a while, but if one more person called him Mr. Hot Tamale, he'd lose it.

He had never really cared about his lack of clear passion until recently. Jaime had been quite content to embrace his anointed title as the irresponsible younger brother, the baby in their dysfunctional family. While Ramón went to Stanford *and* Harvard and laid-back Enrique went to Cal Poly San Luis Obispo, Jaime had been content to kick it at Sonoma State, wanting to get as far away from his family as possible without leaving his beloved California. NorCal was so picturesque and different from San Diego. Instead of clubbing, he'd spent his weekends getting wasted at wine tastings and hiking the trails with earthy vegan feminists. They loved him, and he adored them back. He could easily be tried and convicted as a womanizer, but he truly worshipped and respected females. He loved everything about them—their scents, their soft bodies, their strong minds. Jaime was many things, but a misogynist wasn't one of them. And it wasn't like he was having a series of one-night stands—in college he had been in a long-term relationship. Ever since he graduated, Jaime was open and honest about his intentions—no committed relationships. He didn't like rules and wanted to love freely. Maybe that NorCal hippy vibe had rubbed off on him. And in his line of work, his chillness was definitely an advantage.

But this worked both ways—he wasn't controlling. If a woman he casually dated wanted to see another man, that was fine by him. He wasn't jealous.

Well, that was a lie—but it was only one time.

Alma Garcia.

His college sweetheart. That girl was fire. Physically, she was his dream girl. Waist-length straight black hair, curvy body with a tiny waist, dark eyes, big pouty lips. She was the only girl he had ever made his girlfriend, the only girl he had ever seen exclusively, the only girl he had ever loved.

And he had blown it.

Not by cheating—he wasn't a cad. He was completely faithful until the day he'd said adiós. But with graduation looming, she had decided to stay in Sonoma and become a sommelier, and he had to return to San Diego. As much as he appreciated his four-year break from living near his family, he missed them. He'd loved her with all his heart, but he was just too young to settle down. So, he broke up with Alma, citing long-distance and their ages, and had regretted it ever since.

Maybe that was why he had never had a relationship after that. No one could measure up to her. Top of her class, volunteered in her free time, first person her friends turned to in crisis. And those hips, man. And the way her lips quivered when he brought her to ecstasy.

He exhaled. Where was she now?

Over the years, he'd had to physically restrain himself from stalking her online. He'd blocked her on his socials—one flash of her long lashes and he would become hypnotized by her. And his college roommate, Santi, who lived in her county, knew better than to mention her whereabouts.

Last he had heard, she had passed her sommelier exam with flying colors, which wasn't shocking. She was probably working at one of Napa's top vineyards or at a restaurant in San Francisco. Maybe she was married to a wealthy vintner. Most guys wouldn't be stupid enough to let a woman like Alma slip through their hands.

But Jaime didn't need or want a long-term relationship. He was young—only twenty-five. Look at Ramón and Enrique—both of his brothers' lives were now consumed by their women. They would rarely even hang out with him now.

Jaime was too young to settle down back then—and he was still too young to even get into a serious relationship. He had to make his own mark in the world first.

Even so, his curiosity got the best of him.

He grabbed his phone and googled her name. Stupid LinkedIn popped up. He wasn't dumb enough to click on that link, which would literally send a message to her stating that he was stalking her.

But he didn't need to click. Her name flashed before him above her place of work.

Alma Garcia—owner of Mezcalifornia,
Marin County's Hottest Tequila Bar.

Chapter Two

Alma Garcia gazed out at the breathtaking landmarks in the distance. The Golden Gate, the Bay Bridge, and the Richmond–San Rafael Bridge surrounded her—each unique in their beauty and their horror. From the suicides on the Golden Gate, to the Bay Bridge collapsing in an earthquake, to the high winds forcing closures on the Richmond–San Rafael, the incredible views were tainted. But the tourists, homeowners, and businesspeople in Marin knew that having space with one of these engineering marvels in the background was priceless. And her business looked out on all three.

It was unfathomable to her that she, a poor girl from the Canal, not only operated but also owned the hottest tequila bar in Tiburon, one of the wealthiest communities in Marin County, California. Most days she felt like she was living in a dream, though she'd arrived here from nothing but hard work. And today, Alma needed to focus. The city's top critic was coming into the restaurant. She had to be on her A game.

Especially since respect in the industry was what she lacked. Despite being a commercial success, the male-dominated liquor industry looked down on her, often dismissing her as just a pretty face. She hadn't earned their praise yet since she was relatively new to the tequila world. But was it too much to ask to not have the critics comment on her looks as they did in almost every review?

There was nothing she could do about that. She wasn't going to change the way she dressed to prove herself.

As a female tequiladora in the male-dominated industry of alcohol, she was causally reminded that she was the odd woman out. Not only had she been the only female and the only Mexican sommelier in her courses at the Napa Valley Wine Academy, but she was also now the first female tequila master after an arduous apprenticeship in Mexico. But she'd embraced what some would see as a disadvantage. She had sought out other women leaders in the industry.

Women who harvested their own agave.

Women who bottled their own brands.

Women who distilled their own liquor.

Alma's tequila bar was successful, even if she was constantly being mistaken as just some brand bimbo. Not that she could blame people who assumed she was a promoter—Alma was young, dressed sexy, and was as proud of her body as she was of her mind.

But now that Mezcalifornia was doing so well, she yearned for more. She was financially sound and professionally successful. She craved recognition from the leaders in the tequila industry. But even more, Alma wanted to truly make a difference in the lives of others—others who grew up like her and didn't have the same opportunities. With budget cuts, rising housing costs, and the backlash against bilingual education in California, kids who grew up in her community today didn't have the same opportunities that she had once had. She needed to change that.

She swiped the finest bottle of tequila from her bar and splashed it on her hands. Alma wore tequila the way most girls wore perfume. She inhaled the note—nothing like the pure scent of the world's finest liquor—the sweetness from the vanilla, the spice from the pepper, and the heat from the smoke made her feel like she was on fire.

Her older brother, Carlos, waltzed into her bar like he owned the place, which he most certainly did not, though he might as well have. He often helped her out when she was short-staffed. He was a badass in his own right—a former Division I soccer player who now coached a youth club team in his community in San Rafael. Tall, dark, and handsome. And, like her, forever single.

"Hey sis. What's up?"

"We're just about to open. I'm anxious and nervous as hell—that critic from the *Chronicle* is coming in tonight." She bit her lip.

She already smelled like tequila, so why not indulge? She downed a quick shot. She rarely drank on the job, but a little taste to take the edge off was always welcome.

"You'll smash it," he said, but he glanced behind him, as if his heart wasn't really in it.

Alma rolled her eyes at her brother. "I should ask you what's up. What brings you by on a Friday night? Don't you have some game to attend?" Ever since Carlos had been a little boy, he ate, drank, slept, and breathed soccer. Nothing had changed.

"Nah. Taking the night off." He paused and pursed his lips.

Yup. He was going to ask her a favor. Alma would save him the trouble of working up to it.

"So, what do you want?"

He exhaled. As her only sibling, Carlos was super close with Alma, though they were nothing alike.

"Nothing. Just wondering if you thought more about sponsoring that Cinco de Mayo festival in the Canal?"

She pursed her lips. "Yes, of course I've thought about it. I'll give money for sure, but I don't know if I want to participate in the festival. It seems like pandering. Let's bring the rich residents of Marin out to the Canal one day a year to get drunk and eat tacos and pretend they care about the Mexicans who live amongst them. They only ever went there if they wanted to go bowling because it was our last alley left, and now that it's closed forever, they will never return. It's like we only matter to them if we are scrubbing their toilets or mowing their lawns. I'd rather do more scholarship and outreach work than something like that. The festival is so cringe. And I can't stand all of the influencers who show up."

Influencers. She hated that whole industry. Making money on social media without really doing anything but promoting themselves and products. Alma was grateful that she had found her true calling.

Now it was Carlos's turn to roll his eyes. "You're a piece of work, you know that? It doesn't matter why they come; it matters that they come. And my soccer team will be playing a game at Pickleweed Park. Maybe one of the coaches from the rich-ass private schools around here will show up and give one of my kids a scholarship. I normally can't even get them to look at my boys."

Alma pursed her lips. She appreciated Carlos's passion, she did. Even so, it all felt so performative.

She closed her eyes and said a silent prayer. Carlos was right. It didn't matter by what means she could help members of her community; it mattered that she helped them. Period. And if she had to resort to a day of watching the little boys play soccer while plying the spectators with tequila, she was game.

"Fine. I'm in." She paused. "Are you actually hanging around here tonight? Or did you just make the trip all the way out here to nag me? You can text, you know?"

"I know. It just seemed impersonal for a big ask."

"Ah, you'll make someone very happy one day."

"We will see about that." Carlos grinned. "Since I'm here, I'll hang out and help. What do you need me to do?"

It was nice having a capable, sane sibling she could rely on. He was a good man—a hard worker and not even remotely a misogynist. She had lucked out in the brother department. Her father was awesome too—worked sixty hours a week, always brought her mom flowers, and never missed a game or recital. Men like that didn't exist anymore. Well, they did, but unfortunately, the only men she knew like that were related to her.

She reached behind the counter and tossed him an apron. "Barback. Ernesto called in sick."

Carlos tied the apron on and went to work. No questions asked. No complaints about the unglamorous tasks. That was how they were raised. Work, work, work.

But sometimes, Alma missed having fun.

And now it was time for her to get centered.

The Marin County crowd, especially in Tiburon, was high-end and expected the best. With the median home price in this San Francisco Bayfront community around three million, Alma never thought she would actually live here, especially because she grew up tagging alongside Mamá when she would come to clean houses. Honestly, she had hated this town for years—resentful of its privilege when residents in her nearby community had nothing. But after she became a sommelier at a restaurant in downtown Tiburon on the water, everything changed. This place that had twisted her stomach into knots was a welcome refuge from the stresses of her life. Every morning before her shift, she would walk from her condo on the water to Blackie's Pasture. The cool ocean breeze and the view of dogs frolicking brought such joy to her. After work, instead of hanging with her coworkers at a pretentious restaurant, she would have a drink at the iconic Sam's Anchor Cafe, which was founded in 1920 and had a saloon that was fully operational during Prohibition.

It was at that iconic place steeped in history, between bites of her Dungeness crab and beet salad and sips of her prickly pear margarita, that Alma began her love affair.

But not with a man. No, she had only made that mistake once.

With something stronger.

More potent.

Something that soothed her soul.

Tequila.

For the Mexican-American sommelier, she had to admit it was a bit cliché, but once she had a taste, she became passionate about mezcal.

And now, here she was, three years later, the owner of the hottest tequila bar in Marin.

She couldn't be prouder.

And her bar was a couple of places down from Sam's, where the idea first took hold. Why couldn't she be more than just a worker in this community? Start her own place?

Now, they shared the views of Angel Island, Alcatraz, and San Francisco.

Her own slice of heaven.

She even owned a condo down the street. An oceanfront condo. Who was she? Sometimes she couldn't even believe her success.

Even so, she still sometimes felt out of place amongst the exorbitant wealth.

She had that same feeling years ago—when she had dated Jaime Montez, heir to the Taco King empire, in college.

It was a name she didn't allow herself to think of often. But as she got ready for the evening, preparing to be judged by yet another critic, Alma suddenly couldn't help but wonder where Jaime was now.

Chapter Three

Jaime stared at the words on his phone.

Mezcal . . . ifornia?

He quickly typed *Mezcalifornia* in the search bar.

It was located in Tiburon, Marin County—one of California's wealthiest zip codes. Jaime had often accompanied Alma to her hometown, where people considered her a hero. Raised in nearby San Rafael, specifically the Canal, which was the most segregated part in the Bay Area, she had defied the odds and become not only the first person in her family to attend college but also the first Mexican-American female sommelier.

But why would she switch from wine to tequila? Was it something as simple as being Mexican and feeling a bond with alcohol that was cultivated in her country of origin?

She loved wine. Used to bore him to death about all the different types of grapes and varieties. The taste of a good merlot used to bring her to tears. What a shame to let all that knowledge go to waste.

Jaime gulped. She adored teaching him everything about wine. And he had been so in love with her that he would just listen to her go on and on for hours as he stroked her hair and rubbed her always-pedicured toes.

And now she owned a tequila bar with a name he had to admit was cool as fuck.

Was it a sign that the thought of starting a tequila brand had just occurred to him, then he reminisced about his ex and found out she was now running a tequila bar? Had he manifested this? Damn, Enrique's new age woo-woo bullshit had rubbed off on Jaime.

He flipped through the bar's Instagram. Wow, it was nice—the bar, not the social media feed. He definitely could make it better. In one particular shot, there were rows of hand-painted tequila bottles stacked on the shelves. The vibrant colors were in sharp contrast to Alma, who was leaning over the counter, wearing a black bustier and a sexy smirk.

Damn, she was finer than ever.

Her lips were painted red, and her breasts burst out of her top. How he would love to suck on her titties just one more time. Fine, a million more times.

But he knew he would never kiss Alma again. His soul couldn't take it.

Maybe, however, it was time for a college reunion.

He dialed Santi, who answered on the first ring.

"Jaime, my man! What's up, bro?"

"Nothing, dude. How's Marin?" Santi was a tech bro who lived in Bolinas, which was a beach town in Marin, and developed some app. Jaime had no idea what it did, only that it made Santi a millionaire. Make that multimillionaire. On his own, with no family help.

"Foggy. Just did a hike on Mt. Tam today. Nothing beats that view."

"I remember." Jaime closed his eyes, and a flashback overtook him. Alma loved hiking and had dragged him up there. Everyone in Marin seemed to be an outdoor fanatic. Walks in Muir Woods, surfing at Stinson Beach. One time on a hike at Mt. Tamalpais he'd pulled her to a secret clearing, and they had made love under the stars. That was also the first time he told her he loved her.

The only girl he had ever said those words to.

Probably the only one he ever would. Jaime couldn't fathom falling for someone else.

Now she was probably whispering *I love you*s to another man who wasn't such an idiot to let her go.

"What's on your mind, man? You never call me."

Jaime snapped back into the moment. He was so lost in the memory that he had almost forgotten that Santi was still on the phone.

"Right, sorry. I'm a bit out of it."

"You drunk?"

"No. Not at all. Though I did just have two shots of this tequila. Tom Bluey's new one. Have you tried it?"

"Nah. Most of that celebrity stuff is crap."

Was it ever. "Agreed. They asked me to do some posts about it, but I'm not going to."

"Good decision."

"Anyway, I called because I stumbled across Mezcalifornia, a tequila bar in Tiburon. Alma's bar. Do you know about it?"

He laughed. "Of course I do. Everyone knows that place. Alma is the toast of Tiburon. I would've taken you there last time you were in town, but you told me not to mention her name. Ever."

Fuck. "I know."

"You over her now?"

Jaime ran his hand through his hair. No need to lie. "Never."

Santi sighed. "Don't blame you. She's perfection."

Latent rage pooled inside him. So much for never being jealous. "Don't even think about it, Santi. Anyone but her."

"Relax, man. I would never. I mean, if she wasn't your ex, I'd be all over her ass, but she is, so I won't cross that line."

Jaime appreciated his friend respecting the bro code, but Santi's words made him uneasy. There were plenty of amazing rich men, not that Alma cared about the size of a man's wallet, that were not Jaime's friends who would be more than happy to sweep her off her feet.

"Good. Well, the thing is, getting asked to promote the tequila line made me think. Why don't I start a tequila line of my own?"

Santi laughed. "Oh, I don't know. How about because you don't know shit about tequila? Remember that time in Cabo when you couldn't even handle the tequila flight and ordered a strawberry margarita?"

Yeah, he was a lightweight back then. "How could I not—you won't let me forget it. But how hard can it be? We're Mexican, it's in our blood."

"We? Meaning you and me, or you and Alma?"

"All three of us."

"I spent years of my life being your third wheel. Never again."

They had done everything together. Day trips to music festivals on the Russian River, wine tasting at the hottest restaurants in Sonoma, barhopping in Santa Rosa. Those days were the best.

"Are you seeing someone?"

"That's a negative. I don't have any time."

Now it was Jaime's turn to laugh. Santi was a workaholic, almost as bad as Ramón was before he met Julieta.

"Neither do I. Well, I mean no time for a relationship. I do have time to start a new business, and I have the money. I'm bored, Santi. Sick of doing cheesy brand deals and modeling gigs. Plus, I miss Northern California. Maybe I can come up there for a bit?"

"You're welcome to crash at my place, anytime."

"I'd love to." And what a place it was. Northern California beach towns were in a class by themselves. A totally different vibe. The water was icy as fuck, and you had to watch out for great whites. But in a town like Bolinas—you could almost pretend the world didn't exist. The residents were so protective of their privacy that they would rip down all the road signs leading to the town so it could remain hidden. Too bad TikTokers consistently revealed the location. Even so, you could literally walk on the beach there and see nothing but sand for miles. The town even sequestered itself during COVID and didn't let any visitors into its bubble.

"But somehow, I think you'd rather be in Tiburon. With a certain ex of yours."

Jaime shook his head. "Nope. That's a negative. I'm not going up there for her. Well, not like that at least."

Santi sighed. "What does that mean?"

"I'm not interested in her romantically. I'm too young to settle down, and I could never have a casual relationship with her. But maybe we could be friends. And she could teach me about tequila."

"You're serious, bro? You want to come up to Tiburon and use Alma to teach you about tequila? Are you high?"

"No, I'm not. When you put it like that, it sounds bad. But I wouldn't really be using her. I'd pay her for her time."

"If she has time for you at all." Santi paused. "When you broke up with her, she was crushed."

"I know." Jaime's throat scratched. Their ending had been brutal on her, and he knew it. After telling her it was over, he'd literally vanished from her life.

"It wasn't cool, man. It was so sudden."

"It was. I loved her. She knows that. But we were too young. We have so much history together. Maybe we can reconnect. And I want to learn about tequila from the best. If she owns a tequila bar, she clearly must be an expert." She was incredible at everything she did, so that wasn't too far of a stretch.

"She is the best. Do you even know what she does? She was a sommelier, and then she went to Mexico and studied to be a catadora. She knows everything, all the different types. Her bar has spirits from around Mexico, no additives, small batches from artisans. And these supercool women-only brands. She's brilliant." He paused. "You know you're an idiot for losing her."

"I'm aware." Jaime clicked on a flight reservation. "Just booked it. A one-way to SFO. I arrive in two days. Will you pick me up at the airport?"

"You're crazy. But, of course. Shoot me the details." Santi sighed. "Jaime, Alma isn't the same sweet girl you crushed in college. She's a powerful businesswoman. Top of her game. Every eligible straight man in Marin is obsessed with her. She won't give any of them the time of day. And she's crazy busy. It's pretty arrogant of you to think that she would take time out of her schedule to teach you about tequila. If you want to learn, go to Mexico yourself."

Jaime scrolled her bar's Instagram. She had twenty thousand followers—he had twenty-two million. He could agree to do promotions for her and blow up her social media. He checked TikTok; the tequilería didn't even have an account. Social media. Her Achilles' heel. He would fix that.

"That's where you're wrong, my friend. Her socials are dismal. I can make her huge. It's the one thing I'm good at. I'll make her an offer she can't refuse."

"Maybe she doesn't care about her socials. She's clearly successful without a great presence."

Not caring about her socials? That was unfathomable. "Well, she should care."

"Trust me, bro, she can and will refuse you."

"Want to bet?"

"Sure. I'm game. Hey, since you're up here, can you go with me to this charity event? It's a prom for Down syndrome."

Jaime's heart constricted. "Oh, I'll go with you for sure, and I can make a donation." Santi's younger sister, Leti, had Down syndrome. She used to come up and visit them at college. She was the sweetest girl.

"Thanks man. It means a lot. It's like a ball, and she gets to dress up. It would be amazing if you could be her host. I could, but I'm sure she'd rather dance with you. And that way I can be a host for another student. The foundation is short on volunteers."

"I'd be honored."

"I appreciate it. Well, I guess I'll see you soon. Just don't get your hopes up about Alma. She has money and doesn't need yours. You're going to have to think of something you can offer to her to even get her to consider working with you. Social media exposure won't be enough. It's not going to be easy."

"Nothing in life worth having ever is. Thanks for the insight. I'll see you soon. Bye, bro."

Jaime hung up the phone and gazed back upon the ocean. A sense of calm came over him.

For the first time in a while, something excited him. He was more than a pretty face, a token Mexican model for brands that wanted to be diverse. If he could learn enough about tequila, he could start his own brand, a Mexican-American-owned brand. He would partner with the best artisan tequila makers. And hands down, he would have the most incredible social media.

This was something he could do without his father, who had ignored him and always favored Ramón. He could do this without Ramón's bullshit business advice too. Last time Jaime wanted to start a business under the family umbrella, Ramón demanded Jaime give him a business plan before he even discussed it. Who does that to their own brother? And without Enrique consulting his astrology chart to make sure Mercury wasn't in retrograde. What did that mean, anyway?

But Jaime finally stood on his own. After he quit managing the social media accounts for Taco King, he had surprised himself with how well he had built up his own social media following. And he made a fortune on influencer deals. He had proved that he didn't need his family financially.

Being back up north in the only place where Jaime ever felt he was seen as more than just the youngest Montez brother would be good for him. He was happy to spend some quality time with Santi and go to that charity event with him and his sister.

But most importantly, he couldn't wait to breathe the same air as Alma.

Chapter Four

Alma shuddered. The critic from the other week had been a no-show. But she heard a rumor from another restaurant owner who knew him that he had said he would stop by tonight.

She clasped her hands and said a prayer.

As badly as she wanted him to come in, one negative review could be all it took for her success to disappear.

That was why she needed tonight to go well—so the reviewer from the *Chronicle* didn't blow her up on socials, and not in a good way.

A sharp pain in her arm brought her back to the moment. She shot her brother a dirty look. "Carlos, what was that for?" He had bailed her out tonight when one of her bartenders called out sick.

"You were gazing out at the bay, like some newbie tourist. You okay?"

A smile spread across her lips. "Never better."

Alma focused. She went behind the tall wood-carved bar and straightened the tequila bottles. She loved the colors and designs of the containers—brightly colored, some were even hand-painted. Her favorite bottle was a white ceramic one painted with intricate blue leaves. The shape of the bottle resembled the curves of a woman, and the liquor itself was just as robust, just as refined—truly the intersection of quality and art.

She signaled her bar manager, Lupe, to turn the music on, to which Lupe quickly obliged. The melodic sounds of one of her favorite Spanish ballads filled the air; the singer's deep baritone voice almost as intoxicating as the liquor in the place.

Almost.

A waft from the kitchen danced through her nostrils. Though this was a tequila bar, Mezcalifornia was known for its happy hour. They served mostly the usual fare that you would expect—small carnitas street tacos, fresh-charred corn dressed with a tangy garlic sauce and garnished with cotija cheese, mini ahi tostadas, and of course, guacamole. She hadn't wanted a typical sit-down restaurant with gourmet food and a wine list. Been there, done that.

No. She wanted a vibe. A destination. An experience.

She checked on the rest of the workers and made sure the bartenders were ready to rumble. Carlos happily milled around the bar, helping out where he could. He sliced limes like a ninja, ground various salt and sugar mixtures, which he would use to rim the margarita glasses, and pulled sage leaves off the vine for garnishes.

Her phone buzzed: It was five o'clock. Time to let in the crowds. And hope the critic showed up and loved the place.

Alma straightened her black bustier, tossed her hair so it framed her bare shoulders, and went to the door. The line wrapped around the ferry dock.

The first couple she let in was at least in their seventies, though the woman looked fantastic. Was she Mexican? With her light skin and jet-black hair, Alma couldn't be certain. The couple held hands.

"Table for two."

"Of course. Right this way."

The gentleman pulled out the seat for his companion. Alma's chest filled with warmth. It was so wonderful to see people who were still in love, like her parents were. It was possible.

A bunch of tech bros followed in after them as well as a bachelorette party. The men circled the women like sharks hunting surfers. Wow, what a perfect match between those two groups. Alma escorted both parties to the upper deck.

"Would you like to do a tequila tasting?" she asked the group of women. "We have a tequila flight where you can try blanco, reposado, joven, añejo, and extra añejo. I can teach you the different ways to imbibe them."

The lady with the bridal veil shook her head. "Nah. I'll just order a round of your watermelon margaritas."

Alma smiled. "Good choice. Coming right up."

She didn't blame the girls for picking something fruity and fun, a drink that hid the pureness of the tequila she had handpicked for the bar.

Sometimes, she resigned herself to the fact that she was fighting a losing battle. Not everyone actually cared about the differences in the tequilas like she did. Half the people came to her bar to get drunk and have a good time, and the other half usually used it as a pre- or endgame. She knew her place in this town and was just grateful for the opportunity.

But she had learned so much about her beloved liquor that she wanted to share her knowledge with anyone who would listen. The history of tequila was downright fascinating. She'd spent months working alongside agave farmers, learning everything about how they harvest the plants. Fell in love with the stories of the women artisans who defied cultural norms to start their own brands. Studied glassmaking with the bottlers and learned how important the containers were to preserve the taste of the liquor.

She ran downstairs to get started on the drinks for the ladies and slipped behind the bar. She glanced at Carlos, whose face contorted.

"Did a spider bite you?"

He shook his head but remained silent. She followed his gaze out to the deck, but she could see nothing and no one of interest. Definitely no sign of the critic.

She ignored Carlos and went back to preparing the bar.

His eyes remained glued toward the water.

"I'll be right back."

Carlos darted to the end of the restaurant—peering outside. His attention then turned toward the waiting area.

After a few moments, he returned to the bar.

She tugged on his sleeve. "Carlos—what's going on with you? You look like you've seen a ghost."

"Maybe I have." He turned to his sister and lowered his voice. "Don't freak out, but I swear I just saw Jaime milling around outside."

She gulped. Jaime? No way. It wasn't possible. He didn't live around here, and he had cut off all communication.

"Jaime? My Jaime?" She winced when those words came out of her mouth. He was no longer her Jaime, and honestly, it was doubtful that he had ever been truly hers.

But she had been his.

And she hated to admit it, but in some ways, she still was.

She shook off the thought.

"Yeah. It sure looked like him."

No. No way. "Doubtful. He has never reached out and contacted me. Ever. I doubt he even knows this is my place. Only way he would show up was if he was part of some event here, but I have no media bookings for the night. They wouldn't be filming, so I doubt he'd come."

Did he know she owned the place? He was way too cool, too cocky to friend or even follow her on social media. Or maybe he just happened to be in town, walking along the water, and had no idea she was here.

But his best friend Santi knew where she worked. And though they still saw each other around town and at different events, Santi never mentioned Jaime. Neither did Alma. She just couldn't believe that Santi would set her up—he was cooler than that.

"Yeah, I don't know about all that. But I know what he looks like. And I swear that was him."

Shivers ran through her. Impossible. After all this time, he couldn't be in her town.

Her turn to investigate. "I'll be right back."

She scanned the place for Jaime. First skulking around the bar like a cat, then dashing upstairs to look on the second floor. Nada. No sign of him. And she would be able to see him if he was there. Plus, she would've noticed him coming through the door. She remembered every inch of his shiny black hair, his chiseled face, his muscular body, his hard cock that had filled her with such unbelievable pleasure.

Ah—stop! How long had it been? Alma needed to get laid.

Maybe a one-night stand with a sexy tech bro or the hot ferry captain could banish fine-ass Jaime from her mind forever.

Though it was super doubtful.

After scouring the place for a sighting as if Jaime was some reclusive cryptid, like a Chupacabra, she went back behind the bar. She had to finish making those drinks for the upstairs party.

She placed her hand on Carlos's shoulder. "You're seeing things for sure. Even if he was outside, he's definitely not in this building. And why on earth would he be here?"

Carlos shrugged. "Forget it. He wouldn't be. Pretend I said nothing." He paused and looked into her eyes. "Sorry I even mentioned him."

"Thanks." She was relieved her ex wasn't there. Although she had to admit, she found it a little strange, the way she'd never heard from him again after he dumped her. Wasn't he curious about her?

Probably not. If he was, he would've reached out. He was all over social media. Fine as ever. She didn't contact him because she didn't want to be pathetic. He was the one who'd dumped her. How could he have ended it and never looked back?

It was almost cruel. Did he never care about her? That was impossible—they were so deeply in love.

Once.

A lifetime ago.

Well, only three years ago. But she had been a totally different person back then.

She turned around and went back to making the drinks.

Her hand clutched the neck of one of her beloved bottles of tequila—it resembled a Day of the Dead Catrina.

A sharp pain radiated through her arm. Again. She slapped her brother's hand away. "Dammit, Carlos! Stop pinching me."

His voice lowered. "Alma—turn around."

She slowly pivoted on her foot.

Standing in front of the bar, his shiny black bangs skimming his eyebrows, with a big smile flashing his dimples, was Jaime Montez.

Fuck.

And why was he hotter than hell?

His boyish frame had filled out and his ripped body was visible through his V-neck T-shirt. Those arms were so muscular! Though now they were decorated with tattoos. God, what would it be like to see this man naked, one more time.

Fine, twice. Three times tops.

As she stood there stunned, his eyes raked up and down her body.

"Hey, Alma. Nice to see you again."

Chapter Five

Jaime stood in front of Alma, taking in her beauty. Back when he first met her, she had been the most gorgeous girl he'd ever laid eyes on. But now, he was staring at a sexy, confident woman.

He had imagined this moment so many times, all the while assuring himself that it would never, ever happen. They did not need to meet again. They were exes, didn't share any children, hell, they didn't even have a pet together. She was in his past. And he had no clue what he even wanted in his future. It certainly wasn't any type of serious relationship for a long time, if ever.

But standing there so close to his ex made all those feelings that he thought he would never have again rush back.

She didn't respond to him, just stared with her jaw dropped. Jaime was mesmerized by her lips, which were painted bright red. He put his hand on the bar to get closer to her. The counter between them created some false sense of distance that prevented him from pulling Alma into his arms for one risky kiss. A kiss he would throw away his life for.

A kiss that would never happen.

Say something, pendejo.

"Nice place you have here." God, he was such an idiot. He had to at least acknowledge the awkwardness of the moment. But he couldn't even bring himself to do that. "You look great."

She sneered at him. Okay, complimenting her was not his best move, especially with a lame line like that. And he usually had all the lines and moves.

Her brother, Carlos, narrowed his gaze at Jaime. They had been close once and used to always play soccer together. Carlos was an amazing athlete, but so was Jaime. Jaime used to feel an ease with Carlos that he never felt with his own brothers. Ramón and Enrique loved him and had his back, but being the spoiled baby brother to his older protective siblings was a hard dynamic to break.

"What's up, Carlos?" was the best greeting Jaime could come up with. A fist bump or bro hug was way out of the question.

Carlos just shook his head and turned to his sister. "Want me to handle this?"

She mouthed *No*. Her long hair cascaded over her breasts. "No. I got it."

New approach. "I'd like to order your best tequila, on the rocks."

Her jaw slowly closed, and she narrowed her gaze at him. "On the rocks? Only someone who knows nothing about tequila would order it on the rocks. Why waste my best liquor on someone who can't even tell the difference between a blanco and a reposado?"

He winked. "Easy, babe—*blanco* means white." Uh. He hadn't

meant to call her babe—he had no right to call her that. Even so, the term of endearment slipped off his tongue naturally.

Alma rolled her eyes and exhaled loudly. "I'm not your babe." He could almost hear the contempt that was probably silently spewing in her mind.

Maybe this was a mistake. Not maybe, definitely. Santi had been right—Jaime shouldn't have shown up here like this, unannounced. She had no warning, no way to prepare herself for his arrival. He had ambushed her. He was such an asshole.

He gulped. "I'm sorry for surprising you like this. Can we talk?"

Her beautiful, perfectly symmetrical face contorted. "Talk? About what? I have nothing to say to you."

"Just talk. Catch up. It's been so long. I know you're working right now, but maybe later? When you get off?" He would love to get her off, but he kept his mouth shut.

She tossed up her hands. "You're unbelievable Jaime, you really are. You show up here out of the blue after dumping me three years ago, and now you want to talk? I have nothing to say to you. Nada."

Jaime clenched his fists. "Well, when you put it like that, it sounds shitty. I'm sorry, Alma. I was young." And stupid.

"So was I, but I would've done anything for you. You said you loved me. Remember?"

Her voice rose and Jaime noticed that a few patrons were staring at him. His gut wrenched—he hated making a scene. "I do, actually. For what it's worth—I meant it." In the moment. It was only after he said those words that he questioned them. Not whether he loved Alma—but if he even knew what love meant.

"It's worth nothing."

Ouch. Her words stung, but he deserved them.

She closed her eyes and placed her hands together in a prayer position. After a moment, she slowly opened her eyes and gazed at him. "Jaime Luís Montez."

The way she said his name tortured him—like he was a child being scolded by his mother. Though his own mother had never even bothered disciplining her youngest. He was the baby, neglected by her, and raised by nannies. Jaime got away with murder.

"In case you can't tell, this bar is packed. *My* bar is packed. And I have a very important critic coming in tonight. I don't have time for this drama."

As if on cue, an older man wearing a shiny black suit walked in the front door. He beelined to the bar, straight to Alma.

But her focus didn't leave Jaime.

She raised her voice. "And I have no desire to talk to you. None. Not today, not tomorrow, never. So please, just leave." She pointed her long, manicured nail toward the door. "Now. I'm not asking."

Jaime winced. He hoped the man in the suit wasn't the critic, watching this telenovela play out. He needed to exit now before causing more of a scene and damaging her business. He considered pleading with her, but his gut told him he was fighting a losing battle. He didn't want to make this any worse than it was or disrespect her any further.

But he couldn't bring himself to leave either.

He rubbed his neck and looked right at her and spoke in a low tone. "I'm sorry I came by your work unannounced. That wasn't cool of me. And I'm sorry about what happened in college. I was young and not ready for forever." He pulled his business card out of his pocket. "I'm in town for a month, staying with Santi. I would love it if you would let me take you out to lunch, at least to explain why I was such a complete asshat and ended things so abruptly. But if not, I respect that." He slid the card over to her on the bar.

She picked it up, glanced at it for a second, and then tossed it in the trash.

Alrighty then.

The man in the suit's face narrowed into a scowl.

He definitely seemed like a critic. For Alma's sake, Jaime hoped he was wrong.

Time to bounce.

"Got it. Goodbye, Alma. This bar is amazing. I'm proud of you, and I don't mean that in a condescending way. Just that you've done well for yourself. I'm in awe. Good night."

And with that, Jaime turned and walked out of the bar. The man in the suit followed a few steps behind him and stomped to his car.

Looked like starting a tequila brand wouldn't be as easy as Jaime had first thought. Though it may be easier than what he had just done—leave the only girl he'd ever loved behind.

And now that he had seen her again, he was certain that what he felt for her years ago was in fact love.

Jaime reached into his pocket to grab his phone and shot off a text: You were right. I'm on my way.

He walked down Tiburon Boulevard and made a sharp left into one of his old comfort restaurants—a place that might be able to take the sting out of Alma's rejection.

Sam's Anchor Cafe.

Oh, Sam's. Back when he and Alma were in college, and she would visit her hometown, he would take her on day dates in Tiburon. Life was so carefree then. They would sit on the deck overlooking the water and dream of their future. Even then, Jaime was cautious not to promise her anything. He was always painfully aware that he was a Montez first and foremost, and he couldn't just do whatever he wanted to whenever he wanted to. Though now, with his father's absence, he finally felt free. Not that he was ready for a relationship.

Back then, he admired Alma because her parents had no expectations that she would return home and work on the family business. In fact, it was quite the opposite. Her mother was a maid, and her father was a gardener. They worked so hard their entire lives so their children could have better ones. So, though Alma definitely felt pressure to help out her parents financially, she was free to pursue whatever career excited her.

Her dreams were her own. There was no family business to work for, no decade-long business rivalry to tarnish her company's hard work, no wrongs of her family that she needed to make right.

Growing up in San Diego, Jaime had a blessed life, well, besides his parents' acrimonious divorce. Jaime lived in La Jolla, went to the best private schools, and was coached by the best soccer players. He spent his summers surfing in Baja and his winters skiing in Lake Tahoe, with spring breaks sunbathing in Kaua'i and Thanksgivings hiking in Yosemite. And as the baby, Jaime always had Ramón and Enrique there to protect him. Being the son of a fast-food tycoon also came with perks. His father had introduced the fish taco to San Diego, and later to the rest of California. It had been a rousing success, until his father and Ramón bought the block in Barrio Logan where Julieta's own restaurant was. Turns out that Julieta's mom, Linda, was his father's spring break fling, and his father had stolen the fish taco recipe from Linda. Luckily, Ramón was able to fix things without further damaging the brand.

Jaime had so much privilege, and was completely aware of all the advantages it gave him in life. He didn't have any right to complain when he'd been blessed with so much while others struggled.

But Jaime's life was not without difficulties. He was stifled by his father's and his eldest brother Ramón's expectations of him. He, like Enrique, wanted to make his own way. But it was easier for Enrique—he was so laid-back, go with the flow, and well, cool. Jaime had his father's temper and sometimes rage consumed him, and he couldn't control his emotions. Enrique kept nagging him to go to therapy, but Jaime would rather work in the corporate office with Ramón than talk about his feelings to a shrink. Jaime had never been good at opening up about his feelings and those paralyzing expectations to anyone for fear of sounding ungrateful for his lot in life.

Anyone, that is, except Alma.

She had understood him.

But back then, he'd been just a cocky college student.

And now, he was just a fucking mess.

Jaime headed to the back of the deck where Santi awaited him. Santi laughed and glanced at his watch. "That's gotta be a record. She kicked you out in five minutes flat. Brutal. Not gonna say I told you so, but I did, so . . ."

Jaime sighed. "I know, I know. I should've listened to you. You are right. She hates me."

Santi flagged down the waitress. The peppy blonde approached the table. "I see your friend arrived." She batted her eyes at Santi, who ignored her charms. "What can I get you, gentlemen?"

"I'll have bourbon on the rocks." Santi pointed to Jaime. "And this poor bastard will have a vodka martini with two olives, shaken, not stirred."

Jaime shook his head. "Who am I? James Bond?"

Santi smirked. "That was your drink in college."

"I've grown up." But had he? Jaime shook off that thought.

"Actually, I'll have your best tequila, but not on the rocks." At least he learned one thing from Alma before she kicked him out. "And an order of the calamari."

Santi shooed away a seagull. "And some blue cheese garlic bread."

The waitress returned to the bar.

Thank God Jaime was with Santi and not Enrique, who would no doubt want Jaime to explore his feelings in depth. Jaime didn't want to say a word, at least not until liquor calmed his nerves and food filled his stomach.

The waitress returned with their drinks and their appetizers. She placed a single shot of tequila in front of Jaime.

"Here you go, sir. It's El Tesoro Blanco. It's my favorite and additive-free. But if you really want to get some great tequila, you should try Mezcalifornia a few doors down. That place is fire and the girl that runs it is badass. Her name is Alma. Severe girl crush. Cheers!"

Santi burst into laughter.

Fuck my life.

Jaime put his head in his hands.

The waitress's face contorted. "Did I say something funny? I'm dead serious. She's amazing."

Jaime opened up his mouth to speak but Santi interjected. "No. Not at all. Yes, Alma is amazing. Jaime here used to date her. They were college sweethearts."

Thanks, Santi.

The waitress's mouth dropped. "Oh, wow."

"I was an idiot," Jaime offered up.

The waitress pursed her lips. "I mean, what more could you want than Alma Garcia?"

Santi clapped him on the back. "I tell him this all the time."

Time to change the subject. "I'll have the New York steak, medium rare."

She nodded. "And you?"

"I'll have the cioppino."

She tossed her hair, shot Jaime a dirty look, and left the table.

"Hear that? Everyone loves her."

"Don't start with me, Santi."

"I'm playing."

Jaime inhaled the drink. It was smooth—no aftertaste. But also, nothing exciting about it. No matter how hard he tried, he just had never been in love with tequila. This idea was so ridiculous, especially the part about using Alma to help him.

Maybe the thought of starting a tequila company was asinine. And Santi was right. He knew nothing about it. As annoyed as he was about all these non-Hispanics starting tequila companies, he himself had no business founding one either. Maybe he should start a craft beer line—at least he loved beer. If he was of Russian descent, would he be looking into vodka companies?

The truth was Jaime was chasing another one of his harebrained ideas.

Maybe Enrique was right—Jaime needed to look inward and figure out who he really was first.

At least the food was delicious. The steak was perfectly cooked and the view of city lights, the ferries in the bay, and the bridges in the background was awe-inspiring.

He clinked his glass with Santi's. "Thanks, man, for just being here with me. Sorry, I'm such a fuckup. I wish I had it all together like you do."

Santi put his hand on his friend's shoulder. "It's just an illusion, bro. Sure, my business is booming, but I'm a workaholic. I have no work-life balance."

"Sorry to hear that, man." Sounded like his brother Ramón. Well, before he met Julieta. "I'm clearly not one to give advice, but Ramón was just like you. After he met Julieta, he changed. Maybe you will meet someone and want to stop working so hard."

"Or maybe I won't. Why? Did seeing Alma briefly make you want to find someone and start a relationship like Ramón did?"

"Absolutely not. Well, not now. Maybe one day."

"I hear you. One day in the future." Santi devoured a large shrimp and Jaime's mouth watered. Though Jaime's meal was excellent, he should've ordered the seafood.

"So, are you going to stick around for the month, or have you had a change of plans?"

Jaime shook his head. "No, man. No. I'm here for the month. I need a beat. And I promised you I'd do that charity event with you."

"Thanks for that, man. I appreciate it."

"No sweat. It will be a good time. How's Leti, by the way?"

"Good. She's on the high school cheerleading team, and she even has a boyfriend who is in her class."

"You okay with that?"

"Of course. I just want her to be happy." Santi paused. "Are you going to give up on trying to have anything to do with Alma?"

A bitter taste filled Jaime's mouth. He hated to admit defeat. But there was no hope. "I don't have a choice. I don't want to stalk her. She made it clear she wants nothing to do with me. I get it. I don't blame her. I respect her choice."

"Yeah. You fired your shot, but you didn't have any chance. Does this mean you're going to abandon your ideas of tequila domination?"

Jaime turned up his palms. "It was a stupid idea anyway. All because I got mad that some oblivious celebrities wanted to use me to sell their products."

Santi paused. "I mean, yeah, that was pretty pathetic of them to ask but it's par for the course with these companies. But starting a tequila line isn't the worst idea I've ever heard of." He paused. "You don't need Alma. You could do it alone. Or we could do it together. I'd love to diversify my portfolio."

Yeah, Santi was way too much like Ramón. Jaime didn't understand Santi's and Ramón's calm, practical approaches to business decisions. Or Enrique's spiritual one. To Jaime, it was simple. Did the business interest him enough to capture his attention for a while?

And if he was honest with himself, his interests waned pretty quickly. At least in business. Jaime had always been passionate about soccer. And women.

But his career aspirations had been all over the place. It disgusted him sometimes that he was nothing more than a social media influencer. He didn't want to be responsible for influencing some young kid to do anything.

He had never meant being an influencer to be his career. He was running the social media accounts for Taco King and once took a shirtless selfie of himself eating at one of the restaurants. That picture blew up online. Brand deals came pouring in, and in all honesty, Jaime couldn't resist the money. Once his father was forced out of the company, Jaime told Ramón he didn't want to run the social media full-time and instead Jaime focused on his own career. But after a couple of years, the shininess wore off and his work, while lucrative, lost its luster.

When he was a little boy, Jaime wanted to play professional

soccer. But his father, of course, was completely against that idea. He wanted him to focus on their business and saw his three sons as mere extensions of himself.

So, after he painfully abandoned that dream, Jaime dedicated himself to school. He didn't want business degrees, like Ramón had, or a degree in agricultural science, like Enrique had. He wanted something more liberating.

He studied communications, and it was a natural gateway into digital marketing. His socials blew up in college, which thrilled his father because he wanted Jaime to use his skills to further the restaurants' social profiles. And while Jaime enjoyed it at first, it left him feeling empty.

Which was how he felt right now.

But despite searching for a new passion, he just hadn't found one. So, he spent his days surfing, his nights partying, and occasionally made some posts for some brands. He barely even played soccer anymore.

Maybe he could pick up a game while he was here. He would've asked Carlos, but that was clearly a no-go.

"Well, I'd love to go into business with you. But, no offense, this was something I really wanted to do on my own. I never do shit on my own. Without my family's watchful eyes or control."

"None taken. I totally understand. But Jaime, you don't need to just drop your idea because Alma doesn't want to help you. She never was going to. You don't need her. I have full confidence that you can do this alone."

Jaime ran his hands through his hair. "Thanks. It's nice to hear that someone believes in me." Ramón was always praised for his intelligence and business acumen, and Enrique was always valued for his emotional intuitiveness.

But people usually just measured Jaime's worth by his looks.

He desperately wanted to be more than just the pretty boy.

He wanted to be smart like Ramón and sensitive like Enrique. He wanted to be well-rounded. He wanted to be a good man.

"I mean it, bro. I believe in you. I can help you any way you want, but don't worry, this will be your own thing. You could go to Mexico and study by yourself. Or you could do a course online. Find another mentor. Trust in yourself. You don't need her."

"I'll cheers to that." Jaime raised his glass of water, since his dance with that tequila shot was a distant memory.

Though when Jaime drank the water, he couldn't help but think that Santi was wrong that Jaime could do it on his own.

Maybe Jaime wouldn't lose interest in tequila—he could see himself forming more of a taste for it every time he drank it.

But about the other thing Santi had said.

That he didn't need Alma.

Jaime couldn't help but think he really did.

Chapter Six

The morning sunlight seeped into Alma's bedroom, the rays reflecting off the ocean waves outside her window, but she wasn't ready to face the day yet, so instead, she snuggled under her fluffy rose-tinted comforter with her fawn-colored pug, Tequila. Her pup's name always made her chuckle; she had rescued her at a time when she had just become obsessed with the spirit. And oh, what a journey it had been.

But the sad truth was that Alma had just replaced her previous obsession with Jaime with a newfound passion for tequila—the dog and the liquor.

During the time she had been involved with Jaime, Alma had been focused on wine and had even applied and been accepted to a prestigious program to become a sommelier. She passed the exam with flying colors and enjoyed working at restaurants and pairing wines with gourmet dishes. She was on her way to a lucrative career and, though she loved learning everything about grapes, from planting them, to watering them, to harvesting them, to all the different varieties of wines, she didn't feel a deep connection to them or the work.

A pristine prickly pear paloma piqued her interest in tequila, but it wasn't until she journeyed to Mexico on a girls' trip that her high school best friend Zoila had arranged for her so she would finally forget about Jaime that she really discovered the new love in her life to get her over her first.

Tequila.

Alma laughed at the saying "The best way to get over someone is to get under someone else," but it rang true for her. Getting sloshed in Mexico opened her horizons up to a new career.

But it wasn't just drinking any type of alcohol. It was all about tequila—truly indulging in it. She had taken a wine tour to Valle de Guadalupe and met a vintner who was from Jalisco—the holy land of tequila. But Jalisco was so much more than a tequila state—it was the birthplace of mariachi music, charrerías, the first sombrero, and was even responsible for the beloved Mexican Hat Dance. She loved every fragrant smell that made her mouth water, every brightly colored wall that shone through her sunglasses, and every cobbled street her heels got stuck in. She couldn't wait to go back, but she had been so busy with her bar that it hadn't happened yet.

Jalisco was quite simply heaven for Alma. The gentleman offered to take her and her friends on a tour of his hometown. Though she questioned his motivations at first, being leery of any overly friendly stranger in a foreign country, she gave him a chance, since she felt safe and was in a group, and embraced adventure. It took little more than riding a burro through a blue agave patch and watching the workers harvesting the plants for her to get hooked.

Not just on tequila, but on Mexico, in particular Jalisco's capital, Guadalajara. Rediscovering the country her parents grew up in changed her life. Being the daughter of immigrants in America always made her feel like she didn't belong, but walking through the streets of Guadalajara gave her a sense of pride and an appreciation of where she came from. Her homeland was glorious.

Being there in a place that was on one hand foreign yet simultaneously strangely familiar helped her overcome her grief and anger about Jaime. As much as she was still deeply hurt, Alma understood that there was a huge world to experience for both of them and that he had probably been right when he gazed into her eyes and told her that they were too young to be together forever.

That didn't mean that she didn't still miss him.

But she had found a new obsession. Tequila.

Unfortunately, her former lover and current love collided last night—and she wasn't prepared for that mixture. The smooth spirit was the clear winner in the battle for her heart. Tequila was loyal to her; it would never betray her. Not that she didn't have people who she loved and trusted blindly. Her parents, her brother, her friends. But all those relationships were safer than romantic love.

She could never trust Jaime again.

And she hoped he wouldn't return again to disrupt her world.

Speaking of that, the critic never showed up. Her brother thought he saw a man who could possibly be a critic lurking during the Jaime reunion disaster, but he couldn't be certain. All Alma knew for sure was the man hadn't made himself known to her.

Alma rolled out of bed, let Tequila outside, did her daily beauty routine—which consisted of too many serums, a huge helping of moisturizer, and a copious amount of sunscreen—and got dressed. Lazy mornings were no time for bustiers and tight jeans, so she chose some soft, sage-colored designer sweats and a loose T-shirt. She tied her hair back, leashed up her pup, grabbed her purse, and walked down the street to get some coffee and meet Zoila.

She scrolled through her phone, but a post on Instagram stopped her cold.

> Mistress of tequila berates her customers.

Her stomach clenched. Oh no. Oh no!

Her eyes scanned the attached article.

> Though I was excited to partake in a night of tequila tasting, it wasn't to be. Miss Alma Garcia was in a foul mood and was yelling at a man in the bar. I left without so much as a sip.

The critic was there?

Kill me now!

Alma had been so busy fuming at Jaime that she hadn't even noticed this guy. What a fool! This one bad review could tank her bar! She may never get a chance to impress him again!

Another reason to hate Jaime. Except that wasn't quite fair. He couldn't have possibly known that she was expecting a critic, though he shouldn't have surprised her.

A text came through.

Zoila: Sorry! I'm late.

Alma: No worries. I'm having a shitty morning.

Zoila: Oh no! What's up?

Alma: I'll tell you when you get here. What do you want? I'll order for us both.

Zoila: A vanilla latte and a breakfast burrito. Ty.

Zoila was always late, but getting in and out of Tiburon was no easy feat. Especially on a sunny Saturday, which beckoned all the tourists who would take ferries in from San Francisco or catch one to visit Angel Island. At least tonight would be hopping at the bar.

Alma put her phone in her purse and strolled by the bay.

Caffé Acri was located adjacent to Alma's tequilería. Alma studied the glass case filled with freshly baked pastries.

Joy, the barista, greeted her with a big smile.

"Hey, Alma! What can I get you today?"

"Hi, Joy. I'll have a hot mocha, a vanilla latte, a breakfast burrito, and the Italian sausage omelet." Her eyes lingered over the sweet treats. "And can you add in a chocolate croissant please? Thank you." Her normal cappuccino and grain bowl weren't going to cut it today. She needed some comfort food.

"Coming right up."

What she really needed was a drink, but one of the rules she had for herself now that she was in the liquor industry was that she would never day drink unless she had an event.

Or a crisis.

Seeing Jaime last night qualified as a crisis, didn't it?

Nope, it didn't.

But having a bad post from a critic definitely did.

She had to have some boundaries. Boundaries she wished she'd had when she was dating Jaime. But she had been so young and stupid then.

She exhaled—she needed to give herself grace. She closed her eyes, an image of herself weeping on the sofa after he'd dumped her popping into her mind. Her stomach churned—she had been so pathetic.

But now, pathetic was the last word she would ever use to describe herself.

Once she received their food and beverages, she led Tequila out to a bench overlooking the ocean. The usual Marin County crowd gathered outside the café. A group of female cyclists proudly strutted around after securing their rides to the rack, a young mother fed her toddler a muffin, and a few tech bros huddled in a corner.

People living, loving, experiencing.

A calmness swept over her. She doused her omelet in a few of the Tapatío hot sauce packets she always kept in her purse and took a warm, gooey bite. Pure peace, bliss, and contentment in her life. Living in a charming waterfront downtown that was walkable to her work and cool restaurants and shops was a dream.

So why did she feel so restless? Was it just because Jaime surprised her?

What the fuck did he really want from her, anyway?

He couldn't possibly want her back.

It didn't matter what he wanted. She didn't want him back.

Hopefully, she would never find out why he showed up.

She gobbled down another bite of the omelet and finally turned her attention back to her phone. Where was Zoila?

Zoila's message popped up on her screen.

Zoila: Here! Parking.

Alma: I'm outside on a bench.

A few minutes later, Zoila strolled over, looking as cool as ever. With her dyed purple hair cut in a short dramatic bob, heavy eyeliner, tight black T-shirt, long black pencil skirt, and leather knee-high Docs that covered up her fishnet stockings, Zoila's Mexican goth girl look was always on point.

They embraced, Tequila licked Zoila's face, which surprisingly didn't disturb her makeup, and then Zoila sat down next to Alma, who was taking a swig of her mocha.

Zoila's eyes narrowed at Alma.

"Bitch, spill. Did you see Jaime last night? He posted a video on TikTok that he was at Sam's with Santi. Did they stop by your bar?"

Ugh. Why, Jaime? Why? It was bad enough that he had broken her safe refuge away from him, but did he have to post that he was in her town next to her bar so that all her friends knew that their paths could cross?

"Do you follow him?"

Zoila shook her head. "No, silly. I don't. But it came up on my FYP."

Social media was the worst. Why was her ex so obsessed with it? He had been so passionate in college about wanting to become his own man. It saddened her that after he left her, he just abandoned his dreams and joined his father's business.

"Yes—he came by, but I kicked his sorry ass out. Worse yet, the critic saw me yelling at him and left! I'm so fucked."

Zoila put her hand over her chest. "Oh no, that sucks. Can you call the critic back and explain?"

Alma shook her head. "Doubtful. It took months for him even to consider coming."

"I'm so sorry, girl. That blows."

"It does." She paused. She didn't want to obsess over him, but she couldn't let it go. "Jaime wanted to talk. Can you believe that?"

"Yeah. I can. But girl, he's so fucking hot. I don't care that he's your ex. At least fuck him. Then ghost him. Give him some of his own medicine."

Zoila had a point. One round, or two, or ten, with Jaime would leave Alma satisfied for months. But she couldn't. He wasn't just a one-night stand that she could fuck and forget.

She actually had loved him. Deeply.

"Hard no."

Zoila grinned and her painted-blue lips pursed. "How hard?"

Alma rolled her eyes. Zoila was wild. Why couldn't Alma be more like her? "Basta. Not happening."

"Shit, girl. Where is the Alma I used to know?"

She winced. That Alma vanished once she threw herself into her business.

"She's dead. I'm a drag."

Zoila squeezed Alma's hand. "Sorry—that was harsh of me, but it's true. You've changed. You're so serious now, and that's a good thing. You're focused and determined and you're running a groundbreaking business right here. But if you did want to slow down, take some time for you every now and then . . . that would be okay too."

"You're right. I'll try to be more spontaneous." She paused. Her life was all work now and no play. "It's just so difficult."

"Well, don't be selfish. At least hook me up with Santi. He's fine and loaded."

Both were true statements. Alma knew Santi well—after Jaime dumped her, Santi stuck around for a bit to make sure Alma was okay. And he never hit on her, which was cool because she would never date her ex's best friend and she was sure Santi would also never date his best friend's ex. Santi wasn't a player like Jaime, but Santi was also a workaholic and didn't want to settle down. Ever.

And Zoila just wanted to have fun.

Not to mention Santi was superconservative and Zoila was anything but. Santi spent his days making millions on apps, and she taught bilingual education at a school in the Canal that didn't even have computers.

"Can't. Never seeing Jaime again, so I won't see Santi. And you can't hang with one and not the other—they are like tequila and lime."

Zoila shook her head, but her perfectly coiffed hair didn't move. "Gah. You're no fun. And mind you, Jaime doesn't live here, so they wouldn't be around each other all the time. I'm patient. I'll wait . . ." She dramatically looked at her watch like a real-life GIF.

"Thank God for this huge-ass state." Alma couldn't fathom what it would be like if Jaime actually lived here. Running into him all the time would be a complete nightmare. Marin was small and intimate—definitely not big enough for the two of them.

There was a pause in the conversation. Alma took another sip of her mocha. The dark chocolate deliciousness soothed her entire body.

Zoila broke the awkward silence. "Hey. So, I was thinking of heading back to Jalisco next month."

"Really? Why?" That was so weird. Alma was just thinking this morning of wanting to go back.

"I always wanted to go to the Fiesta de San Isidro."

Alma racked her brain back to catechism class but couldn't remember who he was. "And he's the saint of . . ."

"Farmers. There is a festival, and they bless the seeds, farmworkers, and working animals. Plus, I just love Guadalajara. I had the best time and really want to go again. Come with?"

No. Not now. Not with the bar doing so well. She needed to focus and work harder to ensure its success.

"I'd love to, but I can't. Too busy with the bar."

"Whatever. You're always too busy with your place. Work will always be there. You need a break."

Zoila was right. Alma needed a break. She deserved a break.

Maybe Jaime popping into her life was a sign. Not that she needed to have any sort of relationship with him, because clearly that was never going to happen. But that her life had turned into all work and no play. Seeing Jaime, remembering their carefree times together and how they would drop everything and take adventure days hiking up mountains, made her yearn for that freedom.

"I guess I could use some time off. And I really wanted to go down there and meet with this tequila artisan. When is it?"

"May fifteenth."

One month from now. Could she swing it?

She did have her brother around. And—she quickly checked her phone—none of her staff had requested off for that week, so she could feasibly slip away with minimal disruption.

Could she? *Should* she?

Alma took in a deep breath.

Commit to this. You deserve it.

"I'm in."

Zoila's jaw dropped. "Seriously?"

"Yes, seriously. I can do it since it is after the Cinco celebration. Carlos roped me into some festival. It's a fundraiser for the kids he coaches. But we also have to make a stop in Oaxaca. There is some mezcal mistress that is supposed to be the bomb and I want to check her out and possibly carry her spirit."

"Yay! I didn't think you'd say yes! I'm so excited. Okay. I'll plan everything. Text me the dates that suit you on either side." She looked at her phone. "I need to run to my tutoring job. Thanks for the cafecito and chisme. I'll text later."

Alma laughed. There was no one she would rather drink coffee and share gossip with than Zoila.

"Bye!" They embraced, and Zoila walked down the street.

Alma exhaled and placed her phone back into her purse. As she and Tequila walked back to her condo, she again felt that sense of peace she longed for.

Seeing Jaime, as disturbing as it was, was a blessing. Not a curse. A reminder of what her life had been like back when she had been with him. Fun, flirty, fantastic.

She missed that girl.

But she was going to discover her again.

In Mexico.

Chapter Seven

Jaime woke the next morning with a hangover and a hard-on. How had he so epically fucked up last night? Why hadn't he listened to Santi? He should've never come to Marin.

Jaime tossed back his covers and hit the shower. The hot water cascaded over his body, washing away his shame. After these last few years, he should've gotten over Alma. But seeing her, smelling her, it was as if they had never spent a day apart.

He wanted to be alone with his thoughts. He exited the shower, quickly dressed, and snuck by Santi's room, not knowing if his friend was awake. Honestly, he was probably working. That guy never took a day off. Maybe Jaime liked him because he reminded him so much of Ramón.

Jaime opened the glass doors of Santi's mansion and took in the view. Though Jaime's home also overlooked the ocean, something about the Bolinas landscape wowed him. The water seemed bluer, and the waves were wilder, not to mention the water here was downright frigid. He had packed his wet suit, but didn't want to surf today. He ran down the wooden steps and walked onto the beach. A few surfers braved the cold, but the sand was mostly empty.

Jaime took a few brisk steps on the beach but decided to cut through the homes and head into town. He stopped into a cute coffee shop and ordered a cortado. The barista served it to him in an adorable light-blue cup with a wave printed on the side, but Jaime resisted the urge to snap a shot and upload it to his Instagram.

It was too easy to get back into social media. Tequila or no tequila, he needed a change.

His phone buzzed. He didn't recognize the number, but it had a 415 area code so was from the Bay Area. Could it be Alma?

No. Of course not. Why on earth would she call him after last night?

Normally, he would let it go to voicemail, but he picked up.

"Hello?"

"Hey, Jaime. It's Carlos."

Carlos? Why was he calling him? Based on the way he looked at him last night, they were definitely not on friendly terms. Rightfully so. Clearly Carlos was upset with Jaime for how he had ended things with Alma.

"Hi."

"Hi. I got your number from your business card."

Jaime laughed. "Yeah. I wasn't shocked she tossed it in there. Don't blame her. What's up?" Jaime was dying to hear why Carlos was calling him. It was definitely not on Alma's behalf.

"Look. I shouldn't call you. Alma would seriously murder me if she knew. But I wanted to ask you a favor."

Jaime's interest was piqued. "Ask away."

"I run this soccer program down in the Canal. I know how you love soccer. You were pretty good."

Jaime smirked. "I was great actually. So were you."

"Thanks. I still am. And that's the thing. I was really good. But I never had the opportunities to go professional. We didn't have club soccer back then, and if we did, my parents couldn't have afforded it. They could barely keep food on the table and pay bills."

Jaime thought of the irony that Carlos could've been a top soccer star but didn't have the resources. Jaime, on the other hand, had the resources but had been manipulated into giving up his dreams.

"Yeah, everything has changed since back then. Club sports are intense."

"They are. I have a small club, but we don't have the resources to compete against the top Marin clubs. I mean, their dues are six thousand a year. Most of my kids are on scholarships. So, I was wondering if you would consider doing a fundraiser here in the Canal. We are doing this Cinco event. I could really use your help."

Jaime didn't hesitate. "Of course. I'd love to. I'll even bring up my brothers and we can donate and do whatever you need." He paused. He had to ask. "Will Alma be there?"

Carlos sighed. "Yeah. She will. But don't worry. I'll handle her. Thank you so much for this. It means the world to me and to the kids. We need to fix the field and get equipment. You will be literally giving my team opportunities they wouldn't have."

"Don't worry about it. I'm glad to help. Just give me the details."

Carlos paused. "Actually, could you come by today? To meet some vendors and the organizer?"

"Yup. Text me the details and I'll be there."

"Thank you, Jaime. I appreciate it. And I don't hold any ill will toward you for your breakup with Alma. You guys were so young. I told her it would never last."

Right girl, wrong time. "Yeah. I still feel bad. I shouldn't have shown up there last night like that."

"It's fine. She'll get over it. I'll text you the details. See you later."

"Bye."

Jaime hung up and took a sip out of his cortado. It was smooth and slightly sweet, no hint of an aftertaste.

Maybe he had been called to come up here to see Alma, not for his business, and not to get back together with her. But for a higher cause.

To help some great boys achieve their dreams of playing soccer.

Chapter Eight

Alma didn't have to be back at the bar until four to prep for the night, so she spent her day working out, tidying up, and answering some emails.

As she hit *send* on an email to a supplier about a missing tequila bottle, her phone rang. She leaned across her white cotton couch to pluck it from the armrest.

It was Carlos.

Why was he calling? He stopped by yesterday. They were close no doubt, but they normally didn't see or talk to each other on the daily.

"Hola. What's up?"

"Not much. You good?"

"No. I'm livid. Did you see the critic's Instagram post? He saw me yelling at Jaime and left."

"Can't say I blame him. You were pretty upset. Rightfully so. Do you want to talk about it?"

Alma rolled her eyes. Last thing she needed was everyone interrogating her about seeing Jaime. She was fine. Perfect, as a matter of fact.

"No. I don't. And I wasn't upset. Just shocked. If I'm upset about anything, it's the critic, not seeing Jaime."

He huffed. "Sure it is."

"Carlos, stop. I'm serious."

"I believe you," he said with a not-so-subtle hint of sarcasm. "Just checking to be sure."

"Thanks. I appreciate that. I actually saw Zoila a bit ago. Guess what? We're going to Mexico together."

"Really? You never travel. Ever."

"I know. But this is the new me. Seeing Jaime made me realize how much of myself I lost when he left. Since I studied in Mexico, I have been married to my work. And I need a break."

He sighed. "It's for work, right?"

"No!" Alma protested. "I mean, maybe a tiny bit of work, but—"

"Aha! I knew it! I know you." Carlos laughed. "You wouldn't just go there for fun. You don't do anything just for fun."

"Fine. There is this maestra mezcalera in Oaxaca I want to meet." At his confused pause, she clarified, "A top female mezcal maker. And I wanted to reconnect with some tequila makers in Jalisco. But I'll still have fun."

He laughed. "No doubt about that. Especially if you're going with Zoila. She's wild."

She was wild. Alma *wanted* to be wild. "Yup. She is. Anyway, is that why you called?"

"No. Actually, can you come to the field today?"

"For what?"

He hesitated. "Uh, there are a few teachers and coaches gathering today for the festival. I was hoping you could come too. And the organizer wants to meet you. It would mean a lot to me. At one?"

"Sure, I don't start work until later."

"Cool. See you soon."

She took a quick shower, put on some tinted moisturizer, a touch of mascara, jeans, and a T-shirt. She would do her full makeup routine later when she went to work.

Tequila licked her leg.

"I guess I can take you with me. It is a park, after all." Alma scooped up Tequila, stuffed her into her car, and headed toward San Rafael down the winding Tiburon Boulevard.

A smile spread over her face fantasizing about her upcoming vacation to Mexico. Flashes of the food she would eat, the drinks she would imbibe, the festivals in which she would partake. She was so grateful that Zoila had convinced her to go. Alma really needed to focus a bit more on taking breaks.

Once she turned on the 101, her heart constricted at leaving her idyllic bubble behind her. Though she was still heavily involved in her old Mexican community in the Canal, she had worked so hard to make a life for herself in Tiburon, returning home filled her with a mixture of guilt for the ones she had left behind and fear that she was one disastrous business step away from landing back there. Not that she didn't love the warmth and culture of her hometown, not that at all. The people of the Canal were hardworking, loyal, and kind. But the stark poverty in contrast to the opulence of the rest of Marin never sat right with her. How could a community with so much give so little to its own residents? Most of Marin was shockingly segregated, including Marin City and the Canal. Marin City, which was famously the hometown of the late Tupac Shakur, was 40 percent Black whereas the rest of Marin was only 4 percent.

And the Canal was even more racially divided—90 percent Hispanic versus the entire county at a mere 17 percent.

Both communities had the worst schools in the county, while the elementary school in Ross was one of the best publics in the nation. It wasn't fair.

As she exited to the Canal, her nerves tingled. Thank God Carlos asked her to do this festival. She could raise some real money for the Canal. Give back even more.

She parked at Pickleweed Park, the only green space in the Canal, which had been promised a multimillion-dollar refurbishing. Even so, she still adored it as it was. It was next to a bilingual library and a great recreation center that held quinceañeras and birthday parties. But the big highlight was the sports fields.

Alma wrangled Tequila out of the car and gave her water since she overheated easily. Pugs always had health problems.

She locked her car and enjoyed the cool breeze from the bay.

A familiar revving roared in the distance. *Had to be a Porsche.* After a few years serving wealthy tourists at the bar, it wasn't hard to pick out.

Still, a Porsche? In the Canal?

Sure, there were some exotic car dealerships and mechanics nearby, but that vehicle was an odd choice at this park.

A bright-orange Porsche pulled in next to her.

Santi was in the driver's seat.

And Jaime was sitting next to him.

Fuck my life.

Jaime opened the door. He was wearing a thin Efraín Álvarez LA Galaxy soccer jersey and soccer shorts that showed off his muscular body. That chest, those arms, uh, those thighs!

Alma tried to process his presence again. Did he follow her here? Was he stalking her?

Seeing him twice in two days was too much. She walked right up to Jaime. Damn, why did he smell like cedar and sex?

"What on earth are you doing here? Are you stalking me? Did you put an AirTag on me last night or something?"

Jaime threw up his hands. "What? No. I'm not a stalker or psychopath, Alma. I was invited here for a game."

Like a lotería riddle, this cruel joke suddenly became clear to her.

Soccer. Goddamn fútbol.

Fucking Carlos. She was going to kill her brother.

She exhaled. "By my fucking brother? Say he didn't."

Just as Jaime opened his mouth, her brother's beat-up old Honda pulled into the parking lot.

He parked and swiftly got out of the car. "Dammit. I wanted to get here first, but I'm too late. Alma, I can explain."

Alma seethed. "Late? You set me up. My own brother. How could you do this?"

Carlos tugged her arm and pulled her away from Jaime to the side of an old brick building housing the public restrooms. Tequila waddled behind, snorting.

"Alma, sorry. I had to invite him."

Alma gritted her teeth. "You better explain yourself right fucking now or I'm going to lose it."

"It's my soccer program. We are going bankrupt. The parents can't afford the uniforms or the tournament fees. I know you agreed to help out with the Cinco festival, and I appreciate that, but it's not enough."

"So what? You called my ex? After you saw how I reacted last night? How could you do that? How did you even get his number? Did you know he was coming last night?"

"No. Of course I didn't. I had no idea he was in town, but after I saw him, it hit me. It was too good of an opportunity to pass up. And I got his number from the business card that you tossed in the trash."

That stupid card. She should've shredded it, but if Carlos had wanted that badly to contact Jaime, he would've found a way no matter what. "I can't believe you would do this to me! Your own flesh and blood."

"Dammit, Alma, it's not about you, don't you see? You live in Tiburon in your oceanfront condo with your oceanfront bar and your oceanfront life. Sure, you pop in and out of events like it's cool and donate money, but you don't live here anymore. You don't suffer like we do. Like our community does." He gestured wildly with his arms. "It has only gotten worse since the pandemic."

Her chest heaved. "Don't shame me for working my ass off and enjoying my success. You chose to stay in the Canal. You could leave."

"That's true. I did choose to stay here, and I'm happy with my decision. And I'm proud of you and you have every right to leave. I'm sorry. I don't want to shame you. I know you still care. But we really need the help."

She understood. But still. Jaime?

Carlos didn't stop yapping. "Jaime not only has money but he is also willing to help promote the festival too. And that's not all."

There was more? Alma rolled her eyes. "What else, dímelo?"

Carlos paused and looked away from her. "His brothers are going to come up to help also."

Alma's eyes bulged. "What?"

"They are planning a huge fundraising event. We need this, Alma; our community needs this. Cinco is two weeks away. You can put up with Jaime for fourteen days, can't you? For the Canal?"

Waves of confusion crashed down on Alma. Why was she expected to have to deal with her ex for two weeks for the good of her community? Could she ever enjoy the life she had worked so hard for without the stinging guilt?

She wasn't going to do it. She glared at Carlos, and then reluctantly followed him back to where Jaime was.

A cute little boy no more than four ran up to Alma's dog.

"What's her name?"

"Tequila."

Jaime laughed, but she ignored him.

Alma smiled at the boy. "Do you want to pet her?"

The boy nodded his head. He pet her dog, who grunted loudly.

When he was done, the little boy pointed at Santi's car. "Is this the man who is going to let me play soccer?" he asked Carlos in Spanish.

Tears welled in Alma's eyes.

How selfish was she? Carlos was right. She had left her community behind to assimilate into Tiburon. She had once been a child who lived here who didn't have enough money for after-school activities. Oh, how she'd wanted to try gymnastics, but her parents couldn't afford the lessons. And Carlos would probably be a professional soccer player if he'd had more opportunities when he was younger. It was too late for him, but it wasn't too late for the sweet boy in front of her.

She turned to Jaime and nodded.

Then Alma knelt down beside the little boy. "Yes, yes he is."

Chapter Nine

Jaime looked over at Alma, comforting the cute little boy with the shiny black hair. The boy smiled and hugged her, then pet Tequila. What an incredible woman Alma was—she had put aside her hatred for Jaime for the good of her community.

She had to talk to him—at least hear him out. Before he could even think of asking her to teach him about tequila, he had to do what was right. Apologize for surprising her. Explain why he hadn't been in contact since they broke up, though honestly, that should be obvious. It was still painful for both of them.

He took a step closer to her. Though she had been dressed all sexy at the bar, Jaime preferred her as she was now—wearing a white T-shirt and jeans. It reminded him of how she was in college, where he'd fallen in love with her. Naturally beautiful. He breathed her in—her vanilla scent filled the air.

Damn, he missed her. Not just her body, or the way her hair

cascaded onto her breasts, but her smile, her passion, her warmth, the way she made him feel.

Jaime ran his hands through his hair. "Alma, can we talk?"

She held hers up like a stop sign. "No. I have nothing to say to you. I'm not really involved in the organization of this festival, so if Carlos feels he needs you and your family to raise money for our hometown, that's fine. It's for the greater good and has nothing to do with me."

He couldn't even get a word in to explain himself. "Okay. But please, just talk to me for a few minutes. I want to—"

She glared at him, and in that hard look, Jaime felt the guilt of ending their relationship crash down on him. The pain, the anger, the longing, that sharp stare conveyed it all.

His gut wrenched.

"No. No. I don't want to hear it. I don't want any part of it, of you, or of your family. The festival is big—we won't have to interact. I'm not agreeing to spend time with you—I'm doing it for him." She pointed to the little boy.

And with that, she turned to Carlos and grabbed his arm. She stomped away from Jaime as Tequila waddled after her, and Alma and her brother tossed words back and forth in Spanish. Unluckily, or luckily in this situation, Jaime didn't have a clue what they were saying. They spoke too fast, and he didn't understand more than a spattering of words. Being a no sabo kid really sucked.

Santi put his hand on Jaime's shoulder. "Man, that was painful to watch."

"Yup." Totally embarrassing.

A man with salt-and-pepper hair and leathery skin pushed a paleta cart on the sidewalk. Jaime handed the guy a one-hundred-dollar bill and took a coconut one and gave the frozen treat to the little boy.

The boy's eyes widened. "Gracias, Señor."

"De nada." Jaime's Spanish sucked but he could flub his way through basic communication. A wave of shame flashed over him for not being able to communicate in his culture's native tongue.

Santi's face twisted. "So, I thought you didn't want to involve your family in this tequila idea. Are you going to tell them about it since they will be up here?"

"Yeah, I'll probably have to. They are just coming up for the Cinco festival, not to help me. What I really came here for, to try to get Alma to teach me about tequila, is not even plausible at this point. She fucking hates me."

"I love that song, man."

Jaime shook his head. "Not funny, bro."

"Look, she's in shock. You bombarded her. And now her own brother is forcing you to do an event together, for a good cause no doubt but still awkward."

"Yeah, and it will be even tougher for her once my whole family shows up." It definitely wasn't fair to overwhelm her like this. But Jaime was grateful that his family agreed to help the Canal. Ramón had some serious clout and star power, especially now with all the media attention for his wedding to Julieta, which was at the end of the summer. And Enrique's girlfriend, Carolina, was an icon in the community, ever since the graduation photos of her picking strawberries on the farm where her migrant parents worked went viral. She later bought the farm with money raised from the media attention.

"It could be a lot for her. You guys never spent too much time with your family, did you?"

"I mean, they definitely know her, but we were so young then. Back when we were together, she always said she thought they didn't like her, which wasn't true. I think they both didn't want to get too close to her knowing that I was only in college, and it probably wouldn't last."

Santi grabbed his soccer ball from the car. "Well, clearly they were right."

"Yeah." They were. They were right about everything. And next thing he knew, his brothers would be up here in Marin for the festival. Jaime still hadn't told them he planned to open a tequila line. Why bother? They would just tell him he couldn't do it.

No one ever believed he'd amount to anything other than a pretty face.

Well, someone did once—Alma.

Besides, he didn't need to tell his brothers anything about his plans. He had his own money. They were so busy they would just do the festival, maybe spend a few days up in beautiful Marin, and then leave. After they were gone, Jaime could figure out how to start a tequila company on his own.

The heated Spanish discussion had ended. Jaime expected Alma to take off in her car, but she marched into the park with Tequila in tow and sat down on a bench on the other side of the field. She lifted up her dog and placed her next to her.

Carlos walked over to Jaime.

"Thanks again for agreeing to help us. It means the world." He glanced over at his sister. "Sorry about her."

"Hey man, don't apologize. She has every right to be pissed off. I shouldn't have shown up unexpectedly. The breakup was rough on me too. I never meant to disrespect her or your family."

"No worries, bro. I understand. You were young."

He looked over at Alma, who was writing something in a notebook. "She's staying around? I thought once she saw me, she'd bail."

"Yeah, I told her that one of the organizers was coming over to discuss the event. He's late, so she will be here for at least a little bit, but then she will hightail it out of here. She's so pissed at me for keeping her in the dark, but she does understand it's for the community. It's all good."

"I'm glad." Jaime stared at the field. His heart constricted. All of the years he spent playing soccer had consumed him and he hardly ever did anymore. He really missed it. "So, you still up for that soccer game?"

Carlos smirked. "If you can handle getting beaten."

"By you? Never."

"All that posing on Instagram wouldn't have improved your footwork."

Jaime smirked. "We'll see."

Carlos grinned. "I'll round up the others." Carlos ran to the end of the field where there were some other men playing. Most of them were pretty good, probably other coaches.

Or maybe just men in the community who had immense talent but never had the opportunity to play anywhere other than Pickleweed Park.

Even if Alma never spoke to him again and the Cinco festival was the last time he ever saw her, he would never regret helping fundraise for the Canal.

Jaime looked over at Alma. Her nose was in a book, and she wasn't paying any attention to him.

Hmm. He grinned. He had a plan to pique her interest.

Jaime peeled off his shirt and tossed it in the car.

Santi burst out laughing. "Are you serious? You think your abs will get Alma to talk to you?"

"Yup. I'm desperate. I'll use what I have."

"You're too much."

Jaime and Santi ran toward Carlos to join the team. Jaime stared right at Alma as he passed her bench. Her jaw dropped when she saw him, and Jaime winked for good measure. Alma rolled her eyes, playfully flipped him off, and went back to reading her book.

Alrighty then.

Time to play ball. Jaime always performed better when he had an audience.

Jaime ran toward the goal, dribbling the ball. Carlos was an incredible soccer player. He kicked it to Santi, who advanced the ball farther. Santi passed it back to Jaime, who spiked it in.

Score!

He glanced over to see if Alma was watching. Her eyes would scan the field every few minutes, but her attention remained focused on her book. Jaime closed his eyes and remembered how she showed up for all his soccer games and used to be his biggest cheerleader.

She was silent now.

Even so, it almost felt like old times. Jaime playing ball with her brother was so natural. But today he definitely wouldn't be invited over to her parents' house for carne asada.

For the next hour, his team battled with Carlos's, who came out the winner with a final score of four versus three. During the game, a man, who Jaime figured was probably one of the organizers, spoke to Alma on the bench for a while then left.

But Alma was still there, fanning her dog. That was a positive sign.

Sweat dripped off Jaime's brow.

Carlos fist-bumped him. "Good game, bro."

"Thanks man. It feels good to play. I haven't scrimmaged much lately."

"Well, we play here every day." Carlos paused. "Join us while you're in town." He pursed his lips and looked at a muddy patch in the field. "It would be really nice if we could fix up this field. The drainage is pretty bad."

Jaime stared at the rough grass. "Well, maybe that is something I can assist with. Turf would be nice here."

"Really? It would be awesome, but you're already helping so much. Of course, I wouldn't say no. So see you next week at the meeting for the festival?"

"Yup. My brothers will get in next weekend."

"What are you going to do while you're in town?"

"I'm just going to hang low. I'm going to a charity ball with Santi for his sister. And maybe I'll head up to Sonoma for a few days." He paused. "I'll steer clear of your sister. I've caused her enough stress."

Carlos stood closer to him. "For what it's worth—she never got over you."

He paused. "I never got over her either."

Carlos looked at his sister, then back at Jaime. "She's going to kill me for this, but do you want to come over to my parents' house? They are grilling tonight. Don't worry about Alma—she has to work, so she won't be there."

Hope flowed through his body, followed by dread. Her parents would grill him instead of the meat, but he was willing to take the heat. After all, he'd enjoyed their company once—maybe they could have a pleasant time.

"Sure she won't be there? I don't want to disrespect her."

"Positive. She has to open her bar."

"Okay. Absolutely, I'll come. Thanks for inviting me."

Carlos jumped into his car. "I have a few errands to run, but I'll meet you there. You remember the address?"

"Yup. See you soon."

Carlos took off, his Honda clunking down the street.

Damn, Alma would be even more pissed off when she found out he was eating with her family, but he wasn't going to say no to her brother. And he said she wouldn't be there. What was Jaime to do? He needed to back off with her. She clearly wanted nothing to do with him. He needed to respect her boundaries.

Santi opened his Porsche's door. "You ready to go to Carlos's parents' house? Or you going to throw a Hail Mary pass to Alma?"

Jaime shook his head. "Why not?" He waved to Alma and yelled a final plea. "Nice to see you, Alma."

She turned her head. Alright, game over.

"Let's go." Jaime opened the passenger door.

"Wait!" Alma's voice rang out.

Jaime closed the door. Alma was striding toward him carrying Tequila.

"Jaime, before you go, just tell me why you came back?"

Chapter Ten

Jaime's face contorted. "Why?"

"Yes, why? Why are you in Marin? Why did you show up at my bar?"

Jaime took a deep breath before speaking. If he told her the truth, it could seem callous. Was the possibility of starting a tequila company truly the only reason he had come to Marin? She might not look too kindly on him admitting that he came up here because he was having a quarter-life crisis and wanted to ask her to teach him everything about tequila. And now, after seeing her and witnessing her reaction to him, he believed that it was an asinine idea to expect that after their past together she would be willing to work with him and that he should've never entertained the thought. But since he'd been here, he wondered if his subconscious was trying to tell him something. That he had actually come up here to see her.

Jaime considered lying and telling her that he just wanted to see her. But he took a deep breath and decided to tell her the truth. "I'm not going to lie—I did want to see you again, but that is not why I came up."

"Okay." She rolled her eyes. "So again. Why are you here?"

"I was asked to be part of a tequila campaign for a celebrity brand. It gave me the idea of starting my tequila company. I looked you up and saw you had a tequila bar so I was hoping we could work out an arrangement between us. You teach me about tequila, and I fix your socials."

Her jaw dropped open. "You're serious. Instead of hiring someone or going to Mexico and doing the work, you thought bombarding your ex at her business and convincing her to help you was a better idea?"

Damn. When she put it like that, it sounded awful. "You're right. It was stupid. Santi warned me but I wouldn't listen." Time to pivot. "I did also want to see you."

"Well, you saw me. And stopping by that one night really fucked up my business. Thanks a lot." She turned to leave.

What was she talking about?

"What do you mean by that? I was only there for a few minutes."

"Well, a few minutes was enough to do damage. There was a critic there, and he saw me yelling at you. He didn't even stay to try the tequila. He left and gave me a bad post."

Damn. He bet it was that guy he saw in the suit.

"I had no idea. What's his name?"

"Why does it matter what his name is? He left."

"Because I might know him. I can fix this."

Alma threw her hands in the air. "You're unbelievable. Why do men always think they can fix everything? I don't need your help."

Jaime didn't know about other men, but he could fix this. He would find out the critic's name. He would make this right. It was the least he could do.

"Okay. I'm really sorry about that."

She pursed her lips. "No. It's not all your fault. I should've controlled my temper."

She was so close, he felt like she was almost in his grasp.

Alma put Tequila down on the ground and poured some water from her bottle into a portable dish.

"Wait, Alma. I wanted to say I was sorry for ending our relationship so abruptly. I was dumb and stupid. We were so young, and I panicked. I can never make it up to you—I know that." Everything he said was true. But that wasn't why he showed up.

He wanted to use her. To learn about tequila. His lazy ass wanted to obtain the knowledge without putting in the effort. It wasn't her job to educate him about her life's passion. But at least he was honest with her about his intentions.

None of that mattered anymore. She was standing there in front of him. Their lips were inches away from touching. Maybe his stupid-ass idea was meant to bring him back here. Back to her.

Maybe he wanted a second-chance romance.

No. No. He definitely didn't. He was just caught up in his emotions.

She exhaled and pulled a lock of her hair. "Apology accepted. But I hope you don't have any crazy ideas about getting back together with me. You're hot, but immature as fuck."

Jaime's nostrils flared. "How would you know? You haven't spent any time with me recently. Maybe I've grown into a complete gentleman."

Santi burst into laughter. Asshole. Jaime had forgotten his buddy was sitting in his sports car listening to this train wreck.

"Fine, maybe not. I'm young. I'm allowed to be a little immature. I'm only twenty-five."

"Twenty-five is not young at all. Shit, my parents had two kids by the time they were twenty-two. You're a grown-ass man." She pointed at his shirt, which was tossed on the passenger seat. "Did you really think taking your shirt off would tempt me?"

Jaime raised his brow. "It worked, didn't it? You're at least talking to me."

"I'm not talking to you because of your body."

Her eyes raked him up and down, the heat in her gaze belying her words.

Well, at least she liked what she saw. "Then why, after all your protesting, did you finally talk to me?"

"Because I'm glad you are going to help this community. I talked to the organizer, and he told me about all the amazing programs that will be funded as part of this festival. They will be adding more community classes at the library, they will revamp the playgrounds, provide new equipment and better fields for the sports teams, and have more after-school care for residents. It's really exciting." She paused. "So I want to thank you for participating and getting Ramón and Enrique to come . . . even if your motive was just to see me. Or to start a tequila company. It doesn't matter why—your presence in Marin will be a blessing to the people of the Canal."

Satisfaction filled him. He was trying to make the world better. He was going to the charity event with Santi, he was fundraising for the Canal—he was doing good, and if he got to start his own new business venture at the same time, that'd be a bonus. "Don't mention it. I'm happy to help." He had to do something to extend this conversation. Get her to agree to see him outside this festival. "Can I please take you to dinner?"

She shook her head. "Nope. No dinner. No dates."

"Come on, babe."

She cringed at his affectionate nickname. "Don't call me that."

Fuck. *Babe?* Why had he said that? Again? It just flew out of his mouth.

"Sorry. I didn't mean to say it. It's a habit."

"I get it. Last time we were together, I was your babe. But I will never be your babe again."

We'll see about that.

No. He was crazy about her, but they were in agreement. They could never be together again.

Time to try another angle. "Fine. Then let's have a business meeting. Over lunch."

Her brow rose. "Business? What business do we have together?"

"Well, I'm only in town for a bit, but I'm realizing that I can do a lot of good here, even though I don't live in Marin. So let's see how I can help."

"Are you serious? Is this about you wanting to do a tequila line?"

Yes, Jaime still wanted to learn about tequila. And he wanted to spend whatever time he could with Alma. "I'd love to still talk to you about tequila, but I won't press it. Though I do think I could help you with your socials, and possibly even that critic. Clearly, I want to see you. I miss you. But you've made it crystal clear that we will never be romantically involved again. I respect that. And I agree, because no matter how I feel about you, I am not looking for any serious relationship. I'll take what I can get. We can be friendly right? Friends, even."

She pursed her lips. "That's fine and all, Jaime, but I know you. You don't just want to be my friend. What if I'm dating someone?"

Was she? Jaime clenched his fist. He had no right to ever have any opinion on who Alma dated. But the thought of another man kissing her, fucking her, made his head explode.

His voice lowered. "Are you?"

"Not that it's any of your business, but not at the moment, no."

Thank God. "Look. You were such a huge part of my life. You were all I had at college. You were more than my girlfriend—you were my best friend. I miss you. Maybe we can find something in what's left of us and start something new."

"Honestly, I missed you too. Like a lot. But I don't know, Jaime. You're fire. And I can't get too close to you."

"Why?" He winked. "You won't be able to resist me?"

"You cocky bastard. No, that's not it. I can and I will resist you. It's just—I was a different person when I was with you. I was fun, carefree, wild. I've changed so much. Even Zoila says so."

Zoila? Zoila was her high school friend. She was super fun, but not at all responsible like Alma was. "Zoila? You still talk to her?"

"Yeah, what's it to you?"

"Nothing. You two were just very different."

"She's loyal and has always been here for me. She's a teacher, actually, at a school over here."

Wow. Good for her. "Cool. Glad she's doing well."

"Anyway, I miss who I was when I was with you. I'm trying to figure out now if that was just because I was in college, or if you brought out a less serious side of me. I want to find that girl again." She bit her lip.

"I'm your man." He leaned in closer. He wanted to cup her face and kiss her, get lost in her and forget why he ever left her. Her brown eyes drew him in like a magnet. Ever since he left Alma, he had never felt this pull to any woman. And honestly, he rarely worked hard for anything anymore, not in his dating life nor in his work life. Everything was easy. One swipe and a new girl.

But he didn't want a new girl. He wanted his old one.

What would he do if he got her? Break her heart again probably.

No. He could never destroy her again. Or himself.

She took a step back, and a breeze from the bay accentuated the distance between them.

"No. You aren't. But I'm glad you came up here."

She wanted something from him. To feel more alive. To feel freer. Jaime puffed out his chest.

"Well, I'll extract the fun Alma. But can you do something for me?"

She squinted at him. "And what is that, exactly?"

"Teach me about tequila."

Her face contorted. "Are you that serious about the tequila line?"

"Kind of. It bothers me that all these non-Mexican celebrities have one. And I know nothing about it. It's your entire world." His voice dropped. "I want to discover why you're so passionate about it. I just want to entertain the possibility of starting a company. It's research. And in exchange, I'll work on your socials and help you get attention from that critic. Or other influential critics."

"What do you mean by that? Just running my accounts or advertising my bar? And how can you help me get more top industry reviews?"

"Whatever you want regarding socials. As for the critical acclaim, I know a bunch of restaurant and drink critics. And Ramón's fiancée, Julieta, is an award-winning chef. She also knows many people. You'd like her."

She glanced up at the sky and her face contorted. She considered his offer. After an uncomfortable pause, she spoke. "Fine. But I want to teach you something else, My Fair Señor."

He laughed. "Is this some weird *My Fair Lady* obsession? You used to love that movie. I'll have you know that I'm a perfect gentleman. I even went to Mr. Benjamin's Cotillion class in sixth grade. It was a huge thing in La Jolla."

"No, no, Jaime. You're perfectly refined. And I did love that movie. But if you are going to represent my brand, you need to learn to speak Spanish, preferably without an accent, for my video ads."

His Spanish really did suck. Learning to speak it well would give him some legitimacy in the tequila world. And he would love to have her as a teacher. "Okay. I'm game."

"Seriously? I thought you would put up more of a fight."

"Nah, I'm open to your proposal. I really want to learn more about tequila and speak Spanish, so I'm down for anything."

"To be clear—just until you leave, you will help me work on my socials and get critics' attention, and I will teach you about tequila and how to speak proper Spanish. And at the end of that, we will go our separate ways."

That song by Journey played in his head. "Sounds like a plan."

"Let's shake on it."

She daintily placed her hand in his. He fought the urge to kiss it, kiss her, and gave her a firm handshake.

"So, when can I see you again?" He wasn't letting her leave until they locked in their next meeting.

"I work all week, but I'm off on Friday."

Dammit, Friday. He was doing that charity event with Santi. And he wouldn't flake on him, not even for Alma.

"I'm sorry, Alma. But I can't." A wicked idea ran through his head. She'd said she wasn't interested in him—but just how true was that? "I have a date."

Chapter Eleven

Alma gulped. A scowl passed over her beautiful face and she clenched her fists. "A date, Jaime? You've got to be kidding me. You're a real piece of work, do you know that? Coming back into my life, flirting with me, teasing me by taking your shirt off, begging me to teach you about tequila, all the while you're courting another woman. How long exactly have you been in town? Two days? Fuck you. What the hell is wrong with you?"

He grinned. He enjoyed her hint of jealousy. "Glad to see you haven't lost your fire, though I saw the spark last night at Mezcalifornia."

"Whatever, Jaime. Deal's off. I don't want to teach you about tequila and have you fix my socials. And clearly, you will never be a gentleman and it's doubtful you will ever speak Spanish. If it was important to you, you would already speak it. I can't wait for this nightmare to end. Just show up at the festival and leave."

"Alma, relax. I'm doing a charity event for Leti. You know Leti? Santi's sister."

Alma's face softened. "You are? That's so sweet." But her smile was quickly replaced with a flash of anger. "Why did you let me work myself all up about this? You said *date*. You could've just said 'I have a fundraiser to attend,' and I would've thought you were a lovely human instead of a manipulative narcissistic jackass."

"Because." He leaned in closer. Their lips were almost close enough to touch. Her sweet scent filled the space, the space that kept these two bodies that desperately wanted to connect apart. "I wanted to see if I had any chance with you at all."

She rolled her eyes. "Well, you don't. I'm not interested in you in the slightest. I just reacted that way because I thought it was pretty shitty that you would come up here and reenter my world and immediately flaunt your dating life in front of my face. Not because I want you currently but because you are my ex."

He smirked. "Right. That's exactly why you got upset."

"You're so cocky, do you know that? I don't think it's possible to turn you into a gentleman."

"Anything's possible."

She threw up her hands. "So, Friday's out. How about brunch—on Sunday? We could go to Napa."

"I'll go wherever you want. But let me plan everything, okay?"

She shook her head. "No. I can't. I need to be in control. Let me think about it." She looked at her watch. "I need to bounce. I have to stop by my parents' house for a bit and then head to work."

He smirked, opened his mouth, and then quickly shut it without muttering a word.

"What is it, Jaime?"

"It's just—Carlos invited me to your parents' house. I'm headed there now." He started cracking up. "I swear he told me you wouldn't be there!"

Her mouth gaped open.

His gaze focused on her beautiful lips, how much he wanted to kiss them once again.

"I . . . I can't even. You're everywhere."

He pushed his lustful thoughts aside. "Hey, I'm sorry about invading your life. Tell you what—I won't go to your parents' house. It's too much. I get that. To be clear, I was going to leave you alone, but Carlos invited me to the festival, to the park to play soccer, and to your parents' house."

Her eyes raked over his body. "I appreciate that. I really do. But you should come."

Confusion rushed over him. As much as he wanted to spend time with Alma, he had to get out of there—Santi was waiting for him patiently in the car, and this wasn't how he wanted to reconnect with his ex, though he was happy to take any time he could get with her. Plus, he was intrigued that she wanted to change him. Didn't women know that a man can only change if he wants to?

Did he?

"Why? Do you want me there?"

She shook her head. "No. Not really. But my parents would love to see you. And I have to leave for work in a bit, anyway."

She had the option here to bounce, to not spend a second more of her time with him, but instead she gave him permission to go to her parents' house.

"Don't they hate me? I wouldn't blame them if they did."

"Well, they hated seeing me so fucked-up, but no, Jaime, they don't hate you. They always liked you." She gulped. "I mean, my dad thought you were going to ask him for my hand in marriage and propose to me, not dump me."

Jaime's face contorted. He had never been close to wanting to wed. "We were like twenty-two. I wasn't ready to get married." And for that matter, he still wasn't. Would he ever be? He didn't want to settle down like his brothers had. Ramón was so wrapped up in wedding planning and the catechism wedding classes, he didn't have a second to himself. And Enrique wasn't engaged yet, but Jaime had his suspicion he would be soon.

"Yeah, but they got married young. And they're happy, but it was another time. Anyway, I'm going to take off. I'll see you there."

He lightly grabbed her wrist, electricity pulsing through his body. "Can I ride with you?"

He waited for her response.

She exhaled. "Fine." She hoisted Tequila up and put her in the front seat. "Just have Santi follow us."

Score.

"And put your shirt back on, for Christ's sake."

He smirked. He opened the door to Santi's car.

"You finally done? Did she agree to go out with you?"

"Yes. Brunch next Sunday, but she won't let me plan anything. I'm working on changing her mind about that. But she's letting me ride with her to her parents' house. Follow us?"

Santi nodded. "Sure. See you there."

"Thanks, man. I owe you." Santi was the best friend—they had bonded at college over their love of craft beers and hiking, and Jaime had been there for Santi when his father died. Back in San Diego, Jaime had relied on his brothers for companionship, but now that they were so busy with their loves, Jaime often spent nights alone in his house, watching the ocean hit the rocks.

"Yeah, you do."

Jaime pulled on his shirt, shut the car door, and went to the passenger seat of Alma's Audi Q8 e-tron. It was a raspberry color.

"Nice car."

She rolled her eyes. "I know what you're going to say. But I love the color. It's called Berry Pearl. Get in."

Sí, Señorita.

Jaime placed her dog on the floor, slid into the seat next to her, but it felt odd. When they had been together, he had almost always driven, unless he had been drunk, and she'd been the designated driver. He resisted the urge to slide his hand over and squeeze her thigh.

Her pug put her paws on Jaime's seat.

"You're in her seat. She wants to look out the window."

"Got it." Jaime pulled her up to his lap, opened the window, and she stuck her enormous head out. The air blew in her face, causing sharp, light hairs to fly everywhere.

Alma blasted some Bad Bunny, and they drove through her old neighborhood. It seemed more run-down than he remembered. There were more homeless people milling around and some of the buildings didn't look structurally sound. The only parts of this city that were newly painted were the bright graffiti on the freeway underpass.

A bunch of teens loitered near a store, roughing up some other punks.

"Has crime really increased here recently?"

"Honestly, yeah, it's pretty bad. There are new gangs here from different countries fighting for turf domination. They killed some kid from the high school the other week," she said casually.

Fuck. Were her parents even safe here anymore? Was Carlos? What about Alma when she visited?

Did Jaime even have a right to ask her those questions? No, he didn't. Especially because he couldn't figure out a way to phrase them without coming off like a completely pretentious prick.

"That's horrible. I don't know what to say."

Alma glared at him. "What, Jaime?"

"What do you mean *what*?"

"I mean say what you are thinking."

Jaime shook his head. "You still know me so well."

"I don't know about that, but I know that tone in your voice."

"Fine. It's just, I know this is your community and Carlos and your parents still live here. But you moved away." He exhaled. "Maybe they could move away, too."

Alma pulled her hair on her scalp. "You're unbelievable."

"I'm serious. Your bar is doing well. Maybe you could help them move to Tiburon? Or a different part of Marin."

"Do you honestly think I haven't tried?" Alma shook her head. "Have you met my parents? Or Carlos, for that matter? They would never let me support them. Ever. And Carlos could actually afford to get his own place, but he chooses to stay and help my parents and work in his community. I'm the bitch who moved out and abandoned her family for her oceanfront condo. But Carlos would never, ever do that. He's selfless."

Her voice choked up. Fuck.

He reached over and squeezed her hand. Luckily, she didn't push him away. "I'm sorry, Alma. I didn't mean to make you feel bad."

"No, I know you didn't. It's just so hard. And I feel so fucking guilty. But I want to have my own life. And live where I work. I guess I'm just selfish."

"You aren't. I promise."

She turned on her parents' street and pulled into the driveway. Santi was right behind them.

She wiped her tears away with a tissue. "If Mamá sees my mascara running, she will think I'm crying over you."

Jaime laughed. There was the funny Alma he knew. The Alma he had loved.

"Well, thanks for not trying to make me look bad. And letting me come with you."

He opened the door and rushed around to open hers, but it was too late. She was already out of the car.

Jaime's stomach clenched. He hadn't intended on seeing her parents this trip—or ever again. He didn't want to be questioned for his actions, but he knew he deserved a reckoning.

Alma had said that her parents wished him no ill will, but was that really true? He'd broken their only daughter's heart.

And it wasn't just her parents. Her entire family seemed to be here. Jaime recognized an aunt standing in the driveway and saw an uncle walk inside with a big plate of food.

Hopefully, the next crime in the Canal wouldn't be a revenge murder—of himself.

Santi got out of the car and assessed the scene. "Wow. It's a full family day for you. When's the wedding?"

"Shut up, man. This is awkward as hell. But thanks for being my wingman."

"Anytime."

The scent of citrus and spice from the carne asada soothed his nerves. Dammit—why hadn't he asked Alma to stop at the store to buy her mother flowers?

Alma approached the door, but before she opened it, it flew open. Carlos stood there with a smug grin on his face.

Alma's parents lurked in the background. It was showtime.

"Hola, Señor y Señora Garcia."

"Hola, Jaime!" Señora Garcia pulled Jaime in close to her and squeezed him tight. "Welcome back! I missed you, mijo," she whispered into his ear. "Carlos told me you came back to help our community."

Jaime was grateful that Carlos covered for him and made his intentions for coming back into town seem honorable. But he refused to lie to Alma's mom.

"I missed you, too. But Carlos is mistaken. I'm happy to help the Canal, but I'm afraid my reason for coming wasn't altruistic." That explanation was sufficient—she didn't need the details.

Señora Garcia nodded.

Señor Garcia shook Jaime's hand and looked him dead in the eyes. "Good to see you again. We need to talk."

Great. This was great.

Jaime should've grabbed Santi and hightailed it out of there. This day was already out of hand.

But Jaime wanted to get this awkwardness over with.

"Good to see you, too. Let's talk now."

Señor Garcia's eyes looked toward the backyard. "Follow me." He led Jaime outside. A bunch of Alma's cousins and aunts and uncles were milling around. One of her cousins leveled Jaime with his eyes.

"Hey, Emilio."

Emilio nodded in acknowledgment but remained silent.

Señor Garcia stood underneath a big lemon tree, which was adjacent to a skinny lime tree. "So, you've come back to see Alma. My wife knew you would."

Jaime's throat tightened. Even worse, her family members were staring at them, talking.

"I did, sir. But not romantically. That ship has sailed. She will never forgive me." Jaime spoke the truth. Alma would never forgive him. But Jaime still wasn't sure he wanted to even try to have a relationship with her, if she could find a way to let him back into her heart. He was too young to commit, and he didn't, he wouldn't break Alma's heart again. Not that he even had the option to.

He should've never come to Marin.

"You must be patient. She still loves you. We love you."

Jaime wasn't used to people openly telling him they loved him. His family wasn't expressive with terms of endearment. He tried to tell Señor Garcia that he loved him too, but he couldn't get the words out of his mouth.

He studied the old man's face, the lines deeper, his skin more leathered than Jaime remembered. It was only three years ago that they'd last seen each other. "I have apologized to her about how I left her. I was so young and stupid. And I want to apologize to you as well."

"Apology accepted. Let's go eat."

Señor Garcia placed his hand on Jaime's back. Jaime's heart grew. Why couldn't he have backyard barbecues with his parents instead of pretentious dinners at the latest Michelin three-star restaurant with his mother and her latest boy toy, who was usually Jaime's age? And he hadn't seen his dad in a while. He wasn't even that pissed at him—Jaime knew what his dad had done with Julieta's restaurant was unforgivable, but that had been two years ago now. Ramón had repaired the damage, and the company was stronger than ever. Enrique had seen their dad recently, but Jaime still hadn't talked to him. He had justified it by saying that his father was the one who was supposed to reach out.

But at this point, did whoever would make the first move really matter?

Jaime met up with Santi at the long table full of food. Jaime loaded his plate up with tortillas, carne asada fresh off the grill, beans, rice, guacamole, and pico de gallo.

Santi grinned. "Bro, her parents are cool as fuck for inviting you in."

"Tell me about it."

"I wish I could grill with my father."

"I'm sorry, man." Jaime clapped Santi's shoulder. There were no words needed. Life was short.

Jaime took out his phone and texted his dad.

Jaime: Hey. I'm in Marin. Hope you're okay.

A few seconds later, a message popped up.

Dad: I'm good. I miss you. I'd love to have dinner with you.

Jaime: I'm pretty busy. I'll let you know when I have time.

It was a little cold, but what could his dad expect? They had never been close. By the time Jaime was born, his father had been so wrapped up in his business that he was never around.

Dad: Understand. Thanks for reaching out.

Unease creeped up on him, but Jaime couldn't focus on his father now. He walked over to Alma, who was sitting at a table, eating tacos and chatting with her cousins. She snuck a piece of meat to Tequila, who was snorting and begging under her chair.

She smirked. "Good to see you survived your chat with my father. Sorry, he can be intense."

"Nah, it was good." Jaime paused, fork halfway to his mouth. "I'm sure he's nice to all the men you bring around."

"Ha!" her cousin snorted from the other side of the table.

Alma shot daggers at him.

"What?" Jaime asked.

"She's not brought anyone home since you, bro," Carlos filled in the blanks. "Ow! What was that for?"

Alma shrugged innocently, and Jaime had to smile. She still had that fire alright.

"Have you really not dated since me?" he asked her.

She doused her taco with some Valentina hot sauce and took another bite. "*Dated* is a strong word."

"Got it."

A bitter taste filled Jaime's mouth, and it wasn't from the lime he squeezed over his meat. She said *dated,* not *fucked.* Of course, Jaime wasn't delusional enough to believe that his sexy-ass ex had been celibate since he left her. He most certainly hadn't.

But the thought of Alma naked, riding some other man, screaming his name, was almost too much for him to bear.

He forced himself to come back to the present. After their horrible reunion, she was not only speaking to him but was sitting next to him eating tacos at her parents' house. That was major progress. He had to focus on the present.

She shoved the last bit of food down her throat and then licked her lips. "I've got to run. Need to be at the bar at four."

Jaime positioned his knee to rub against hers, and she didn't move away.

"So, can I get your number to set up brunch next Sunday?"

She gazed into his eyes. The space between them was ripe with tension.

"Sure."

He handed her his phone and she typed in her number.

"You're really a good man for doing that fundraiser for Leti. I mean that."

"Thanks. I love Leti. It's a prom—I'm not her date, but I'm her host to make sure she has a good time. Every girl should have a prom. She has a great date, per Santi. Another boy she goes to school with."

Her face crinkled, and she leaned into him. Her voice lowered to a whisper. "Why, Jaime, do you have to be so sweet? It makes me remember why I loved you."

"When was I ever sweet?"

"When we first fell in love. You were always going out of your way to do kind stuff for me. Rubbing my feet when I studied, taking me to expensive restaurants you knew there was no way I could afford, so I could taste the wines on the list, believing in me."

"I still believe in you, Alma. What you've accomplished is so inspiring." He paused and pushed a lock of her hair off her face. "You don't need me. You never did."

She pursed her lips. "That's where you're wrong. I did need you then."

Jaime was careful to notice that she did not say that she needed him now in any way, shape, or form.

"I'm going to bounce. But you can come and take me to brunch next Sunday. Pick me up at my bar at ten."

Yes, score. "Where are we going?"

She pressed her lips against his cheek. "I'll let you know. But it will be dog friendly. Tequila comes with me."

"Sounds like a date."

"It's most certainly not a date. It's a business meeting. I'm glad you're back, Jaime. I missed you."

It was so simple, so easy to be around her.

Alma stood up and left the backyard.

Carlos stole Alma's chair. "You two seem cozy."

"Yeah. We're having brunch next Sunday."

"Impressive. So, I was thinking, I know you're staying with Santi, and who can beat Bolinas? But you could spend some time in the Canal."

"Sure. When?"

"We can hang out here, and I can show you the neighborhood. I think you could make a real difference, and I know I only have you for a limited time, so I'm going to milk it for all I can get. I want to take you around so you can meet people."

No. Jaime's initial thought was a hard no. He had planned to spend this break learning about tequila and hanging with Santi on the beach.

But he couldn't turn his back on the Canal. Not now.

He could go to the schools. Talk about Taco King and social media. Help Carlos coach soccer. Raise money.

And it wasn't just for Alma. It was for Carlos. It was for the boys like Victor, the little kid he'd played soccer with earlier that day.

"I'd love to."

"Cool. One more thing. Do you want to come over tomorrow night for Sunday family dinner?"

Jaime exhaled. He didn't even want to ask if Alma was coming. Carlos said family dinner, so the assumption was there.

He wanted to say no, give Alma some space.

But at the same time, he wanted to spend as much time with her as possible and their planned brunch was a week away.

"Absolutely. But this time, please, at least tell Alma."

Chapter Twelve

Alma paced around her parents' house and looked out the window at the gorgeous landscape that her father had cultivated with love. The roses bloomed in pale shades of pastels, a lime tree was ripe with luscious fruit, butterflies flitted on the milkweed, and a hummingbird and a sparrow waded in the brightly colored Talavera birdbath he had purchased and installed for Mamá. A perfectly glorious spring day.

It could've been just a lovely family dinner at home, but tonight would be awkward at best and disastrous at worst. Well, maybe not. At least this time Carlos had told her that he had invited Jaime to dinner. Carlos explained that he wasn't trying to set them up, just that he was trying to show Jaime around the Canal so he would hopefully become a long-term donor to the community. Alma understood his rationale and accepted it. But that didn't make this entire scenario any less strange.

And unfortunately for Alma, there was no chance that Jaime

would flake. He honored his commitments, and she had always known him to be a man of his word. As heart-wrenching as it was, she almost understood why he had dumped her many moons ago. They had been committed to each other when they were mere teens, and he wasn't ready to settle down. He could've strung her along long-distance for a while to keep her on call and cheat like some other men would do. But Jaime would never cheat on her after what he had gone through with his parents.

Alma couldn't believe that he had agreed to come to her parents' house not once but twice, nor could she believe they had asked him to come. He'd never even wanted to spend the night at her parents' house when they were actually dating—not that she could blame him. But his reasons back then were because he felt uncomfortable staying in their home knowing he was sleeping with their daughter.

Alma was grateful for how wonderful and progressive her parents were, despite their traditional backgrounds. Though they were immigrants who were both born and raised in Mexico, they weren't particularly old-fashioned like many of their friends were. They had no problem with her dating and had never made her feel any shame for spending the night with Jaime. In fact, she had been quite open and honest with her mother about her entire relationship with him. It helped that her parents had a loving and equal relationship. Both of them worked outside the home and they shared the domestic chores around the house, which Alma thought was pretty evolved, considering how they both had grown up.

She was blessed to have such a warm, close family, including her overprotective brother, Carlos, though she still couldn't figure out why he was acting so chummy with Jaime. It could just be because he wanted help with his festival, but Carlos was a mystery. He was fiercely private about everything in his life.

Alma extracted herself from the living room because having Jaime catch her staring out the window and waiting for his arrival would definitely not be cute.

She walked into the kitchen. The scent of cumin wafted through the air, mixing with the sweet citrus that Mamá had plucked from the backyard trees. Mamá's apron was decorated with splashes of salsa, and Papá diced onions on the chopping board. When he finished, he washed his hands and then patted Mamá's bottom. Mamá tapped him with her wooden spoon. Alma's eyes teared up, and it wasn't from the onions. How had she and Carlos been so lucky to be raised in a household full of love and equality? And as much as she had refused to let herself think about dating since she had been so focused on her business, she had to admit that she wanted what her parents had.

Ay. That was it!

It hit her like a chancla straight to her head. Were her parents plotting to get her back together with Jaime? Sure, Carlos wanted and needed his help for the Canal, but did her parents have an ulterior motive?

"Mamá? Why exactly did you ask Carlos to invite Jaime to dinner?"

Her father answered instead. "He's like family. It's not just about you—I once thought he would be my son. And he was also Carlos's friend. He's helping your brother with this festival of his to raise money for his team. The least we could do is open our home to him and serve him a home-cooked meal. The poor boy is probably staying in a cold hotel."

Alma let out a chuckle. "He's not staying in a hotel—he's

staying with Santi, who just happens to be filthy rich and lives in an oceanfront mansion in Bolinas. Oh, the horror! How could Jaime ever slum it like that?"

Mamá's eyes narrowed into a glare. "Jaime never had a close family like we have. Home-cooked meals, love, warmth. Money isn't everything."

Alma wasn't going to press, but she had to know why her parents didn't even seem to care that Jaime had hurt her so greatly.

She clenched her fist. "So it's just like old times? Full-on forgiveness? Did you forget how comatose I was after he dumped me?"

Papá placed a warm hand on her shoulder. "Mija, of course not. What Jaime did was hurtful. But you were both so young and still are. Men mature slower than women. We never expected it to last. Especially with him."

Ah, great. Even her own parents knew he would dump her. "I guess everyone saw the end coming but me." She didn't want to discuss this further with her parents. "I'll go set the table." She grabbed some plates from the cupboard next to the sink and brought them into the dining room.

Maybe her parents' odd behavior could simply be explained by the fact that she hadn't had a serious boyfriend since Jaime, and they wanted her to be happy. And Alma couldn't fully discount her parents' traditional upbringings despite the way they had adapted to American culture. Maybe they couldn't fight the notion that Alma, at the tender age of twenty-five, was an old maid. That stuff is deeply ingrained.

Carlos finally ambled in from wherever the hell he'd been. She glared at him. Had he never invited Jaime to the Cinco festival, then this dinner wouldn't be happening. Yes, yes, for the greater good. But still, it was messed up.

Carlos leaned against the dining table.

"Nice of you to show up. I'm stressing here."

Carlos laughed. "Relax. I don't know why you're so nervous—Jaime is the one who should be anxious."

"Whatever, Carlos. It's weird. You know it is. Plus, why does he have to have dinner here? The charity event is bad enough."

"I think Mamá and Papá just wanted him to feel like they've forgiven him."

Alma rolled her eyes. "It's not their forgiveness he should seek."

Carlos grabbed her hand. "I know what he did hurt you. But you are one to talk about inviting him over. Didn't you agree to teach him about tequila and how to speak proper Spanish in exchange for some help with critics and posts?"

Wow. Good news travels fast. Thanks Jaime. "I did. But that's different. It's between us. I don't want my entire family involved in my business."

Carlos burst out laughing. "You realize that you are Mexican, right? You need to get over that privacy fantasy real quick."

He had a point. "Fine. You're right. It's just, he broke me."

Carlos hugged his little sister. "I'm sorry. But you can live in the past or try to see him as the man he is now."

Was her entire family conspiring to get them back together? "I don't want to get back together with him. I can never trust that he won't break my heart."

"It's not about getting back together with Jaime. It's about forgiveness and healing. So you can move on—with someone—someday. That's the thing—you haven't moved on. You still love him. If you didn't, you would've found someone new. You're stunning and smart and successful. How many dates have you been on since he left?"

A lump grew in her throat. "I plead the Fifth."

"Right. So all we're trying to get you to do is to be open. We all see that whatever is going on with you two, the final chapter hasn't been written. Even if he is just here in town so you can finally have closure on the past and move on, then that will be worth it."

Alma exhaled. Carlos was right. Maybe the reason Jaime had appeared in her life wasn't an opportunity to get back together with him, but so she could finally forgive him and be able to move on.

Because she really needed to. She yearned to be held, to be kissed. She had closed that part off in herself for so long. But now, seeing him had stirred up all sorts of feelings and desires.

The doorbell rang. Alma's heart constricted.

Let the evening begin.

Alma slowly walked toward the door; her breathing quickened. Why was she so nervous? She had just seen him yesterday.

She opened the door and Jaime stood there holding two bouquets of flowers—zinnias in vibrant shades of violet, yellow, orange, and white. But Alma's gaze quickly left the blossoms and locked with Jaime's.

It was almost like she was seeing him for the first time.

Laugh lines bracketed eyes full of sunshine. His jawline, so strong, so pronounced, was the perfect underscore for the fullness of his lips. His shirt stretched against broad shoulders. Had he always been this handsome?

That answer was yes.

Maybe this was a turning point.

But Alma could never forget the past. Forgive, she could try. But her harrowing recovery made moving forward with Jaime an unlikely possibility.

His eyes danced up and down her body, and he grinned. "Hi. You look beautiful." He pecked her on the cheek.

What surprised Alma most was that even though they had been apart for so many years, the chemistry between them was still electric.

Mamá emerged from the kitchen, trailed by her husband and son.

"Hola, Señora Garcia. Thanks for inviting me to dinner. I brought these for you." He presented her with the flowers.

Mamá hugged Jaime as if he was her son-in-law. "Mijo, thank you for coming."

Carlos high-fived him, and Papá shook his hand.

Her brother showed Jaime this new video game he had just bought, and Jaime sat next to him on the sofa. Alma milled nervously in the background.

After a few minutes had passed, she decided she'd had enough of the awkward greeting shenanigans. It was time to start this evening. She would begin with the most important part. The beverages.

She was tempted to run to the outside bar and make them by herself, but she had decided to show Jaime how it was done since he wanted to start a liquor line.

"Jaime, I'm going to make margaritas outside. Want me to show you how?" she asked in Spanish.

His face contorted. "I understood margaritas."

Ay! How did he still not know Spanish? It wasn't his fault exactly for not being raised bilingual, but he could've taken the time to learn. Alma vowed to only speak to her children in Spanish.

"Do you want to learn how to make margaritas?"

Jaime stood from the couch fast, like a Marine called to attention.

"Sure. I'd love to."

He followed her to the patio. Alma made sure to swing her hips as she walked. She wasn't trying to tease him—just torture him a bit for good measure.

They stood alone in the backyard, her body just inches from his.

She grabbed a knife from the bar—she needed something to cut the tension.

"So, we're going to make a spicy jalapeño margarita. I'm using a high-end tequila blanco with one hundred percent blue Weber agave, but any tequila can work for this drink because it's really the flavors of the cucumbers and jalapeños that shine. This is something easy that you can whip up in advance for parties."

He tugged on her hair. "So, what you're saying is you think I buy cheap liquor."

Alma laughed. "No, I'm not saying that at all. I personally know how flashy you can be. When we go to my bar, we can do a tasting so I can show you the different intricacies of the higher-end tequilas. I wanted to make this one tonight because my mom loves everything with a kick—even her drinks."

Alma took down a clean large mason jar from the shelf. She had built this outside entertaining space for her parents once Mezcalifornia became a success. "You can chop the jalapeños."

"Seeds or no seeds?"

"I like it hot. Leave in a few."

Jaime licked his lips, and Alma's own lips quivered in response. She wanted those lips on her again. And not just on her mouth, but on her neck, on her chest, on her breasts, on her—

Focus!

The blade of the sharp knife sliced into the jalapeños quickly and efficiently. He chopped them into tiny, symmetrical pieces with finesse. "I'm impressed with your knife skills."

"I spent my entire life working in restaurants, remember?" he teased.

She pursed her lips and nodded. Mexican restaurants. Then why didn't he pick up Spanish? Didn't he want to communicate with the other cooks? The dishwashers? She wasn't going to bring it up. Yet.

"I do." The restaurateur and the tequiladora. They could collaborate.

Ay. Stop.

It was getting hot outside, and it wasn't from the sunshine. She distracted herself by doing some prep work. "I'll slice the cucumbers."

She loved pepinos and the way they cooled off the heat from the jalapeños. She very thinly sliced them up and tossed them into the jar. "Okay, so you add those jalapeños in with the cucumbers and tequila. And then you muddle them." She offered him a spoon.

His hand brushed against hers, and he grabbed the utensil. "Muddle?"

"Yes, muddle. Pretty much mashing them. The crushing helps to infuse the liquor with the other ingredients."

He stared at her old wooden spoon. "Don't you have a fancy tool for that?"

"There are many expensive muddlers and I have plenty at the bar, but at home, I just prefer an old-fashioned spoon."

"Why?"

"I don't know. Probably because I first learned how to make drinks using a spoon. I used to make cocktails for all my dad's friends and my relatives. There's something nostalgic and simple about it."

He brushed a lock of hair off her face.

Her breath hitched.

"I love that."

"What?"

"That you found a way to do something you love that originated as something you did for your family."

Alma gulped. She had never thought of her journey like that. Jaime almost made it seem predestined that she would end up where she was now. She liked his idea—it almost romanticized her life.

"Thank you."

He stared at her for a moment, smiling. "You're welcome."

She poured tequila into the jar, and Jaime began to muddle. He was doing an okay job, but he kept missing a corner of the glass. She resisted the urge to take over. His brow was furrowed, and he was trying so hard. She didn't want to micromanage him.

She took the lid and sealed the jar. "Normally I would let this sit for up to eight hours, but let's just make it now so we can have it with dinner."

"Sounds good to me. I'm starving. I've been craving your mom's cooking."

"She is a great cook. Well, the margaritas won't be as good as they could've been."

Jaime stared into her eyes. "They will be great. What's the next step?"

"You can strain everything. And I'll mix the liquor." She squeezed some limes, fresh off Papá's tree, into a bowl and grabbed the bottle of orange liqueur. After Jaime strained the tequila, she poured it, the orange liqueur, and the lime juice into a cocktail shaker, which she had filled with ice. She vigorously shook the drink, Jaime staring intently at her hands wrapped around the shaker.

She took out five glasses, ran a lime around the rims, and dipped them into her mixture of sugar, salt, and Tajín. She filled each glass with ice, poured the cocktail, and garnished each with a wedge of lime and a coin of a jalapeño.

Jaime picked up his glass. "Salud."

"Salud." They clinked the glasses and took a sip.

Jaime closed his eyes briefly. He inhaled and then exhaled and opened his eyes. "Wow, this is incredible."

Alma smiled. "Right? And they were so easy to make!" She studied him. Though they had been together for years, she didn't know too many of his childhood stories. He had never really wanted to talk about his past.

Maybe he would open up to her now.

"Do you have any fun family traditions you remember from when you were a kid?"

Jaime winced. "No. Just my parents yelling at each other."

She placed her hand on his shoulder. "I'm sorry."

"Thanks. I mean, we used to go to the Padres games together. It was fun. They were good at putting on a public face."

Alma's heart constricted. That was so sad. Her mind was racing to offer some word of comfort.

"Dinner's ready!" her mom yelled out.

Thank God.

They carried all the drinks into the dining room. Jaime pulled out her chair, and she blushed. She didn't remember him being so chivalrous. Maybe he was trying to impress her since she had given him a hard time about being a gentleman.

Her mother went into the kitchen and returned with a platter of enchiladas. Carlos and Papá brought the remaining side dishes.

Mamá served everyone enchiladas, with a huge helping of beans, rice, and salad. A simple meal, cooked to perfection by both Mamá and Papá.

Carlos said grace, and then it was time to eat.

"So, Jaime," her father started in, "I hear you want to start your own tequila company."

Jaime made strong eye contact with Papá. "I do. My father had already started Taco King when he was my age, and I really want to create my own path."

Papá nodded. "That's admirable. But why tequila?"

"So many non-Hispanic celebrities have tequila lines and ask Mexican influencers like me to promote them. The liquor is part of our heritage, and I figure why can't I do it myself?"

Alma perked up. "Wow, Jaime. I didn't know you thought about stuff like that."

He winked at her. "Stuff like what?"

"You know. Cultural appropriation."

He grinned. "With all due respect, Alma, we haven't talked in years. I've changed."

Alma pursed her lips. Had he changed? Not just when it came to relationships, but in life?

Of course he had. They were older. He'd just been a college kid then.

People can change.

Carlos relaxed into his chair. "Jaime, remember when you stole that donkey for your fraternity?"

Alma's jaw dropped. "What? I don't remember this."

Jaime burst out laughing. "Do I ever. I was dared to do it. I stole it from the mission."

"Ay, Dios mío, Jaime. From the mission? Which one? San Francisco Solano?" Alma quickly did the sign of the cross.

"No, the one in Sonoma."

She rolled her eyes. "That *is* the one in Sonoma. Didn't you take fourth-grade history?"

"Yeah, down in San Diego. I don't remember much. Anyway, I went in the middle of the night with Carlos in my truck and we stole the donkey."

Mamá swatted Carlos with her napkin. "You stole from the mission?"

"Relax, Mamá. We brought him back the next day. No one knew he was even gone."

Jaime downed the rest of his margarita. "I thought about it the other day because Enrique conned me into doing this Las Posadas event with his now-girlfriend, Carolina, and they had a donkey strolling with them."

Between bites of sumptuous food and sips of the spicy margaritas, the conversation flowed effortlessly, almost easier than it had in the past when they had actually been together. Alma's knees brushed against Jaime's leg more times than she would like to admit, and she wasn't even sure herself if it was accidental on either of their parts. She couldn't ignore their magnetic chemistry.

Memories from their past, holiday celebrations, and family chisme were shared with love. The awkwardness that Alma had expected at this dinner hadn't happened, and it couldn't have been a more lovely evening.

But that was the problem. It had been too normal. Almost like they were back together, which they certainly weren't. Even though he had changed, it could never work between them. Besides the long distance, which could possibly be resolved, they had a fundamental flaw. He didn't want to settle down. And she couldn't have a casual relationship with him.

Papá brought out Alma's favorite dessert, tres leches cake. Alma was so grateful that her mom would take the time to make it for her, because Alma never baked herself. Moist with three different types of milk, it literally melted in her mouth. Jaime devoured his slice also and went back for seconds. How did he keep his eight-pack abs?

"I gotta go. Tequila needs me."

Jaime looked perplexed. "Why didn't you just bring her?"

Mamá stroked the fabric on her armrest. "I don't want all that on my beautiful velvet sofa."

"Wasn't she here yesterday?"

"Yes! And I had to clean all day."

Alma rolled her eyes. "What about you? Are you heading out?"

Jaime shook his head. "I drank a bit too much. I'll wait until it wears off."

Mamá's eyes lit up. "You can stay here. I'll prepare Alma's room."

Jaime turned to Alma. "Is that okay with you?"

Alma nodded. "Yeah. If you don't feel safe to drive."

"I don't. But I can Uber."

"No. Just stay here. I don't mind." She looked at her Apple Watch. "Okay, I'm off."

Jaime stood up. "Let me walk you out."

She hugged her parents then quickly embraced Carlos despite the smirk on his face.

Alma went outside onto the porch with Jaime.

He took her hand, an electric shock jolting through it. "That was fun. Better than I expected it would be."

"Yeah, it was nice." Her throat tightened. "Too nice."

"I know this is weird. But I don't regret coming here."

She lowered her voice into a soft tone that hopefully only he could hear in case her parents were listening. "I just don't want to get used to you again. It's so easy between us. I'm going to miss you now, when you leave."

Jaime stared at her. "Alma, I—"

She placed her finger on his lips, silencing him. "Good night, Jaime."

Alma stepped away. But he pulled her back to him. His hands cupped her face. Was he going to kiss her? Did she want him to?

He leaned in and she closed her eyes. His lips pressed softly on her forehead.

"Good night, Alma."

Chapter Thirteen

Jaime watched Alma drive away from her parents' home, which was bizarre since he was used to being the one who'd leave.

The night had been pleasant, better than he had expected, but still made him uneasy nonetheless. He was getting closer to Alma, and he was learning more about tequila—but was he falling for her too?

He walked back into the house. Señora Garcia was waiting for him with a kind smile on her face. Jaime's heart tightened a bit. He almost never saw his own mom, nor did he even want to. He couldn't remember the last time she'd made him a home-cooked meal, and smiles were few and far between, though the judgment was rampant.

Señora Garcia handed him a fluffy folded-up blue towel. "This is for you. I have your room all prepared."

"Thank you, Señora Garcia. For dinner and for offering to let me stay here."

"You're welcome, mijo." She paused and pursed her lips.

Jaime knew that look—he'd seen her daughter make it many times. "Do you have a question for me?"

She clasped her hands in a prayer position. "Yes. I do. Why did you come back up here? It was for Alma, yes?"

Jaime exhaled, loudly enough that she could hear. He had actually come up to Marin to see Alma, but not to get back together with her. So a yes wouldn't be a lie, would it?

"I did. I wanted to see her." All true.

Señora Garcia hugged him. "I knew it. I just knew it. I told Juan that you would return. He didn't believe me. I even lit a candle."

Jaime forced a smile. A candle? Was Señora Garcia doing some Mexican candle magic love spell on him and Alma? He didn't even understand what that entailed, though Enrique had dragged him once to a curandero in Escondido. That Mexican soothsayer had been a trip. The guy had reeked of sage and weed and wore a ridiculous colorful serape. Enrique had forced Jaime to get a reading done, but the curandero didn't speak a word of English, and both Enrique and Jaime were too embarrassed to admit they didn't understand anything that he'd said.

"What kind of candle?" Jaime leaned gently against an old grandfather clock Alma's father had won on *The Price is Right* in the eighties. He must've watched that VHS tape of her father winning at least twenty times when Jaime came over to her parents' house.

"A love candle. Ven a mí."

Jaime stared at her, completely lost. His brain searched his high school Spanish knowledge for clues but came up empty. "What?"

"Return to me. But not to *me*—to Alma."

Great. Fucking great. Here Jaime thought he'd had some control over this situation, but apparently this entire idea of coming to Marin, which he'd thought originated while he was drinking tequila in La Jolla, had been all destined by some type of bruja-ha.

Should he ask her more about her little love spell? Did he even believe in this stuff? No. Definitely not. But he would still tell Enrique and ask him to explain. Later.

He needed to clarify his intent. "I don't want to mislead you—I did want to see Alma. I came up here to see her. But it wasn't to get back together with her. I wanted to learn more about tequila. I'm sorry."

She cupped his face with her hands. "That is what you told yourself. To make it easier on you if it didn't work out. But I believe you were guided back to her by that fake reasoning. Because you two are meant to be."

Her eyes were so hopeful. He couldn't crush her. "Maybe."

"Not maybe, mijo. Definitely."

Jaime gulped. Time to make his escape. "Good night, Señora."

"Good night."

He walked into Alma's bedroom. It was odd that he was sleeping in her childhood room, especially without her. There was a giant poster of Selena on the wall and another of Diego Luna. He was about to shut her door when he saw Carlos lurking in the hallway.

Might as well get all the family talk over. "Hey, man. What's up?"

Carlos shook his head. "Nada." Carlos stared at Jaime. "Actually, can we talk?"

"Of course."

Carlos walked into the bedroom and closed the door behind him.

Carlos sat next to Jaime on Alma's small twin bed, covered with a crocheted blanket her mom had made. Jaime nervously looked out the window at the citrus trees. What did Carlos want? He hoped it wasn't another guilt trip about Alma.

"Sorry again about roping you and your family into the festival, and even more sorry about giving you so many drinks that you had to stay here. I know that's super weird."

"It is a bit, but don't worry about it."

"And my mom is a piece of work. She's a die-hard romantic. And Alma hasn't been serious about anyone since you broke up so in Mamá's head she feels you are meant to be."

"I get it. It's fine. As long as Alma and I are clear. I don't want to mislead her."

"Good. Then we won't have any problems."

Carlos looked at his feet.

Jaime had been pretty close to him years ago, and he had never seen him this nervous. "You okay, bro?"

Carlos nodded. "Yeah. I am. I just wanted to ask you something."

"Anything. Shoot."

"Look. I know you are already going to fundraise and donate for the park. And I hate to beg. But my soccer program is bankrupt. The parents can't afford the dues or uniforms. You saw our field—it's shit. There are so many talented players down here, and they honestly don't have a chance. It's not fair."

Jaime exhaled. Carlos was right. "It isn't fair."

"And, I haven't told Alma this, but I'm not going to be able to continue being a coach. I need a job. I can't keep living with my parents, even though they say they don't mind. I'm twenty-seven. One day, I want to have my own family and my own house. Which probably won't be possible in Marin."

He was right about that. Gentrification had taken over San

Rafael. There were hardly any homes under a million. It was impossible for most families to ever dream of owning a home in the community they grew up in.

"I'm sorry, man. I don't know how I can help."

Carlos turned to Jaime, his eyes pleading. "Don't you have a foundation? I mean, doesn't the Montez Group?"

"We do. There is a board of directors. We do mostly charity in San Diego. Restaurant worker funds. Food shortages. That kind of stuff."

"That's great. And really important. But I know how much you love soccer. And you are super talented, not just saying that to butter you up. It's true."

"Thanks." Jaime lived to play soccer when he was younger. He'd had all the resources to make his dreams a reality. But his father didn't want him to pursue being a professional. Jaime wished he had pushed back.

Carlos stared into Jaime's eyes. "I'm asking you to consider funding a world-class club soccer program here in the Canal. Pay for top coaches. Buy uniforms and equipment for the kids. The children here are so talented and can go all the way. But they don't have the opportunities. I don't know anyone else to ask. And I know you have already done so much but I'm going to shoot my shot."

A burst of hope flooded Jaime. He could do this. He could make a proposal to the board and fund this. Something he loved. Something he was passionate about.

But he didn't want to overpromise and underdeliver. If he told Carlos he could do this, he needed to be a man of his word.

"Bro, it's a great idea. And I will do everything in my power to make it happen. Let's talk the logistics tomorrow."

Carlos beamed. "Thank you. I'd like to be the director if possible. I'm more than qualified." He laughed. "And maybe, if you're interested, I'll hire you as a coach."

Jaime smirked. "I'd like that." And it would be one way for him to stay in town.

Near Alma.

"Night."

"Good night. Thank you."

Jaime got ready to sleep, lying down in Alma's bed. He felt a sense of peace wash over him.

And for the first time in a long time, he was proud of himself.

He hadn't always just been a vague pretty boy—once he'd had substance, he'd been someone others found friendly and nonjudgmental. That was worth being happy with, and he could make a difference in so many people's lives.

Jaime smoothed the lapels of his black tuxedo. Tonight, he was hosting Leti and accompanying her to her dance.

He thought back to his own prom—which he didn't even attend. He and a bunch of his buddies hijacked the limousine his dad had rented and headed to Mexico. They partied at this nightclub on an abandoned ship in Ensenada, dined on lobster in Puerto Nuevo, and then drank all night on the beach. His father was livid when he found out where they had gone. He'd grounded him for a month, but that didn't stick. Jaime just waited for his dad's next business trip and went back to his usual antics.

Man, his high school years were nothing like those of his friends in normal, stable families. What would his life have been like if he had ever been given rules and boundaries and had punishments enforced when he broke them? Maybe he wouldn't have turned into such an entitled prick.

Maybe he never would've broken Alma's heart.

But tonight he was going to this prom. He would make sure that Leti had a great time.

Jaime pulled up at Santi's mother's house, where she was standing outside with her son.

For a moment, Jaime imagined Santi's dad standing with them. He would've loved to see his daughter go to prom. It was so unfair that cancer had taken him away from his family.

Jaime climbed out of his car and joined them, hugging Santi's mother.

She hugged him back. "Jaime, you look so handsome. It's been too long."

"Yes, it has. I haven't seen you since graduation." Another milestone Jaime's dad didn't make it to. He was on a very important business trip. "How have you been?"

"Good, I guess."

Santi slapped his hand, and they engaged in a bro hug. Santi held a fancy-looking camera. Jaime guessed his latest iPhone wasn't going to cut it for tonight.

"Thanks again for doing this, man. She's so excited."

"My pleasure." He clutched the sweet-smelling corsage he'd bought her, a mix of white roses and baby's breath. "Where's Leti?"

"Inside with her date, Ben. He's a nice boy. She can't wait."

"Awesome."

Jaime followed Santi and his mom into her home. She lived in a sprawling ranch in Sleepy Hollow, in San Anselmo. They had a stable full of horses that Leti loved to ride. Santi had actually taught Jaime how to ride during long weekends away from college.

It was so peaceful and serene out here—definitely different from his San Diego beach house, where tourists, influencers, and grifters hung out on his front lawn.

A teen in his tux stepped into the hallway.

"Hi. I'm Ben."

Leti's date extended his hand to Jaime, who gave him a firm handshake. "Hi Ben. I'm Jaime. I'm an old friend of Santi's. Are you excited?"

"Yes. It will be so fun."

Santi's mom offered Jaime something to drink but he declined. After a few minutes, the light tapping of heels on the tile alerted them to Leti's arrival. Dressed in a long pink ball gown that was adorned with sequins, she had a big smile on her face when she saw Jaime.

"I didn't think you would come."

"I wouldn't miss it. You look beautiful, Leti."

She twirled around in her dress. "I feel like a princess. This is better than my quince."

Jaime placed the corsage on her wrist. "Hope you like it. I've actually never bought one of these."

She lifted the flowers to her nose and inhaled the scent. "It's so pretty and smells so good. I love it. Thank you."

Jaime glanced at Santi's mom, who was dabbing her eyes.

Santi put his arm around his sister. "I wish Dad was here. You are so pretty."

They hugged. He may not have been close with his family, but at least they were alive.

Maybe Jaime needed to do more. Maybe he needed to try harder with them.

Santi escorted everyone out the door. "Have a good time." He lowered his voice. "Thank you."

"Don't mention it."

A flash went off, and then more. Santi was snapping photos like he was a paparazzo. Jaime grabbed the camera from him and took some family photos.

Leti's best friend, Tanía, showed up with her date, John. Santi would be hosting her. Santi took some more pictures of the girls dressed up together.

The limo took the group to a restaurant in Mill Valley. The prom was held in the banquet area, and it had been transformed into an under-the-sea theme. Lights twinkled on the ceiling like stars in the sky and the floor was lit in an aquamarine tone and had holograms of fish swimming projected over it. Absolutely spectacular.

What had his prom been like? His date had been so angry at him for wanting to go to Mexico that she went to the prom without him. It had been downtown in some fancy hotel. Looking back, he regretted not going.

Jaime didn't mind hosting Leti at all, but he did feel a little bit awkward being surrounded by so many high school kids.

A dance song blared through the speakers.

Ben and John had wandered off.

"Do you want to dance?" Jaime asked.

Leti took his hand before he had a chance to take hers. "Yes."

He took her arm and led her in a West Coast Swing. She followed wonderfully.

Those ballroom classes his mom had forced him to take had really paid off. He did a rock step and then threw her into a small dip. She laughed and threw back her hair. She didn't miss a beat.

"Wow, Leti. You can dance."

"Yes! My mom put me in lessons. I'm on the cheerleading team. I love dancing." Joy graced her face.

She was having so much fun and honestly so was Jaime.

The next song was a ballad. Ben had returned and cut in. Ben and Leti swayed to the music at a close but respectful distance.

After a few more dances, Leti and her friend Tanía went outside. Jaime walked over to the refreshment bar and grabbed a cup of punch for himself.

A girl walked up to him. "Excuse me, are you Jaime Montez?"

"Yes."

Her eyes widened. "Oh my God! I told my friend it was you, but she didn't believe me. What are you doing here?"

Jaime didn't know how to take that question, since the answer was obvious, but gave the girl the benefit of the doubt, that she wasn't being rude and was just curious. "I went to college with Leti's brother. I'm happy to escort her."

"Wow. That's so cool that you would do that. I never thought someone like you would do something so cool."

Jaime paused. "What do you mean?"

"Oh, you know. I mean, I follow you on Insta. You just seem to be a typical influencer. Like you only do something or post something if you're getting paid."

Jaime winced. "I can see how you would think that. Good night." He wasn't mad at this girl. She was right. Normally, he didn't do anything he wasn't paid for.

He had been a douche. And though he'd come up to Marin to learn about tequila, and he'd had an ulterior motive for going into Alma's bar, Jaime had agreed to escort Leti to prom because he had wanted to. It was as simple as that.

Maybe there was hope for him.

Leti waved at him, and she and Tanía walked over to have

some punch. Tanía, Ben, Leti, and John danced a few more songs.

Santi nudged his sister. "Save a dance for your brother?"

She nodded and he led her to the dance floor. Jaime took out his phone and captured some pictures of them.

After they were all danced out, the girls took their dates to the dessert table, with Santi and Jaime following. It was filled with pastries, cookies, cakes, and mini pies.

Leti chose the chocolate cake, and Tanía had a mini apple pie. Ben and John made root beer floats.

"Is it good?" Jaime asked Leti.

She smiled and forced him to eat a bite of his own cake. "Jaime, only think of the cake."

Jaime inhaled and enjoyed the dessert. He focused on the bitterness of the chocolate, the moistness of the cake, and the sweetness of the whipped cream. He didn't think about anything else but the taste.

At the end of the night, the limo took them back to Santi's mom's place, where Santi and Leti's mom, Tanía's mom, Ben's mom, and John's mom were all waiting. Jaime opened up Leti's car door and walked her inside.

"Good night, Leti. I had a great time."

She wrapped her arms around his neck in a tight hug. "I did too. It was the best night of my life." She ran inside and started talking to her mom in the kitchen.

Santi bid Tanía, Ben, and John goodbye and sat on a swing on the front porch with Jaime.

Twinkling stars lit up the sky like jewels. Horses neighed in the background and Jaime could've sworn he heard a distant coyote bay. The fragrant smell of orange trees from the grove filled the air.

Santi put his hand on Jaime's shoulder. "Thanks again, man."

"Seriously, don't mention it. I had fun. I was shocked what a good time I had."

Santi shook his head.

Jaime looked at him. "What? I did."

"Oh, I don't doubt that. It's just you."

"What does that even mean?"

"You. You're this great guy, Jaime. Like you really are. But you are so hard on yourself, and you think you're such an asshole. You aren't. You had a rough family life and you fucked up with Alma, but you can't keep beating yourself up about it or living in the past. You have to move on. Allow yourself to be happy."

Jaime rolled his eyes. "Pot, kettle. You don't enjoy your life. You work like a maniac—dare I say more than Ramón used to."

"Fair. I'm a workaholic. But since my dad died, I support my family. I don't have a trust fund like you do—I have to work and make sure they are provided for, and that Leti gets the care she needs. Next year she will be going into an assisted-living program, and they will help her get a job."

Jaime understood circumstances were different for Santi. He was creating a first generation of wealth like Jaime's father had, whereas Jaime did work and provide for himself, but he'd always had his family money to fall back on. Since college, he'd also received all his opportunities based on his name—well, and his looks.

He yearned to be more than just a pretty face. More than just a fuckboy.

He desired to be a good man. "You're right. I've just been believing the narrative that I'm an asshole and embracing it. I'm better than that."

"You coming back to my place tonight?"

Honestly, he wanted to be alone. "No. I'm going to check into the Lodge. But I'll come by your place when my family gets in."

The Tiburon Lodge. He checked to see if they had a room, and he lucked out. He quickly booked it. The hotel was a block from Alma's bar. And her place.

He wasn't planning on bothering Alma. No. He would give her space. But just being in the same town as her comforted him.

"Sounds good. I can drive you?" Santi offered.

"Nah. It's okay. I'll Uber so you can spend time with your family."

"Thanks. Night, man."

"Night."

Jaime ordered the ride. Once in the vehicle, he relaxed on the drive from San Anselmo to Tiburon, and reflected on the night. He loved being around Leti. She lived in the moment and her joy radiated. She was happy just dancing and talking. Jaime was always living in the past or the future.

His whole reason for this trip was future motivated. But what if he lived in the present?

Maybe he could change now.

Maybe he could be as happy as Leti if he could just try to let go.

Damn, he sounded like fucking Enrique.

Jaime's driver dropped him off at the Lodge. He checked in and entered the room. It wasn't a luxury hotel, but Jaime liked its simplicity. And he loved the location.

He looked at himself in the mirror. The night was still young, and he wanted to take a stroll on the water, get some fresh air, and look at the bridges. He didn't have any clothes with him, so he had nothing to change into even if he wanted to. It was the tuxedo or a hotel robe, so to not get arrested for indecent exposure, he opted for the formal attire.

But Alma's bar was on the pathway of his walk, and she could never resist him in a tuxedo.

Dammit. He promised himself he wasn't going to stop by her bar.

He left the hotel and walked toward the water. A few older couples were walking hand in hand. Tiburon was such a safe, quaint town; it almost had a magical feel to it.

After strolling around the block, he ended up at Alma's bar after all. He took a moment to watch her work. She was chatting with her patrons and racing around the bar. A few guys were checking her out, which shot a spark of jealousy through Jaime. The thought of another man touching her, kissing her, licking her, fucking her, was excruciating to him.

He had pushed those thoughts out of his head for years. But tonight, it became clear.

He wanted Alma back. Not just for tonight.

But possibly forever.

He'd sworn he wasn't going to walk in, but he couldn't resist. She was like a magnet.

He couldn't not see her.

Jaime took a deep breath and opened the door.

Chapter Fourteen

The door to her bar opened and Jaime sauntered in, though for some reason he seemed less cocky than usual. Alma's heart beat rapidly when he stood in front of her. His eyes raked over her body, and she shuddered under his gaze. She felt so exposed, as if she was naked in front of him.

Or maybe she just wanted to be naked. Desperately. Being near him was always so intoxicating, like the finest tequila. He was strong, spicy, delectable.

Damn, that man was fine. His strong jawline, his adorable dimples, those lips! And he was wearing a goddamn tuxedo, for Christ's sake. The black fabric stretched over his broad shoulders, his defined chest puffing out of his vest as if it were made for him.

What was he doing? Trying to kill her?

Alma took a deep breath, trying to be cool. "Wow, Jaime. You clean up nice. I haven't seen you in a tux since that Young Hispanic Leaders Gala you dragged me to in college."

He smirked. That sexy stupid smirk she hated and loved at the same time. "I remember that night. Every man had his eyes on you. But you were all mine."

Were was the operative word. Were, was—all in the past.

But she no longer wanted to live in the past. She wanted to be present. *Be Here Now* like the guru Ram Dass said. She had clearly grown up in Marin, a former hot tub–hippy enclave in the Bay Area that had esoteric spiritual leaders. Many of her non-Mexican friends in grade school had parents who'd raised them in his commune, which had horrified her Catholic mother.

"They did. But the only one I wanted was you." *Was that too strong? Dial it down woman.*

She changed the subject. "How was prom?" She poured a shot of tequila for an anxious patron at the bar and slid it to him.

Jaime whipped out his phone and showed her some pictures of him, Santi, Leti, and her friends. "It was wonderful. Leti is so sweet, and she had such a great time. I'm glad I could take her."

Leti looked lovely in the pictures. This simple act of kindness Jaime displayed toward Leti made Alma soften toward him. He couldn't be a complete jerk if he was willing to escort her to prom with no ulterior motive.

"She looks beautiful. That was nice of you to escort her and her date."

"Honestly, I had fun. It feels good making others happy."

Nothing he said sounded like a line that he was trying to use to impress her. He seemed, well . . . genuine. She reminded herself that this wasn't some guy who was trying to pick her up at the bar. This was Jaime. The only man she had ever loved. She had always thought deep down he was a good guy, just a bit of a mess, but who wasn't?

He sat down on a stool in front of her.

"Do you want a drink?"

A guy yelled at her. "Hey lady, can I get another shot?"

Alma was reminded that they were not alone. "Coming right up."

She was still running a bar full of people. And unlike the first night that he had come in, she wasn't going to bring her personal life into her business life. She winced, remembering how she'd yelled at him in the crowded room, dramatically tossing out his business card. She still hadn't heard from that critic, but either way, she never knew who was in her bar, and with everyone having cell phones, she was most certainly not going to make another scene.

And she had finally accepted the fact that it wasn't Jaime's fault that the critic left. She had screwed herself and might never get that opportunity again. Yes, Jaime had surprised her, but she should've been able to control her temper. It wasn't professional of her. Alma planned to make an appointment with her therapist to deal with her anger.

She served the man a drink, and then turned back to Jaime. "Drink?"

A patron pointed a camera toward her. Maybe the girl was just filming the bar, but maybe she was filming Alma. Her luck, she would go viral on TikTok for drooling over her ex.

She instinctively wiped her mouth just in case she was actually drooling. Her red lipstick stained the cloth. She imagined that red tint marking up Jaime's shirt, his chest, his abs.

Stop!

Jaime glanced at the back wall behind her, giving an impressed nod. "I'd love one. What do you recommend?"

"Our special is our blackberry margarita."

“I’ll take that.”

“Coming right up.” She muddled the fresh blackberries, the dark juice tinting the glass. Then she added the rest of the ingredients and finished making his drink, placing it in front of him. “Anything else? Are you hungry?”

He bit his lip. “Actually, I see something I’d like to snack on.”

She tilted her head to the side. “What did you have in mind?”

“You.”

She laughed. He was just flirting, clearly not serious. “I’m not on the menu, but nice try.” She grabbed a laminated menu from behind the bar, wiped it down, and shoved it in front of him.

He perused the menu. “Actually, I’d like to do an official tasting tonight. Tequila tasting, I mean.”

She glanced at her watch. Quarter until midnight. Two more hours on the clock. “Maybe after hours. I can serve the flight, no problem, but I won’t have time to explain everything to you about the tequilas. Not with all these other people to serve. We’re understaffed tonight.”

“No worries, then. I’m good for now.”

A man in a white collared shirt flagged her down from the other end of the bar. She motioned toward Jaime. He took a sip of the margarita and licked the salt from the rim. Ay, she was jealous of the salt.

“I need to get back to work. I hope you like your drink.”

“It’s delicious, thank you.”

She escaped from the bar, and from the sexual tension, and walked over to the customer. After attending to that party’s needs, she checked in on a few other groups, went back to the kitchen to order some more appetizers, and then returned to Jaime. A few beautiful girls at the bar were staring at him, tossing their hair and batting their eyelashes in his direction. She honestly couldn't blame them.

Alma tossed her own hair. Jaime winked.

She was doomed.

"About that tasting." He licked his lips. "How about we do it when everyone else goes home tonight? You and I, alone. Then you have all the time to teach me about tequila."

Her hands shook. She'd be alone with him. Truly alone. For the first time since they'd broken up. Sure, she had been alone with him making margaritas at her parents' house, but in her restaurant, a block away from her king-sized bed in her condo seemed different. Like there was no going back. This was the point of no return, and for once, she was being honest with herself about what and who she wanted.

She wanted Jaime.

Tonight. She craved the way he'd once made her feel, the pleasure he'd given her, a joy that she had not experienced since and wasn't sure she ever would with that intensity again.

"I'll think about it." She paused. If he was going to sit here all night and wait for her to get off—er, get off *work*, then he could help out. He grew up in the restaurant business; he had to be useful.

She threw him an apron that was tucked behind the bar.

He scratched his jaw. "What's this for?"

"If you want that tasting tonight, you're going to have to work for it. It's only midnight. We don't close for a couple more hours."

Jaime hopped off the stool, grabbed the apron, and tied it around his muscular body.

He walked behind the bar and whispered in her ear, "What would you like me to do?" His hot breath blew on her neck, and she melted.

Me? Here? In front of all these people?

Ah, the thought of him taking her, going down on her on the bar, everyone watching, excited her. What had gotten into her? She'd never had an exhibitionism kink before.

Her mind was wild. Time to focus. What had he asked her?

Oh, right, how to help. She scanned the bar. Little green orbs beckoned.

Limes! Limes are good. She knew from the previous night that his knife skills, like all his skills, were impeccable. She handed him a sharp knife. "Okay, please slice some limes and these jalapeños."

"Sí, Señorita." He washed his hands in the sink and then stood behind the counter.

She placed a chopping board in front of him and he went to work. She tried not to hover over him and watch him, but he fascinated her. His slicing skills were on point. Hell, she'd hire him. Not that he needed a job. Or lived here. Or that them spending any more time together was remotely a good idea.

Two weeks ago, she'd been completely focused on her job and on hopefully getting a great review from that critic.

And now, her mind was all over the place and she was fantasizing about her ex fucking her in her bar in front of her customers.

She forced herself to pretend he wasn't there and went back to making cocktails and chatting with patrons. On this spring pre–Cinco de Mayo day, the bar was busier than usual, for which she was grateful. Another party of gorgeous women walked over to the bar and beelined straight for Jaime. Alma greeted them and asked for their orders, but they ignored her. *Alrighty then.*

One of them pointed at Jaime. "He can make my drink."

Alas. A flash of her getting so jealous when they were younger after girls would hit on him in front of her. But this time, she just smiled. "He's not a bartender. I am. But I'll make sure he personally slices your garnishes. Now what can I get you ladies?"

The girls ordered a variety of fruity margaritas. One stared at Jaime, but he didn't even meet her gaze. Alma served the ladies the drinks and they went to their table.

One of her other barbacks, José, pointed to Jaime. "Who is that? Did you hire someone new?"

"No. His name is Jaime. He's just . . . helping me tonight."

José cackled like a hyena. "Helping you with what?"

"José. Do you have something to say?"

"Nada, mi jefa."

But she knew José could see right through her.

Jaime glanced up once or twice toward Alma from his prep station and smiled but didn't lose his focus.

Alma sighed. Jaime had crushed her at the end of their relationship, but the one thing she could say about him was that he had never cheated on her nor had a wandering eye. And he'd always made her feel like the most beautiful woman in the world.

And she still felt like that in his presence.

Right after the clock hit two, Alma escorted the last guests out. "Good night!" The brisk bay air blew into the bar. José and her other remaining employees closed up the bar, cleaned up, counted the till, put misplaced items away, and swept the floor. Finally, when they finished, Alma quickly shut the door and locked it after her employees left.

Now she was alone with Jaime.

He slowly walked toward her, his gaze on her lips, and she was certain he was going to kiss her, but instead he sat at a table overlooking the ferries, which were draped in lights and docked outside.

What was she doing? Did she want to hook up with him? Could she handle it?

"So, how about my tasting?" he asked.

Right. The tasting that she had promised him.

The earthy scent of agave permeated the room from all the tequila she had served. Alma was high on the fragrance that mixed with Jaime's masculine scent. "Coming right up."

She went behind the bar and put together a tray of six different types of special glasses designed for each type of spirit. She placed some accoutrements, some of which Jaime had chopped himself, in a few bowls and brought the platter to the table.

Jaime smiled as she walked toward him. She also placed an assortment of bottles of tequila on the table.

"Tonight, My Fair Señor, we will be tasting six types of tequila. Blanco, joven, reposado, añejo, extra añejo, and cristalino. Each sip will take you on a journey through Jalisco, a chapter in our country of origin's rich history."

His voice dropped to an intense, deep tone. "Why don't we actually go to Jalisco?"

"What?" Did he know she was planning to go with Zoila?

"It would be fun. I've never been there."

"Well, I'm actually planning to go in a few weeks for business. But it's a work trip."

Jaime paused. "Alone? You're going to Mexico alone? I don't think that's a good idea."

"Okay, Papá."

He clenched a cloth napkin. "That's not what I meant, Alma. Don't twist this."

Breathe. He was just being protective. "I appreciate your concern but I'm not going alone. I'm going with Zoila."

"A work trip? With Zoila?"

"Yes, with Zoila."

"Whatever, Alma. I just want you to be safe. Promise me you'll be careful."

She appreciated his concern even though it was totally misplaced. They were no longer together. "I'll do my best. Back to the tequilas." She pointed at the glasses.

Jaime relaxed back into his chair. "You're so fucking sexy. Do you know that?"

"Pardon, Señor. This is a dignified tasting," she teased.

He rubbed his hands through his hair. "I apologize. Continue, please." He undid his bow tie, so it hung around his neck, and undid the top few buttons on his shirt. A wisp of chest hair peeked out and she gulped.

He grinned and undid one more button.

Alma pulled herself together.

She raised the first bottle; the clear liquor caught the reflection of the moonlight. "To start, we have the blanco." She poured a small amount into his glass. "If you notice, the shape of this glass is tall and slender, which is supposed to funnel the sensation to your mouth."

He took a small sip. "This is exquisite."

"Enjoy the floral notes; it's sweet and soft." She took a glass from behind the bar and poured her own sip. She was off work now. What was the harm in partaking?

Jaime's eyes closed for a moment. They opened and met hers. "I was taking a beat to enjoy it. It's light."

Alma gleamed. She had rarely met anyone, man or woman,

who seemed to appreciate tequila as much as she did. She was constantly rattling on and on about her love of this spirit, and most people she encountered just wanted to get drunk or drown out the liquor, either blended with fruit or masked by some other alcohol.

But as far as she could tell, Jaime seemed to truly enjoy the object of her affection.

And now they were both enjoying her favorite blanco together. "This is best in a margarita or a paloma. It can be aged, but often goes from the still to a tank to the bottle. That is why it's white or silver in color."

Jaime downed the rest of his glass, and she drank hers too. When in Rome. Or Mexico. Or Tiburon.

"For our next tequila, we have the reposado, which means rested. It is aged in barrels, which gives it the golden hue. This one is smoother on the palate. You can use it in any recipe that calls for blanco, but I like it simply with a slice of lime and a sprig of basil. And notice this glass—it's shorter so it directs the aromas of the drink to your nose so you can smell the elements."

Jaime lifted the drink, swirled it around the glass, and inhaled. "Smells heavenly." He took a small sip. "I've never tasted anything like that. This one is woodsy."

"Yes! That's the oak notes!" Her mouth widened into a smile.

He took another sip. "It's so exciting to taste them the way they are meant to be savored."

"It totally is. And now, we have the joven, which means . . ." she prompted Jaime. His Spanish sucked but he should get that one at least.

"Young, Alma. I'm not an idiot."

"Not saying you are. Not learning Spanish isn't your fault—it's part of generational trauma."

Jaime rolled his eyes. "You sound like Enrique."

"Oh, I didn't know he was so in touch with our cultural issues."

"Yeah, he's really into that stuff. He sees a therapist every week. It's not really my thing—I spent enough time in therapy as a kid."

Alma winced. She had hoped over the years that Jaime would seek therapy for his complex family issues, but she realized it was rarer for a man to get mental help than for a woman. It wasn't her place to nag, but she couldn't help but try to encourage him.

"You should go to therapy again. Seriously. It's super helpful for me." She put a hand on his.

He squeezed hers. "It's not my scene, but I like talking to you."

He leaned closer to her, their lips so close.

She pulled away. Tequila. Tequila.

"So about the next type of tequila. This is joven. Yes, it's young. It is blanco mixed with reposado. It's a sipping tequila. Some cheaper tequilas will have additives and will present as joven or gold, but you wouldn't want to sip them, or you'd have a headache."

He laughed at her joke and took another sip. "That one is nice."

"I like it. It's a good blend and a gorgeous color."

He raised his brow. "You're gorgeous."

Alma twirled her hair. She knew the look that he was giving her. He wanted her. He was going to make his move. And she didn't have the willpower to say no.

And she didn't want to say no. She wanted to say yes, yes, and oh, yes.

But they still had more tequilas to taste, and she was enjoying this foreplay. "Jaime. Pay attention. You begged me to do this."

"I'm sorry. Go on."

She downed another shot. She wasn't drunk by any means;

over the years she had built up her tolerance to alcohol. She was buzzed but she was in complete control of her actions and desires.

"And now, we have the añejo. To be an añejo, it has to be aged for at least one year, up to three. The shorter glass is so you can appreciate it with all the senses. This one can also be sipped or can be used like a whiskey in an old-fashioned. You will taste some vanilla and bourbon notes."

He raised his glass to his lips. If she could be that glass. Gone was the boy she fell in love with, the one she hated, the one she'd cursed. Sitting across from her was a man. A mature man who was interested in her and her work.

"This is my favorite so far. I've never thought to substitute it for whiskey."

"Most people haven't. I love the sweet flavors in it. Okay, so next we have the extra añejo, which has been aged over three years. This one is rich and luxurious. It's a bit bold. It does well in a Manhattan."

He locked eyes with her and sipped. "Wow. That one is strong."

"It is. It's an acquired taste, but I love it."

He brushed her face. "What else do you love?"

You. No. She had to love something else. "My dog. Tiburon. My life."

"I love the life you built, too. I'm so proud of you, Alma."

"Thanks." Man, it was hot in here. "And our final tequila is the cristalino. It is white like a blanco, but it is actually an añejo or extra añejo that has been filtered with charcoal, which strips the color. You can sip this one pure or mix it. It's kind of the best of both worlds."

He lifted the glass to his mouth and drank. "Now this is my

favorite. I knew there were so many different types of tequila and had read about the differences, but it's nothing like tasting them."

"Yes, it's so important to really try them. And tequila is just the beginning. Then we can get into mezcal."

"I have a confession, Alma."

She crossed her arms. "What?"

He stood up and stepped toward her. She didn't step away. Then he came closer, and closer, challenging her.

Alma didn't back away.

"I've been watching you all night, counting down the minutes until I could kiss you."

Ay, this man.

Jaime slammed Alma against the wall, pressing his hard cock to her stomach.

His mouth took hers and she welcomed it.

This wasn't their first kiss. Far from it. Maybe it was their thousandth.

But Jaime had never kissed her like this.

Every day that they had been apart made Alma kiss him harder and deeper.

She never wanted this kiss to end.

From tasting tequila to tasting Jaime, their night and their relationship had evolved into something that was as rich and complex as the finest añejo.

Chapter Fifteen

Alma forced herself to pull away from him, but she didn't want to.

She wanted to lean in for more. More kissing. All the kissing. Jaime's tongue in her mouth, licking her body, tasting her—

Jaime's eyes were wide. Hopeful.

"Alma, I, we—"

This is what she had wanted all night. To be with him, to sleep with him, to reunite and experience the passion they shared.

But now that it was right in front of her face, she couldn't do it.

She wanted to so, so badly, but she couldn't give in when she was still so hurt.

"Jaime. I think you should go. Now, please."

He nodded. "Can I at least walk you home? It's late."

"It's safe here, Jaime. I don't need you to walk me a block. I do get myself home every night after work perfectly fine."

Jaime shrugged his shoulders. “Okay.” He walked toward the door. Alma hated to see him leave but knew it was the right choice.

He turned back toward her. “Are we still on for brunch on Sunday?”

Alma should’ve said no. This, whatever this was, had gone on long enough. She should limit their interaction to the festival. He could honor his commitment to help her with her socials, but he didn’t need to be around her for that. And he could easily arrange to get that critic to come without getting her involved. She had already taught him a bit about tequila tonight; a simple Spanish lesson for when he promoted her bar should be sufficient, right?

There was no need to go to brunch on Sunday.

But she wanted to.

“Yes. You can pick me and Tequila up here at ten.”

“Did you make reservations?”

Dammit. She had totally spaced. “No. But I can now.”

He squeezed her hand. “Let me take care of it.”

She exhaled. “Okay. That’s fine. Good night, Jaime.”

He exhaled. “Great. Good night, Alma.”

He left the bar, and she locked the door behind him. She quickly cleaned up the tequila tasting, wiped the countertops. She rubbed her eyes. It had been a long night. She locked up the bar and walked the quick distance to her home.

On Sunday morning, Alma milled around her condo frantically. She should’ve canceled this brunch when she had the chance. But she couldn’t deny how much fun she’d been having with Jaime. Maybe this day would give her the closure she needed to move on . . . or move forward.

She curled her long hair so it framed her face, applied her makeup in natural tones with just a hint of sparkle, and spent a full hour choosing a dress, finally settling on a white sheath that was slightly transparent, without being too tacky, and flowy, not form-fitting. She still wasn't sure what she wanted, if anything, from Jaime, but either way she wanted to make his mouth water.

She had to admit that his reemergence in her life was exciting. Lately, she had been in such a rut. She had one focus, making her bar the best. She wasn't proud of the fact that this had caused her to withdraw from her family and friends. Just being involved in the festival would be a welcome change from her daily routine.

Jaime would be on his way to pick her up at her bar. Why had she not only agreed to go out with him but also suggested brunch? She could've said coffee. Coffee was easy and quick. Brunch was not a quick day date, well, definitely not with Jaime. Back when they were together, they would drive somewhere in the wine country, have long, luxurious meals complete with lots of wine and indulgent desserts. Then they would spend their days shopping in the cute local boutiques and finally check into a hotel and stay up all night making love. It had all been so easy, so effortless. She was so in love with him back then that their past seemed like an endless stream of dates and decadence.

She secured the leash on Tequila's pink harness, checked her reflection in the mirror one last time, and locked her condo door. As she walked the block to her bar, her refuge, she saw Santi's orange Porsche drive up the street. But Santi wasn't driving nor was he anywhere to be found; not that she had expected him to show up. It was Jaime who was in the driver's seat.

There was no turning back now. She was about to spend significant time with her ex.

He pulled up to a loading zone near the turnabout, stopped the car, and opened the door for her. He wore a perfectly fitted blue suit with no tie. He looked like a movie star.

"I told you to meet me at Mezcalifornia."

"I know. But I saw you walking so I thought this was easier, and I didn't have to park. Unless . . ."

"Unless what?"

"Unless you want to actually give me a tour of your condo."

Alma studied him. He was so handsome. His black hair skimmed his brows, and his cheekbones were chiseled. He had lost a bit of his boyish looks that she had fallen in love with, and now he was all man; not that she was complaining.

"Maybe later." She slid into the slick leather car seat and placed Tequila on her lap. "I hope Santi likes pug hair. That was nice of him to let you borrow his car."

"He's the best. I really missed him." He gazed at her and winked. "And you."

Alma ignored the wink that caused her core to burn for him. "Where to? There are some great new places in Marin. Or we could go to San Francisco."

"Alma, I said I got this. We're going to Sonoma."

Her hands shook. This was her fault for not making a local reservation and then agreeing to let him handle it when he asked the other night. She had worried that Sonoma was where they were headed. The romantic wine country. How could she possibly return to the area where they had fallen in love and resist his charm? Did he really want her back? The kiss Friday night said he did, but maybe it was just an in-the-moment kind of thing with the tequila flowing. In what way could this ever work? Was this some power trip just to see if he could get her? There was no way Jaime wanted to settle down. He was only twenty-five. She didn't know if he would ever settle down. Hell, Ramón didn't settle down until his thirties.

They drove back through downtown Tiburon, past the dog park, and alongside Blackie's Pasture. With the top down on the convertible, it was hard to carry on a conversation, which was probably a good thing. Tequila's tiny ears flapped in the wind. Maybe the long drive might be too much for her precious, sturdy-yet-fragile pug.

Alma tapped Jaime's leg. "Can you put the top up on this car? I don't think the air is good for Tequila's eyes."

"Sure." Jaime pressed a button in the convertible and the top went up. "When did you get her?"

"A few months after we broke up. Pugs N' Roses, a pug rescue, had her up for adoption and I couldn't resist her wrinkly face. And let's face it—I needed someone to cuddle with after you dumped me."

Jaime exhaled. "Alma, all I can say is I'm sorry. Unfortunately, I can't go back in time. I know how I ended things abruptly was fucked-up. I thought just doing it suddenly would actually hurt less than dragging it out and having long conversations about it. I loved you—though we both know we were too young to settle down. That sounds awful but it's true. I don't want to continue living in the past."

"Neither do I. Hence why I was so surprised when you showed up in my bar!"

Jaime sighed, his lips turning down. "I apologize again for showing up here and invading your life, but I don't regret it. I missed you. And your family. Is there any way we can move forward?"

Forward? "What does that even mean?"

"It means we start fresh today. Here. Now. Forget about our

past and see if we have anything between us today that we can build on."

Hard no. "I already told you I don't want to date you. That kiss last night, though enjoyable, was nothing but confusing. And this *friendship*, or whatever it is, is awkward at best and painful at worst. You don't even live here. I can't imagine ever being friends with you. I have to trust my friends."

Jaime just nodded and looked at the road.

Maybe Alma was being too hard on him. They had been so young. And they were still young. She hadn't expected him to marry her at age twenty-two. She was just so heartbroken that she couldn't let go of the pain.

Alma tried to focus on the present. Maybe she could be more zen and start meditating. Zoila was always obsessed with that new age crap. But Alma had taken some of the messages to heart too. Live in the present. Maybe she could be happier if she lived for today.

It was a glorious spring day in the bay. The sun shone brightly in the sky, and cautious excitement replaced Alma's nervousness. What would it be like to return to the area where they had fallen in love? Would her feelings toward Jaime soften? Would she be lost in their past and blind to the problems they would most definitely have if they considered a future?

As the grand mountain in the distance came into view, Alma's heart leapt. Napa was so magical. She had been such a shy, nervous girl when she had moved here to start college. She had never been away from her parents' house and was a first-generation college student, and it had been so surreal for her to be on her own. Then Alma had met Jaime the very first week in school, at one of those Latino student get-togethers. She had fallen fast in love with his dimples and his charm.

As Jaime took a familiar exit, there was no doubt. He was taking her to their favorite café in downtown Sonoma.

The landscape was decorated with glorious vineyards and rolling hills. A beautiful place for some other couple to rekindle a romance—but not them. Alma couldn't be swayed by looks, whether they belonged to the gorgeous wine country or the man by her side.

Jaime parked and Alma lifted Tequila out of the car. Her dog peed on a nearby bush and Alma poured some water into her portable bowl, which the pug lapped up eagerly.

Alma smiled as she glanced across the road at the rustic café filled with plants. It was the same one they used to frequent. "Wow, we first came here seven summers ago. Remember?"

He reached out and squeezed her hand. "I'll never forget. You were wearing that yellow sundress." He lowered his voice. "With that matching lace bra and thong. I couldn't wait to take you home, eat your pussy, and fuck you."

Whoa. Alma's cheeks heated. He'd been overly polite since they had reunited, but hearing him remembering her in such a sexual manner rattled her. But since that kiss, it was clear that he wanted her again, at least sexually.

And she had to admit—she wanted him too.

Jaime checked in with the hostess, and she led them to an outdoor table. The café was decorated with rustic charm. There was a trellis dripping with vines and thick-cut wooden tables. Jaime pulled out her seat. He was really coming in strong with his gentleman act, well, minus his dirty talk.

The waitress brought a doggy menu for Tequila and read the specials. Jaime ordered a gourmet hamburger with all the fixings and Alma chose the smoked trout and ordered a bowl of steak and rice for Tequila.

Jaime perused the wine list, but Alma took it from him.

"Allow me." But she didn't order any wine—she ordered a blood orange margarita with mezcal and a Tajín rim and a blackberry margarita with tequila and a black salt garnish.

Jaime licked his lower lip. "Excited to taste the drinks you ordered."

"I love mezcal. It's smoky."

"Until you gave me that tasting, I didn't really take the time to learn about it. I would just drink it to get drunk."

"Oh, it's so good. And there are so many new opportunities for it. Tequila is only from the blue agave plant and mezcal can be from any type of agave plant. Also, the cooking process is different."

Jaime's eyes lit up. "How so?"

Alma's heart beat rapidly. The years between them seemed to dissolve. "Well, the blue agave piña is steamed in a brick oven. Most tequilas will have somewhat of a consistent taste because they are made in similar ways, though the good brands are cleaner. With mezcals, the agave plant is roasted by the mezcalero or in some places the mezcalera. It's put into the ground to cook, which is why it tastes so smoky. There are so many amazing artisan batches and mezcaleros."

"How did you get into this? Why did you leave wine?"

"I don't know. With wine, I loved it, but I didn't feel called to it. I don't know if it's because I'm Mexican or not, but I felt a deep connection to the people who made these spirits." She leaned back in her seat, enjoying the warm sunshine. "I went to Mexico after we broke up, and we met someone whose family made tequila. Once I saw the process and met the makers, that was just it for me."

Jaime relaxed into his chair. The waitress brought the drinks and placed a drink that reminded Alma of the Sonoma sunset in front of him.

He sipped on the blood orange margarita.

Alma studied his expression. "What do you think?"

"It's wonderful. Like a barbecue aftertaste."

"Well, that's one way to put it. Try mine."

He popped a blackberry into his mouth and then sipped the drink. "This is closer to what I'm used to. Very clean."

"Yeah. That one is more standard. We can do a tasting of the different mezcals back at the bar." She stopped. What had she just said?

He winked. "So, I get another date?"

A blue bird flew over their heads. She focused on it for a moment, trying to gather her thoughts. "I guess. I'm just confused, Jaime. I feel like we're talking in circles. I can't lie and say that I'm not having strong feelings sitting here across from you. If I forget about the past, this is just easy breezy. You and I, having lunch in Sonoma, drinking, just like old times. And that kiss was incredible. But I don't want to get hurt."

"I'd never hurt you again, Alma."

Ugh, this man. "So, what does that mean? Listen, Jaime. Don't even try to kiss me again, unless you mean it. I got over you once, but I don't think I can do it again. Let's just keep this friendly."

He took her hand across the table. "If I kiss you again, you'll be the last woman I ever kiss."

Alma couldn't help but roll her eyes. "Are you serious right now? Don't give me one of your lines. I'm spiraling here, Jaime.

Sorry that I sound so pathetic, but seeing you, hanging out with you, kissing you, has really rattled me."

"I'm sorry. I don't know what to say to that."

The waitress walked over with their food. "Can I get you anything else?"

Just a lobotomy. "No, we're good, thanks."

Alma focused on her food. The fish was buttery and fragrant. She sipped her margarita and got lost in the moment. When was the last time she went out just for fun and not for work? This day, even though being with Jaime was challenging, was blissful.

Jaime downed his drink. Alma didn't bother telling him it was best sipped slowly.

"So, did you know your brother wants me to donate to his soccer club?"

Alma gulped.

"Really? I can't believe he asked you that. You don't have to. I'm so sorry." She had always known Jaime was rich. Crazy fucking rich. But she never wanted him to think she or her family was interested in his money.

"Don't be. Carlos wants the students to have great opportunities. And he deserves to be paid well for his work. I want to help. I'll talk to the foundation board."

"Don't feel guilted into helping the program. We appreciate you and your family's help at the festival. But you don't need to do this."

"I know. But I want to. It's important to me to support things I care about. And I care about soccer. And your family. I'm sorry. I know it's awkward." He wiped his mouth with the napkin. "Just wanted to give you a heads-up."

"I get it. He wants you to raise money for the Canal and his program."

Time to change the subject. "How are your brothers?"

"Well, Ramón is getting married to his fiancée Julieta this summer. She's great. A super-talented chef. She has a really close-knit family. Randomly her mom, Linda, and our dad used to date back in Mexico when he was there surfing over spring break years ago. Linda actually made him his first fish taco, which inspired our taco business."

"Wow. That's random. And a bit creepy."

"Yeah, that's what I said. Linda hated my dad. He told Ramón that he returned to Mexico to propose to her but saw her with another man, who was Julieta's father."

"Oh, that's so sad. How are they both now?"

"Linda still hates my dad because he and Ramón tried to gentrify the block Julieta's taco shop is on. Ramón, of course, saved the day because he's a hero, but Linda hasn't forgiven my dad. But I hope they will be civil one day. They will both be at the wedding."

The wedding. Alma used to fantasize about a big, beautiful wedding to Jaime. Now, she only dreamed of finding success in business. She could wear a fancy white gown to an awards ceremony sometime.

"When is it?"

"In August. In Coronado." He paused and stuffed a french fry in his mouth. "Want to be my date?"

Alma shook her head. "Don't play with me. I can't be your date to your brother's wedding. That's too intimate."

"Why not? You know my entire family; they will be here to promote the festival." He gazed at her dress. "And I'd be honored to be there with you."

"Wouldn't you rather be single at the wedding? Pick up one of the beautiful bridesmaids?"

"Nope. None would be as beautiful as you."

"Ay, Dios mío, stop teasing me. I can't take it."

"Maybe I'm not teasing you, Alma. Maybe I'm dead serious."

"Well, maybe isn't good enough." She finished her food and purposely didn't give him an answer. He didn't deserve an answer. Her seeing him up in Northern California on her turf was one thing. But down in Southern California, in his hometown, where he was a socialite and seen as a king, was a whole other issue. Not to mention, there would be some type of press at this wedding. Would there be pictures of them together? She couldn't fathom the level of hate she would receive on her socials for dating California's most eligible Mexican. With Ramón engaged and Enrique in a serious relationship, Jaime was the lone Montez left. For years the media hailed the trio as the sexiest Latinos, and with Jaime's looks, he had endless thirsty women commenting on his every post. Alma wanted nothing to do with the hate she would receive if he committed to her, even though she had been his one and only, once.

They shared a crème brûlée, Jaime paid, and they left the restaurant. Alma walked Tequila in the nearby park, where she chased after and barked at the ducks.

As they sat on a bench, Jaime put his arm around Alma's shoulders, cautiously at first. She didn't pull away and he squeezed her tighter.

His hand felt so lovely against her. She felt safe, at peace, even loved.

"I'm glad they haven't changed this park. I love the ducks. So does Tequila."

"Yeah, it's so beautiful here. I forgot how much I loved it up north. It's so much cooler and laid-back."

"You used to get bored up here."

"Yeah, I did, but I was younger. I've done a lot of living, and I want to slow down."

With her? Alma was careful not to read anything into his words. "I get that."

"Alma, I can't change the past. But I've never found any woman as incredible as you. Would you at least open yourself up to not hating me?"

"I don't hate you, Jaime. It's the opposite. I'm just scared."

"I'm scared too."

He put his thumb under her chin and lifted it. What was he doing? And why was she letting him do it?

She tilted her head toward him, her heart wanting to kiss him, but her head screaming at her to stop. He closed his eyes, and she did as well. Their lips met in a soft kiss. It was nothing like their first kiss ever, which had been after a boozy night at a party in the dorms. He had slammed her up against her door in a passionate fit and she had kissed him back with abandon. Back then, she was full of lust and wonder; now she was filled with cautious hope and trepidation.

Or like their last kiss at Mezcalifornia, which was like scratching an itch of longing and sexual tension to the reunited lovers.

This soft kiss turned more urgent, as his hand cupped her face. She wanted more of this, more of him.

She finally pulled away.

His words rang in her head.

If I kiss you again, you'll be the last woman I ever kiss.

That could never possibly be real. Alma knew it in her heart and Jaime probably did also.

But for a second, Alma held on to the hope that those words were true.

Ay, what had she done?

Chapter Sixteen

Jaime's head was woozy but not from the mezcal. It was from Alma's scent. He could still taste her on his lips, in his mouth, on his soul.

Fuck. He had cheesily told her that if he kissed her again, she would be the last woman he ever kissed. What the fuck was wrong with him? Why on earth would he say something like that? How could he make such a stupid fucking promise? He hadn't even meant to say it as a line—in that moment, he was caught up in his feelings and he believed every word he said. But the kiss at that point was still a fantasy, not a reality.

Was this just some sick game to see if he could get her back? Enrique was right—Jaime needed a therapist. Badly. Unfortunately, it was too late for this mess he made. He hated himself.

At least his brothers would fly into San Francisco today. Ramón would set his ass straight and Enrique would help him clarify his actual feelings. Jaime should've never come here. He was trying to prove to himself that he didn't need them. What a fucking joke.

Back when he and Alma were together, Jaime would regularly book a hotel room overlooking the plaza. But tonight, there would be no romantic getaway. There would be no more careless kisses. He would take Alma back home, meet up with his brothers at Santi's house, and then spend the next week preparing for the festival. He had already honored his commitment to Leti, and as a man of his word, he would participate and promote the Cinco de Mayo–palooza or whatever it was fucking called.

And learn all he could about tequila from the woman who was its mistress.

Cinco was such a stupid holiday—just an excuse for gringos to wear sombreros and get drunk on cheap tequila promoted by non-Mexican Hollywood douchebags.

Then, he would leave the Bay Area with no plans to return. But not because he didn't want to. He literally would leave his heart in San Francisco. The longer he stayed here, the more he would hurt Alma.

And possibly even himself.

Alma's dog was huffing and puffing under a bench. She was an odd-looking thing—wrinkly, pudgy, and comical. Pugs clearly were not meant to travel.

He didn't want this day to end but he needed to create some distance between them since he wasn't thinking clearly. "We should get back."

"You're right. We should."

She rubbed his thigh and his cock jolted to attention. "Do you want to stop by my bar again? We did a tequila lesson but maybe we could work on some Spanish for your promos? And I can show you more about my favorite tequila brands."

Yes, he wanted to. So desperately. Learning about liquor was the full reason he came here in the first fucking place.

But he had to start doing the right thing. Everything up until these dangerous kisses and that stupid-ass line had been questionable, but he hadn't crossed any lines.

Just say no.

"I'd love to, but I can't. My family is coming in tonight. We need to start figuring out what to do for the festival."

She pulled on her hair. "Yeah, about that. Carlos will take care of everything. Don't stress out. Just show up and we will be good."

Jaime wished it would be that simple. "Well, I'll see what he has planned."

She planted a quick kiss on him. He was doomed. She was his kryptonite. He could not resist her.

A pit settled in his stomach. This could end badly. And it would be his fault.

Jaime drove back to Marin with his head spinning and it wasn't from the one cocktail he'd had. Jaime cared enough about others and himself to never, ever drive drunk. He wasn't even buzzed. Well, that wasn't true. He was high on Alma.

She was smiling and laughing and singing to Becky G songs blaring on the radio that Jaime did not know the lyrics to. It was just like old times. Except it wasn't. She wasn't his girlfriend, and he wasn't her boyfriend. They were awkward exes with tension between them and debilitating desire. The pressure built in his chest. This was an impossible situation. He craved her, he still loved her, but he wasn't ready for a serious relationship. And he definitely wasn't ready for forever. They couldn't just have a fling.

Or maybe that is what they both wanted?

She had never said, not once, that she wanted to get back together. Quite the opposite in fact.

Maybe she just wanted to have a fling also? No, that wasn't it at all. Jaime was clearly misinterpreting her actions. She was clearly still deeply hurt by their past, but they both had unresolved feelings.

They needed to have a mature adult conversation. But not now. He needed to be sure what he wanted first.

He pulled up in front of Alma's bar.

Her hand caressed his cheek. "Are you sure you can't stop in, just for a little bit?"

No, he wasn't sure. He wanted to throw her over his shoulder and carry her into the place like a caveman and take her from behind while she was pressed up against the bar. "I'd love to, babe. But I really do have to meet my brothers. I begged them to come to the festival, and they dropped everything to fly up here."

"Okay. Totally. I understand. No worries. Come by the bar later and I can give you another lesson."

Or maybe he would give *her* one.

"Sounds like a plan. See you later."

Her pink fingernails lightly scratched his jaw, causing the hair on his arms to perk straight up. Their lips met yet again, but this kiss felt different. It was an old-school kiss, as if they hadn't just lost three years between them.

But Jaime couldn't listen to his lips or to his heart. He didn't think he was ready for a relationship, and he didn't want to lead her on.

The kisses weren't a mistake, but a gift—one he hoped to repeat.

He would talk to her later and make sure they both wanted the same thing before it went any further. He refused to hurt her again.

Jaime arrived at Santi's house. He walked in the front door.

The full clan was there. Ramón, his fiancée, Julieta, Enrique, his girlfriend, Carolina, and her sister Blanca, Julieta's mom, Linda, and Julieta's cousins, Tiburón and Rosa were all there waiting for him.

Thank God Santi had a huge house. At least Jaime's mother wasn't here. That would be a supreme nightmare. He was dreading Ramón and Julieta's wedding. Not the actual ceremony and the reception of course. Julieta was in full-on bridezilla mode, and it would be a blast. But the guest list gave him major anxiety. Their dad and mom who barely communicated without a lawyer present, their mom's pretentious friends who would no doubt try to marry off Jaime and Enrique, despite the fact Enrique had a girlfriend, Julieta's mom and eccentric tías—there was no telling what kind of crazy town would ensue. Take that back—it actually should be a blast.

Jaime smiled. "You guys made it."

Ramón walked over to Jaime and gave him a strong hug. "We took an earlier flight so have been here for a while." His voice lowered and he whispered in Jaime's ear, "What the fuck are you doing here, man?"

Jaime stammered, "I don't know. It's a long story."

Ramón shook his head. Gone were his days of buttoned-up suits and shiny shoes. Ramón's attire now consisted of polo shirts and long shorts. He had completely changed since being with Julieta. In a good way. Jaime was still anxious around his big brother and always wanted to please Ramón, but Julieta had definitely chilled him out.

Enrique was sitting on Santi's bright-orange modern velvet sofa. "Sit down, bro. Tell us what's going on. I'll make some tea."

Tea? Jaime needed tea-quila. Lots of it.

But there was no escaping this family talk.

Ramón sat next to Julieta. "Jaime, tell us everything."

Julieta placed her hand on Ramón's thigh. "Jaime, what he means is, are you back with Alma? We didn't mean to bombard you. I consider you a brother already, and I just wanted to be there for you. Ramón told me that this Alma woman is the only girl you've ever loved. And she's so badass. I can't wait to meet her."

Great—next thing Jaime knew Julieta would be partnering with Alma for some tequila–taco bar collaboration.

"She's pretty busy. She wasn't too excited to see me, so I don't know if she'll want to hang out with my future sister-in-law's family."

Rosa let out a cackle. "Then I've got to meet this poor chingona. Two years ago, I would've been jealous. But now I'm just glad I'm not her."

Fucking Rosa. Their friendship had started out flirty until Ramón had forbidden any hookups. Rightfully so, because they were soon to be family and that would be messy. Rosa was gorgeous like her cousin, though they had very different styles. Rosa dressed like a chola with her tight sleeveless sweaters and loose Dickies pants that cinched at her waist. But Rosa and Jaime learned early on that they were too similar. Both wild and carefree. Watching both of Ramón and Enrique's relationships with their women, Jaime realized that it was better to have some sort of balance in place between partners.

"If you all really must know, I was asked to be a brand ambassador for Somos Tequilas. Tom Bluey's latest endeavor."

Julieta scowled. "That jackass has a tequila line? Who doesn't have a tequila line these days?"

"I don't. We don't. We are Mexican. We have more rights than he does to profit off tequila. So, I came up with the idea to start one."

Enrique shook his head. "You have a point, but I don't like where this is going, bro. Alma has a tequila bar, so you came up here to ask her to help you?"

Carolina playfully smacked him. "Like you didn't do the same thing with my farm."

Enrique threw both his hands up. "You're right, I did. But you weren't my ex. You were just some beautiful girl I admired. Jaime and Alma have a lot of history together."

Tiburón exhaled. "Do all you damn Montez brothers only meet women that can help you with your careers? It's fucked-up, man." He turned to Blanca. "I don't want nothing from Blanca but to spoil her and have her carry my babies." Blanca kissed Tiburón.

Jesus. "I hope this love thing isn't contagious. You're all nauseating."

Santi laughed. "Agreed. I may rescind my offer for you all to stay. This is a bona fide bachelor's pad."

Linda stood up. "I'm still single. Happily. And I'm going to make dinner." She walked toward the kitchen, with Santi trailing behind her.

"No, you don't have to. I can order food," Santi pleaded as Linda ignored him.

"Don't be ridiculous. It's Sunday. And on Sunday we feast as a family."

Right. Sunday Montez–Campos family dinners. The food was always delicious but the chisme was exhausting.

Jaime looked at all the luggage. "There are too many people here. I can stay at the Lodge."

Ramón raised his brow. "Next to Alma?"

"Yes, actually, but not the reason. At least I'm not staying at her parents' home." He paused. No point in lying. "Again."

"Again?" Ramón blurted out. "Why would you do that?"

"They asked me to stay over after I drank too much. And I couldn't say no."

Ramón took a step toward his brother. "You dumped this girl, right? Three years ago? Suddenly ended it and devastated her? What's happening right now?"

Jaime's anger got the best of him. "I don't know, okay? I fucked up. I thought that I could come up here, learn about tequila, start my own line alone, without the two of you nagging me about business plans and astrology charts. But you're right, I'm a dumbass and didn't think it through. I never think anything through. I didn't consider Alma's feelings. Santi even warned me, but I was too stubborn or delusional. Not sure which one. Probably both."

Ramón patted his brother on his back. "Stop being so hard on yourself. I'm sorry we always give you shit. You're our baby brother. I've spent my life trying to protect you, and I can't turn it off sometimes. But I love you, man."

Damn, Ramón. Always had to be the nice guy. "I love you too. I just can't seem to do anything right. I wanted to create something on my own. Without your help, with my own money from influencing. Be my own man. And now I involved Alma. I don't want to hurt her. Again."

Enrique's brow cocked. "How would you hurt her? You're just doing this festival that you told us to come up for. Right?"

Jaime didn't want to lie, and since this was the closest he would get to a therapist and his family was all up in his business anyway, he decided to spill. "I took her to Sonoma today. Just to reconnect.

It was friendly at first. But then . . . I kissed her. Actually, I also kissed her the other night."

The entire room collectively gasped except for Tiburón, who stood up and high-fived Jaime.

"My man! She's fire!"

Carolina swatted her sister. "You don't care that your boyfriend is saying another woman is fire?"

Blanca shook her head. "No, my man is obsessed with me. But he's human and can appreciate beauty. I saw a picture of Alma. She is fire."

Rosa glared at Jaime. "Do you want her back?"

Jaime looked at his feet. "No. I still love her, but I don't want to settle down. But she seemed into it and didn't even ask about the future. Maybe we can just have fun."

Rosa burst out laughing. "Ay, Jaime. You're an ass clown. You know that?"

He had to admit, Rosa was right.

They came to see him, but he needed to be alone tonight. To think. The hotel room would be a good refuge. Fuck family dinner. Jaime had to figure out what he was going to do with, or to, Alma.

"I need to go. I'll get room service at the hotel." Jaime had to get out of here. Far away from his family.

He went to the room he had been staying in and packed up all his belongings. Santi's house was sick. Sleek and modern with massive windows looking over the rocky coast. Though nothing could beat the surf in La Jolla, Bolinas had its own vibe. With the hidden town, the icy water, and the laid-back locals, this place was special. But he needed a break. Well, it was better than being interrogated all night by his family.

Santi walked into the room. "Here. Take my car again."

He tossed Jaime his keys. "What? No, man. I can't do that. I'll Uber."

"Don't worry about it. I have others. I'll just drive my Rivian this week." Santi sat on the bed. "Why'd you kiss her? Twice."

Here, away from his family, Jaime could try to make sense of his foolish actions to his best friend. "I had to kiss her. She's fucking hot."

"I know that. That's not what I meant. *Why* did you kiss her? You do have self-control."

"I don't know. It's just easy being around her. She understands me, she doesn't look down on me, she doesn't expect anything of me. When I'm with her, I think I can do anything. It was always like that with me and her." Back in college, Jaime would stay up all night after procrastinating, trying to study or write papers, but he just couldn't focus. Alma would sit with him, not nag him or make him feel bad, and just be in the room doing her own work. Somehow, her level of calm would rub off on him.

"So, why are you so against having an actual relationship with her?"

Jaime's eyes widened. Why was he so resistant? "Because I'm only twenty-five. And I don't live here."

"So what? Twenty-five is an age. Just a number. Don't focus on all that."

Emotion welled up in Jaime. "I don't have any idea what a healthy relationship looks like. Sure, Ramón is now with Julieta and that seems functional, but Ramón is older than me and a workaholic. Enrique and Carolina had a rough time but now they seem to be good. My parents fought and fought nonstop. What if we end up like that?"

"Did you and Alma ever fight when you were together?"

No. They didn't. It had been four years of fun, sex, love, and friendship. They had stupid disagreements about spending time together and issues with communication, but never any all-out spats. "Surprisingly no. Never."

"So, it seems to me like you're capable of having a healthy relationship with her."

"Right. I guess."

"Is that why you left her? Because it scared you?"

Jaime sighed. "Probably. I was so young. I'm *still* so young."

"Take it from me, just be open to any possibilities. My parents had a wonderful marriage. They were affectionate and kind and respectful. I've never dated anyone like Alma, but if I did, I would consider moving forward. You don't have to make any decisions about the future. Just enjoy the time you have together. Go with the flow, and don't make her any promises you can't keep."

It seemed so simple the way Santi explained it. Maybe Jaime was stressing too hard. Alma had enjoyed the kiss as well. Why did a kiss have to mean forever?

Tonight, he would clarify his intentions toward her.

Chapter Seventeen

Jaime checked in to the hotel and ordered room service. He turned on the TV and counted down the minutes until Alma's bar closed.

The minutes turned into hours, and Jaime couldn't wait any longer. He brushed his teeth, dabbed on some cologne, and walked over to her bar.

He didn't bother her when he first entered, instead picking a spot upstairs so he could let her work. She delivered a drink upstairs and finally noticed him. She didn't say a word, nor did he. He winked, she smiled, and she went back to work.

Finally, the night was dying down and he made his way downstairs to a small table. After the final guest left, she and her staff cleaned up quickly. When her employees went home, they were alone at last.

She walked over to him.

"So, Jaime, what exactly did you come here for tonight?"

He narrowed his gaze on her. "You. I want you."

"Jaime, I—"

He stood up and pressed his finger to her lips. "Alma, if you want me to go, just tell me now. But you said you wanted to be free and have a good time. I'm the man for that. We don't have to talk about tomorrow or yesterday. Let's just enjoy ourselves while I'm in town."

Alma paused for a second. She would certainly kick him out.

But instead, she opened her mouth. "I want you too. I want you now."

Jaime's hands grabbed Alma's wrists as his lips covered hers. He couldn't believe how fucking sexy she looked tonight, in command and control of the bar. She was wearing what he considered to be her uniform, a tight black velvet bustier and even tighter jeans. He had watched her in her element—everyone in the bar admiring her, worshipping her, wanting her. It was so fucking hot. *She* was so fucking hot. He had wanted her so desperately the other night while she was preparing the tequila. He had imagined her plump ass pressed against his cock behind the bar. How hot would it have been to take her in front of a roomful of clients, so everyone knew she was his?

And tonight, he would fuck her like she was his. Forever.

For all he knew this could be the last time he would ever be with her. Maybe she just wanted one final fling to get him out of her system.

Even though she would never be out of his.

Didn't matter. At this point, he would take what he could get.

His lips made their way down her chest and settled in her ample cleavage. He buried his face in her tits and undid her corset with his free hand, which actually would've been quite hard to do, if not for the fact that he was a pro. He sucked one of her nipples between his lips, and she let out a sweet little moan.

God, how he'd missed her moans.

Alma's mouth opened; her words breathy. "Oh, baby . . . Just like that. It feels so good."

Alma never used to talk during sex. He loved how confident she was now, only wishing she had been that secure before. But they had been so young. And he had been her first. Was he still her one and only?

He would never dare ask her that. He had no right to know. He'd lost that privilege when he tossed her aside.

And he had definitely not been a saint since he'd left her. But he had never been in love with any other woman than the one he was kissing right now.

"You like that?" Her skin tasted spicy yet sweet. Just like her.

"Yes, baby. Don't stop."

He threw her over his shoulder and carried her to the bar, where he placed her on her back. He pulled off her jeans, revealing her black lace thong. Man, she was perfection. He spread her legs open wide.

He took a moment to appreciate her beauty . . . her curves were even more kicking than he remembered, and her skin was tanner. She had filled out in all the right places; she was no longer the eighteen-year-old cute girl he had fallen for. She was a brilliant, sexy, and accomplished woman.

He hitched in a breath at the sight of her eyes. In her dark brown orbs, he saw something different from what he had seen in the past. Something that he'd never noticed before, maybe because he hadn't looked or maybe because it hadn't been there. Confusion lingering in her soul.

Jaime would flush out the uncertainty and replace it with ecstasy. At least for a moment, she could escape with him to paradise.

He forced himself to pull away from her and move around the bar.

"What are you doing?"

He shook his head. "Relax. Time to create my own tasting."

He grabbed a bottle of tequila—a blanco—some salt, and a lime.

Alma's mouth widened into a smile. They had been kids in college and had grown up and explored each other sexually, but Jaime was the first to admit he had been inexperienced back then. His knowledge of sex had been from awkward experiences as a teen and watching way too much internet porn. Since their split, he'd learned a few things, and he was more than willing to give her a glimpse.

"Open your mouth, babe."

She licked her lips and parted them. Jaime placed the rind of the lime in her mouth, so its flesh pointed toward him, sprinkled salt on her chest, and then poured the tequila in her belly button.

"This is the way I like to drink tequila."

She spit out the rind. "Oh, aren't you the expert. Maybe you *should* open your own tequila line," she said teasingly.

His throat tightened. He was grateful that he had been honest with her about why he came up here in the first place. Maybe he would make more progress on the tequila line before he left town.

It'd be so damn hard if he never got to do this again. He swirled his fingertip over her nipple, unable to resist teasing her while she waited for him. He kept his gaze on her eyes as he licked the salt off her tits in long, slow movements, and smiled when her breaths became a little erratic. She wiggled, causing a drop of tequila to spill down her side, but he bent and licked it off before taking the small shot from her belly button.

He was still smiling when he took the lime from between her lips.

"Maybe I should add this tasting method to the menu. I could charge a lot for it," she teased. "Though I question your choice of tequila. Honestly, I would've gone with an añejo."

"Smart-ass," he growled. "And don't you dare. It's only for us."

She laughed and arched her back, which made her knees pull up a bit.

Jaime climbed up onto the bar and gave himself an even sweeter taste than anything he had sampled in the bar.

Her.

He kissed down her body, lavishing attention on her belly until he reached her panties. She let out a deep moan when he pressed kisses over the delicate lace, which was already wet. He pulled them off and stopped to stare at her beautiful pussy. Her skin was tan and soft, and her hair was waxed into a perfect landing strip.

He planted kisses on her thighs, inhaling her sweet scent, teasing her for as long as he could hold himself back. Then, spreading her legs wide, he licked her, and she gasped. God, she tasted as sweet as he remembered, like pure honey. He licked her like she was an oasis in the desert, like she was the first woman he'd ever had the pleasure to be with, like she was the last woman he would ever taste.

"Oh, Jaime. That feels so amazing, baby."

She ran her fingers through his hair as he devoured her, her scent making him high. After all these years, she still tasted the same, the one taste that he was addicted to. Jaime loved eating her pussy, making her feel good, watching her react to his tongue and knowing how much she loved it.

He cupped her beautiful ass cheeks in his hands as he ate her for all he was worth, sucking on her clit, changing his rhythm to see what she liked.

Her breath came in spurts, and Jaime knew she was close. He reached up and pinched her nipples as he kept his mouth on her pussy. He slowly inserted his finger deep inside, and she gasped. She started thrashing on the bar, but he wasn't done with her yet. He flipped onto his back.

"Come here, baby, and sit on my face."

"What?" She put her hand over her chest. "I . . . we've never—"

"There's a first time for everything."

She gave him a devilish smile but quickly obliged and straddled his mouth.

Jaime was in heaven with the beautiful view of her breasts and the taste of her pussy on his lips.

This was so fucking hot. She placed her hands on the sides of the bar and rocked back and forth, all over his tongue. Her moans got louder and louder, and he didn't care if the tenants in the nearby restaurant or the community patrol heard her.

He gripped her ass and sucked her clit.

"Oh, oh my God . . . oh, baby."

Her body constricted as she let out a breathy moan before coming in his mouth. He lapped up every sweet drop. He couldn't get enough.

He didn't give her time to come down from her high before he was turning her over. He took a moment to admire her incredible ass as he spanked her, and then with quick, borderline frantic movements, dropped his pants, took himself in his hand, and pressed his cock to her slit.

She melted against him, throwing her head back and gripping the bar top. "Yes, baby! Fuck me."

Damn, he wanted to raw dog her, but he knew that wasn't okay. They weren't in a committed relationship. He pulled a condom out of his wallet and rolled it on. She didn't comment but smiled.

He growled and entered her slowly, inch by inch, wanting to take her hard, but he also wanted to savor this moment, the taste of her pussy on his lips, the bliss of being inside her, fucking the only woman he'd ever loved.

He increased his pace, rubbing her clit, wanting her to come again, come with him, share the pleasure she was giving him. Her pussy clamped around his cock, pushing him closer to his own orgasm.

"Jaime, yes!" she cried as she shook her head, her long hair draping over her naked back.

He couldn't keep himself in check anymore. He slammed into her over and over again. He needed her, needed this moment, needed this connection.

He could feel her orgasm approaching again, and he drove into her harder. His own pleasure was exhilarating, and every nerve inside of him was completely euphoric.

"Alma, fuck!"

He waited for her to orgasm, and she screamed in ecstasy, causing him to come so fucking hard, and for a moment, he was lost inside her.

"Wow. That was better than I remember."

He slapped her on the ass. "You haven't seen anything yet." Would there be another time?

His heart rate returned to normal.

When he released her, reality again came crashing down beside them.

This was too intense. Was he even capable of having a fling? Not with her.

How was he ever going to let her go?

After a few minutes of recovery, she finally spoke. "I can't believe we just did that."

"I can. I've wanted to since the second I saw you again."

"Of course you did. I'm hot."

He laughed. "Yes, you are."

"But I can't say the same. I didn't want to see you at all when you arrived." She gave him a cheeky wink. "But I have to say . . . I'm sure glad you're here now."

"There's nowhere else I'd rather be."

She kissed him on the forehead. "I'll be right back."

Alma hopped off the bar, gathered her clothes, and ran to the bathroom.

Jaime also got up, gathered his clothes, and ran to the men's bathroom. He disposed of the condom, cleaned himself up, got dressed, and went back out to the bar.

Alma emerged a bit later, fully dressed and armed with cleaning supplies.

"Don't you have a janitor service?"

She rolled her eyes. "I do, actually. But I'm not going to have them clean this up. My mom was a maid, you know. I can clean."

Jaime grabbed a sponge and dipped it in the hot water. "I can help."

She hugged him. "Aren't you so progressive? I've never seen you clean anything. Didn't you grow up with maids? I bet you still have one."

"I did and I do," he admitted. "I'm not above hard work. I'd clean up every day if we could have another night like we just had."

Alma pursed her lips and remained silent. They sanitized the bar until it was sparkling clean.

"So, are you going back to Santi's?"

"Nah. My family took over the place."

"Oh, I understand." She paused. "Did you want to spend the night with me?"

Damn, did he ever. But he couldn't. Sex was one thing. Spending the night in her place, in her space, was too intimate. He really needed to figure out what the fuck he wanted to do regarding her before this all blew up in his face.

Earlier, he'd decided to live more in the moment—and during sex with Alma, he'd been all about the present.

But there was a difference between being real and being reckless. He needed to think of what would happen tomorrow—and the next day and the day after that.

"I'd love to, babe. Thanks for offering. But I got a room at the Lodge."

"Oh. That's better." She looked down.

He put his finger under her chin. "Hey, it's not better. I need to be real with you, Alma. I'm such a fucking mess. I'm confused. I'm crazy about you, you know that. I always have been. Tonight just solidified that for me. But what are we fucking doing here? I don't live here. And you have a bar—a successful one. I don't want to do long-distance." That wasn't the real reason, but he threw it out there to see her response.

"You could move. You can start a tequila line anywhere."

Yes. He could.

And he'd love to do it with her.

"This is true. That isn't an obstacle. But I just don't know if I can commit to you. It's not you—you're perfect. It's me."

"I know, Jaime. You think you are too young. But you aren't."

"Maybe not. But I was in college, and I'm still figuring my life out. I can't apologize enough for dumping you back then. I was a fool, I know this. But it was because I was too young to settle down. I'm a bit older now but I still haven't fucking figured out my life. Look at you! You're a successful business owner, and I don't have a clue what the fuck I'm doing. I kissed you the other night and at brunch because I couldn't resist you. And I made love to you tonight because I'm obsessed with you. My heart is saying one thing, and my head is saying another. I just think spending the night at your place will make this more confusing. I will be leaving in a few weeks."

She gulped. Was she going to cry? Great. Perfect end to a night. He was such a dick. He hated himself.

"No, no, you're right." Her voice cracked. "I wanted to sleep with you too. God, it was amazing. It's been so long since—" She stopped talking.

"Since . . ."

"What, you have to make me say it?" She smiled coyly. "Since I've had sex."

Jaime wanted to ask her so badly if she'd been with anyone since him. But he couldn't.

"In case you're wondering, you're the only one I've ever been with."

Jaime's heart quickly soared with pride, and then just as rapidly sank. It was true. He had been right. He was her only lover.

Guilt swallowed him. It wasn't fair. She hadn't been his first, and though he had always been faithful when they had been together, he had been a manwhore in recent years.

Such a fucking double standard. The machismo had benefited him clearly, but it didn't sit right with him.

Plus, even if he had wanted to commit to her, which he couldn't trust himself to, it wouldn't be fair to her if he was the only man she'd slept with. What if they got married and one day, she was curious. Another reason why they couldn't be together. As much as it pained him, she should date other men before she committed to him.

But it had been three years, and she hadn't.

"May I ask why?"

"I mean, it wasn't because I was pining over you or anything. I just put all the focus I had into my business. I went on a few dates here and there, but nothing ever sparked. Don't flatter yourself."

Jaime tried not to, but he had to admit—he loved that she had only been with him. He was definitely a jerk.

"Don't you want to be with another man? See what it's like?"

Alma rolled her eyes. "That's such a man thing to say. Sex isn't like that for me. It's incredible and all, but it was so great with you because I loved you."

He cupped her face in his hands. "I loved you too." Did he still? He kissed her sweetly.

He helped her lock up the bar. "I'm going to walk you back—it's late."

She didn't protest this time. They walked along the dark water, a few homeless people milling around. He clutched her to his side. "Do you always walk home alone?"

She nodded. "Yeah, it's only a block. And Tiburon is very safe."

His gut clenched. "Sure, it is. But you work until at least two—anything can happen."

"Ay, Jaime. I've lived here for a while and I'm fine."

Jaime resisted the urge to press further. He didn't feel comfortable with her being alone here, but he had no right to tell her what to do, just like he didn't have the right to tell her not to travel to Mexico alone.

They arrived at her front door and her pug barked. Damn, Jaime had forgotten about her dog.

"My poor baby. She misses me when I work."

"I can watch her, while I'm in town."

She tilted her head. "Thanks, but no need. My neighbor walks her sometimes, and she has a back patio. She's a good girl."

She unlocked the door, knelt down, and kissed her dog. Jaime peeked into Alma's place. It was cozy but elegant. She had a bright painting on the wall, and a bar full of tequila. He wanted a tour but knew he needed to get back to his room or he would never leave.

Alma put the leash on Tequila, and they headed outside. After Tequila peed on a bush, she led Alma back to her door.

Jaime put his arms on Alma's shoulders. "Good night, Alma."

He cupped her face in his hands and gave her a gentle kiss good night.

"I'll see you at Cinco fest."

Yes, that was a week away. Would he see her before then? His family was in town, and she would be busy. It was probably best if he kept his distance from her.

Could Jaime handle another few weeks in Marin, knowing that Alma was so close? And then what would happen next between them? Would he honestly consider moving here to be with her?

No. No. His dad and mom married young and look how they turned out.

"Yup. Look, I'll be busy this week with my family, but I'll see you then."

"Good night, Jaime." She shut the door.

Jaime walked back down toward the bar on the way to his hotel.

When he finally arrived in his room, he collapsed into the lounge chair and placed his head between his hands. He was so overwhelmed after being with her again. He couldn't imagine never seeing her after the next few weeks. Was he making the biggest mistake of his life by planning on going back home?

Honestly, nothing was keeping him in San Diego.

But he couldn't shake the feeling that he still wasn't ready for a relationship with Alma.

Chapter Eighteen

Alma woke the next morning with nausea filling her stomach. Though the sex had been incredible, Jaime couldn't have gotten out of there fast enough. She'd thought for sure that he would accept the offer to spend the night at her place.

But no. Despite the intimate moments they'd experienced, he'd bounced the second he could, even though he couldn't resist nagging her about walking alone back to her place.

Alma brushed her teeth and took a long hot shower. The steam filled the bathroom—great for her skin, not so wonderful for her hair. But she didn't care about frizz in her locks when it was her life that was frazzled. She had to be honest with herself. She had not slept with Jaime hoping to get back together with him. She just wanted to have sex with someone who knew her body and could make her feel good. That was it, right? It was simple. Sure, she could please herself or, over the years, she could've had a one-night stand, but she wanted to sleep with someone with whom she felt comfortable and could truly enjoy herself.

So, she had used Jaime.

Whatever she had to tell herself.

And it wasn't like the fling would last long. He would be returning to San Diego soon, and she would finally get the break that she needed and go to Mexico with Zoila. Since she and Jaime clearly didn't have a future together, maybe their encounter would enable her to finally break free from the chokehold he had her in.

Picturing herself sunbathing in Mexico, lounging by the pool and sipping a spicy margarita that she didn't have to make, did the trick. She exhaled—her daydreams calming her down.

Her doorbell rang.

Was it Jaime? Apologizing? Maybe bringing her some flowers? He was staying only a couple of blocks away at the Tiburon Lodge.

She wrapped herself in her robe and went to the door and peered through the hole.

It was not Jaime. It was Zoila, holding two coffees and a pastry bag from Caffé Acri.

They hadn't planned to meet. That was bizarre. Zoila never showed up unannounced.

Alma's heart sank.

It could only mean one thing—those were guilt pastries.

She opened the door and let her friend in.

Zoila handed Alma a coffee cup. "Hi! Sorry to bombard you. I was in the neighborhood and thought I would stop by."

Alma laughed. "The neighborhood? No, you weren't. You wouldn't have driven here and gone through all the trouble to find parking. What's up? Spill."

Zoila flopped down on the sofa. “Girl, please don’t kill me, but I can’t go to Mexico with you.”

Alma squeezed the coffee cup and luckily didn’t spill any coffee on herself. “Please. No. I need this trip. Don’t do this to me!”

“I feel awful. I do. I would do anything to avoid it. But there is this special project I was asked to do last minute at my school and we’re up for a grant. I can’t miss it. I’m so sorry. I can go during the summer though. I was trying to swing it in the school year, and it had been approved, but I can’t let my school down.”

Alma couldn’t blame Zoila for focusing on work. After all, that was why she wanted the trip herself.

No. That wasn’t true. Yes, she would do some work on the trip and meet some tequila makers. But she wanted, no, she needed this trip to relax.

“I understand. I was so excited to take this trip. It was your idea!”

“I know.”

Alma sipped her coffee. It was lightly sweetened with a hint of vanilla and a touch of cinnamon. Zoila had tried her best to make up for her shitty news. “It’s fine. I’ll go alone.”

Zoila shook her head. “No. Oh my God, no. You can’t travel to Mexico solo. Are you crazy?”

“We aren’t supposed to call people crazy. That’s rude.”

“Stop. I’m serious. It’s not safe to go alone.”

“Mexico is safe. It’s all propaganda. There are parts of America that have way more crime.”

“You could get kidnapped and sex trafficked.”

Why was everyone on her about security? Sure, it could be risky, but so was walking home at night. She had to live her life without fear. “You sound like Jaime.”

"Jaime?" she smirked. "Have you been spending time with him?"

Alma pulled a chocolate croissant out of the pastry bag and sat on her sofa. "Yeah. Actually, I slept with him yesterday."

Zoila's jaw dropped. "YES! Finally, an end to your dry spell. I need details. All the details."

"It was super hot. I gave him a private tequila tasting Friday night, then we had brunch in Sonoma on Sunday. Later that night, he stopped by and we fucked on the bar."

"Woman! You are the coolest. Was it like old times?"

"Even better. But then it got weird. I asked him to spend the night, and he said no. He went back to the Tiburon Lodge. I haven't heard from him since."

Zoila shrugged and took a sip of her own coffee. "See! He hasn't changed. Look, I'm glad you got laid, but you shouldn't even think of getting back together with him. He left you once—he can do it again. Now this should force you to get back out there, with someone else."

Zoila did have a point.

But Alma had a plane ticket to Mexico and even though she acted like she felt safe, she really didn't want to travel by herself.

"I'll consider it." There was no future with Jaime. But still, she couldn't imagine being with someone else. "It's not like we're getting back together. It's just hot sex. He is leaving town a few weeks after the Cinco festival."

"Oh, cool. I can't wait to go. Will Santi be there?"

"Yes, he should be."

"Awesome." She clasped her hands in a prayer position. "Sorry again about Mexico. I really wanted to go for the Feast of San Isidro."

"I know. But it's best to cancel it. We can go next year."

Zoila picked up Tequila, who was begging for a bite of her pastry, which was not going to happen because chocolate was toxic to dogs. Light-colored pug hair blew everywhere like willows in the wind. "Or . . . I don't think you should get back together with Jaime, but maybe you should ask him to go to Mexico with you. You even said he was concerned about your safety. You could have fun and great sex. Then you can return home and move on with your life."

When she put it that way, it honestly didn't sound that bad. Alma had had a blast in Jalisco when she went with her girls, but she had been so sad from the breakup. Seeing couples together, walking through the streets, had made her miss Jaime even more.

Being there with him, she would feel safe. And it would be nice to have a crazy no-strings sex vacation with someone she trusted.

"Fine. You're right. I'm going to ask him."

Zoila high-fived Alma. "Deal. But no love, just great sex."

Alma finished getting dressed, then they took Tequila for a short walk. Alma had the entire day off and she knew that Jaime was only a couple blocks away at his hotel. She resisted the urge to text him. She would see how she felt in a week and possibly ask him to join her in Jalisco when she saw him at the Cinco festival.

She tucked herself under a blanket, pulled Tequila beside her on the sofa, and settled in to watch the latest true crime documentary on Netflix. Something about safely viewing these horrors from the comfort of her home calmed her.

Damn, she was so messed up.

Her phone rang. It was Chuy from work.

Oh no. This was her lone day off. She needed this break.

But as an owner of a small business, she was always plugged in.

"Chuy, this better be important. I'm watching that show about the mom who vanished in the middle of the night but was found a month later with her ex."

Chuy, one of her employees, chuckled. "Sorry, Alma. I wasn't going to call you, but I thought you would like to know what is happening."

"And what is that exactly?"

"The critic is here."

Holy shit. "Are you sure? How do you know?"

"Evelyn recognized him as the guy who came in and left that night. I just wanted to let you know. We have it under control."

Chuy was the best and Alma didn't doubt his capabilities for a second. But this was her shot. "I know you do, but I'm on my way."

She turned off her television, kissed Tequila before placing her on the ground, quickly freshened up, and darted out the door.

Why had he returned? Usually, critics gave one chance and one chance alone. She had already blown that by yelling at Jaime.

Jaime.

She stopped cold a few feet from the bar.

Had he actually come through for her and got the critic to come see her?

He was a man of his word, so she didn't doubt that it was possible for Jaime to arrange it.

She exhaled and stepped into her bar.

Chuy greeted her and then pointed to the back of the restaurant.

And there, dressed in a black shirt and gray slacks, was the critic.

She gulped. Was it too obvious if she just walked over to him and gave him her best tequila?

Yes, yes it was.

"Chuy, did you take his order?"

Chuy nodded. "Yes, of course I did. And I prepared him his first drink. He sipped it and said it was wonderful."

Alma bit her lip. "Good. I'm sure you did it perfectly." Should she make the critic a flight? "Did he order anything else?"

Chuy scrunched up his face. "No, he didn't."

No. She needed to chill and let him call the shots.

Why was it so hard to give up control?

She slid behind the bar so she could pretend she was busy and not intently staring at the critic.

After a few moments, the critic's hand went up.

Be cool, Alma muttered to herself.

She sauntered over to his table. "Hi, sir. I'm Alma Garcia, the owner of Mezcalifornia. Is there anything else I could get for you?"

He grunted. "I'll have a tequila flight. And some elote."

"Good choice sir. The street corn is delectable. Coming right up."

She slowly walked over to the bar and exhaled. Showtime.

Alma put together the best tequila flight that she had ever made. She chose top-of-the-line tequilas that she herself rarely drank unless it was a special occasion.

The kitchen prepared the elote and Chuy brought it to her. She carried the drinks and food to the critic, and Alma explained each tequila to him, then returned to the bar.

The man sipped the tequila, but Alma wasn't close enough to see if he was smiling or not.

Did he like her place?

The suspense was killing her.

She walked over to the table again, scanning the critic's face for some type of signal as to what he was feeling.

But it was blank.

Breathe.

"Can I get you anything else?"

He shook his head. Alma's heart dropped. "No. Just the check."

"I'll be right back." She turned and walked to the register.

Hated it. He must've hated everything.

She calculated his bill and returned to the table. "Here you go, sir."

He opened the check, gave it a quick glance, and handed her his card. But his fingers grazed hers. "You're doing a great job here, kid." He winked.

Alma gulped. "Thank you, sir!" She tried to contain her excitement and not go overboard, but she had no chill.

She processed his payment in her handheld machine and it printed a receipt. She ripped it out and gave it to him. "Would you like to try one last special mezcal? On the house."

"Sure."

She grinned and dashed back to the bar, quickly but thoughtfully prepared her signature smoky blood orange mezcal, and then ran it over to the critic.

She bounced around the room. She would be getting a good review. She knew it! This critic had been notoriously stoic.

She couldn't wait to thank Jaime.

She grabbed her phone and texted him.

Alma: What room are you in?

Jaime: 302

"Chuy, thank you! I'm going to split, but you're amazing."

"Anytime, boss."

Alma walked out of her bar and crossed the street twice. She strode straight toward the Tiburon Lodge. The elevator opened to the third floor, and she knocked on the door.

Jaime opened the door.

Alma's jaw dropped. He was shirtless, his arm perched in the doorframe.

"Did you get the critic to come?"

He smirked. "Maybe."

Alma licked her bottom lip, pushed her way into the room, and shut the door.

She dropped to her knees in front of Jaime.

"Thank you."

Chapter Nineteen

Jaime gasped. The sight of Alma kneeling in front of him while she tugged on his belt was almost enough to make him come without her even taking him in her mouth.

But he wanted to savor every bit of their encounter.

It might never happen again.

However, he didn't want her to think she owed him anything.

"Hey," he said in a whisper. "You don't have to do this. I wanted to help you."

"Oh, I know. I want to though. I've been dying to since I saw you. Please, let me."

Well, if she insisted.

She undid his belt with a single motion, and his shorts dropped to the floor.

He stood there before her and her hands grazed his black boxer briefs.

She teased a little, like she used to. A few kisses on the elastic, her fingers stroking him.

Damn how he wanted her. How he needed her.

"Baby." He stroked her hair, and their eyes met. "Suck my cock."

She didn't say a word but nodded her head. Her hands squeezed his ass, and she pulled down his underwear.

Jaime closed his eyes. This was happening, they were happening again. She initiated it. She wanted him.

And he never wanted to let her go.

She kissed around the base of his cock. Jaime couldn't take the torture.

"Stop teasing me, babe."

She licked down his length and grasped him firmly. Stroking him with her soft hands, she kissed his tip a few more times before taking him deeply into her mouth.

Jaime exhaled and ran his fingers through her hair.

"That's it, baby. Did you miss my cock in your mouth?"

"Sí."

Her mouth bobbed up and down, taking him deeper and deeper.

Pulses of pleasure jolted through his body. This intimate act felt different with her than with any of the other women he had ever been with.

Why?

Was it that he had once loved her?

No time to think about that now.

Jaime took control. He pulled her head into his waist.

"Damn. Your mouth is so hot."

She dug her nails into the sides of his thighs as he thrust his cock deeper into her mouth.

"I'm going to come, baby."

He tried to pull away, but Alma wouldn't let him. She sucked him so hard, so deep. He grunted and filled her mouth with his hot cum, and she lapped up every bit and then swallowed.

"Alma, baby. That was incredible."

She wiped her mouth. "Glad you liked it."

He laughed, pulled up his boxer briefs and then embraced her. "Liked it? I loved it."

A wave of emotion flashed over him. Was he just in the afterglow?

He could've sworn that his feelings had come back to him.

He loved her.

No, no. It was just that intense high from the pleasure.

And despite her showing up tonight, she hadn't given him any indication that she wanted to date him again.

But he had made a decision.

He wanted her.

More than just a fling.

He'd been thinking about it, about them, nonstop. Yes, he was still young, and yes, he wasn't sure what he was going to do as a career. But he wanted her. Maybe growing up meant taking a risk even if it will fail, both in business and in love.

And what if they could start something together? Not just personally but professionally. He could start a tequila brand with her.

It wasn't the right time to tell her now. Not until they spent more time together. Not until she could see for herself how much he had changed.

And that he was serious about her.

After they both went to the bathroom, Jaime relaxed on the bed in his room. She cuddled up next to him, her head resting on his chest.

"Seriously, thanks for getting the critic back to the restaurant. It meant a lot to me."

He laughed as he stroked her hair. "Ha. If I knew that would've been my reward, I would've done it sooner."

Alma playfully smacked him. "Stop."

He pulled her into him. "No, I'm joking. Your bar is amazing, and you deserve all the success in the world. It wasn't fair that I ruined your chances to have a good review."

She looked up at him and batted her eyelashes. "Thank you. And I'm sorry for going off on you that night. I was so shocked. I never thought I'd see you again."

"Honestly, I didn't plan on seeing you again. Ever. I did just come here selfishly because I wanted to start a tequila line. I wanted to see you, of course I did. But I wasn't planning on rekindling anything."

But I am now.

He kept his thoughts to himself.

"I have a question for you."

His breath hitched. "What?"

"What are you doing in a couple of weeks?"

"Oh, I don't know. Why?"

She pursed her lips. "Nothing. Just curious."

Jaime didn't press. Back when they were dating, Alma had always been cautious and slow to open up. She would tell him what was on her mind when the time was right.

They had a quiet night in. Ordered room service—juicy cheeseburgers and crispy french fries for the win—and watched some cheesy rom-com on the television.

"I should get back. Tequila needs me."

Jaime hesitated. He shouldn't push but he couldn't help himself.

Alma glared at him. "What? Do you want to walk me back?"

"I do. But what I really want is to spend the night with you."

Alma's eyes widened. "Okay."

Jaime beamed. "You sure?"

"Yeah, it would be nice."

He gathered his toiletry bag, and they walked to her place. She opened the door and gathered up Tequila.

"Make yourself at home."

Jaime nodded and took in the room. It was cozy and warm. Big throw blankets, family pictures on the wall, a few pieces of brightly colored art.

She returned from her dog walk and got ready for bed.

Jaime did as well and snuggled in beside her.

He kissed Alma on the forehead. "I wanted to stay with you last night, but I didn't want to overwhelm you."

She grinned. "This is really great Jaime, but I want to be clear. Let's just enjoy ourselves while you're in town, and then when we say goodbye, we can both finally move on."

Jaime's throat tightened. He turned his head away, trying to conceal his emotions. "Right. Exactly what I was thinking."

"Cool. I'm glad we're on the same page."

"Yup. Night."

He closed his eyes and tried to go to sleep but it didn't work. He was up most of the night watching her sleep.

How had he been so stupid, allowing himself to find feelings he thought he had lost forever?

She woke early in the morning.

Jaime needed to bounce.

"I'd love to stay and have breakfast, but I have to meet my brothers."

"Oh, totally. I have to get to work." She kissed him softly. "I'll see you at the Cinco festival."

"Yup. See you there."

Jaime bolted out of her place and walked back to his hotel. Once there, he finally crashed.

When he woke up, it was early afternoon. He texted his brothers.

Jaime: Sorry I've been absent. Can you meet for lunch?

Ramón: Yup. We're at the Depot now.

Jaime: On my way.

The Depot was close by in the neighboring town of Mill Valley. It was a historic train stop that had been turned into a bookstore and café. He and Alma would often go there and study together when they spent weekends in Marin.

Jaime arrived. The place looked exactly as he remembered it. People playing chess, skateboarding on the concrete, reading underneath trees. It reminded Jaime of Europe.

Europe.

Jaime had planned to surprise Alma with a graduation trip to Europe as she had never been. But he had broken up with her instead.

Had she ever gone?

Ramón and Enrique were sitting at a table, drinking coffee. Their women were nowhere to be found.

Ramón stood up and hugged Jaime. "You look like shit. Rough night?"

Jaime nodded. "Yeah. I'll tell you all about it. Where are Santi and Tiburón?"

"You know Tiburón. He convinced Santi to take him joyriding in one of his many cars."

"Sounds like him. I'm going to get some food."

Jaime walked into the café and ordered a breakfast burrito and an iced vanilla latte with a double shot of espresso.

While he waited for his food, he perused the books. The store was small with a curated collection of cookbooks, YA books, and some literary fiction.

He paused over a book with cocktail recipes. He picked it up and browsed through the pages.

Alma should write one about tequila.

He wanted to text her right away, but her words rang in his head.

She wanted this to be casual.

He didn't, but he hadn't told her that.

Nor would he.

His food finally arrived, and he took the plate and glass over to his brothers.

Enrique patted him on the back. "So spill. What have you been up to?"

"You know the answer. Alma. We slept together. And I spent the night with her last night."

Ramón's eyes widened. "Not shocking at all. I'd be more shocked if you hadn't."

"I know."

Enrique shook his head. "So you plan to end it and leave?"

Jaime's voice lowered. "That's the thing. I think I want to get back together with her."

Ramón's mouth dropped. "No you don't."

"I do though. But it won't happen. She made it very clear she is only interested in a fling."

"Maybe she's saying that out of fear," Enrique said. "Did you tell her how you feel?"

"Of course not."

Ramón leaned into his youngest brother. "Look. I never thought I'd be in a happy relationship. Neither did Enrique. But we are both in healthy partnerships. You hurt Alma greatly. She's probably scared. You have to tell her what you want."

Jaime sipped his latte. His brothers were right. His soul knew that Alma still cared about him. He had to tell her that he was willing to try out a real relationship with her.

With no expiration date in sight.

Chapter Twenty

The air was alive with vibrant energy as the sun shone on the Canal, casting a warm golden hue over the bustling Cinco de Mayo festival. Brightly colored papel picado fluttered in the gentle breeze, and the intoxicating aroma of sizzling street tacos and elote filled the air. Families, friends, and couples wandered through the streets, laughing and enjoying the festivities that had taken over the town park. It was so heartwarming to see a community that suffered so much come together and be part of so much joy.

Amidst the crowd, Alma strolled through the maze of booths, her smile reflecting the joy of the celebration around her. After she had gotten over her initial anger of being manipulated into attending, she'd looked forward to this event for weeks, and now that it was finally here, the anticipation had been worth it.

The journey through the festival was a sensory delight. The measured beat of live mariachi music enticed her to watch a group of dancers in a lively circle, swaying and twirling to the infectious rhythm. Kids' laughter mingled with the music as the little ones attempted the intricate steps, occasionally stepping on one another's toes, but always recovering with grace.

Alma checked on her stand. The town had approved her liquor license for the event, and she had created a small tequila-tasting booth that also served her famous spicy margaritas. She mixed up some cocktails and helped her bartender. Carlos had told her that they had already raised over one thousand dollars to support the community's programs.

Jaime walked up to the booth. She hadn't seen him since the night they'd spent together. He hadn't reached out and she hadn't seen a reason to either since she knew she'd see him here.

She wanted to ask him to go to Mexico with her.

She said hi to José, who filled her in on the sales. Then Alma turned her attention to Jaime.

"Hey," Jaime offered with a head nod.

"Hey."

"How's it going over here?"

"Good. We've raised some money for the community."

"That's great. It's a wonderful event."

"And you? What does my brother have you roped into?"

Jaime laughed. "It's not too bad. Julieta has a taco stand, and Ramón, Enrique, and I are judging some Miss Canal contest. But I guess more women than registered showed up, probably to meet Ramón."

Alma laughed. "Ha, just Ramón? You're the one with a zillion followers."

"Alma, you know that means nothing. You're the only one I want following me." He stepped closer, caging her in on the outside of the stand. "About the other night—"

She held up her hand like a stop sign. "Don't complete that sentence. We don't need to define what happened."

Jaime sighed.

Was that a hint of disappointment from him? Did he want to clarify their relationship?

Well, she didn't. "For now, I just want to focus on my tequila." Though she wanted to ask him to go to Mexico with her, now wasn't the right time. It was so crowded, and they were in public. But being that close to him, with uncertainty in the air, was unbearable. Besides, he lived a million miles away—and there was no guarantee he wouldn't break her heart again.

And she wasn't even sure she wanted to be in a relationship. That critic had printed the review, and she was already fielding calls from press.

She was going to mention that to Jaime, but she had already thanked him the other night.

"Got it. Sorry I bothered you." Jaime walked away toward his brothers. She could see them look at her and then pat him on the back. Then Carlos escorted them to the stage to judge the contest.

This was for the best. She just wanted this event to end, and then she would ask him about Mexico. If he said yes, they could have a great time on their trip, and then when they returned, Jaime would leave Marin. And who knew what would happen after that? But Alma couldn't give him the power to break her heart again.

As the sun dipped lower, the lights strung across the park began to twinkle, illuminating the festivities. The scent of churros and tacos mingled in the air, making her mouth water. She wanted to try Julieta's famous tacos but didn't want to have a conversation with her about Jaime, so she sampled other delicacies as she walked along. She bit into a crispy churro, the sugar rush taking over her body.

She sat on a secluded bench behind a vendor. There—a moment of peace.

After the contest concluded, Jaime found her stuffing her face with a tamale.

"Can I sit here?"

"Sure. How was it?"

"It was fine. Hard to choose. So many great women."

"Isn't that your motto?"

Jaime shook his head. "It's not like that. I can't even think of any girl but you."

"Really? I haven't heard from you this week."

He clenched his fist. "I didn't call because I wanted to give you space. I'm having real feelings for you, but I *am* leaving. I was trying to do the gentlemanly thing, so we don't complicate this further. I thought I could do the fling thing but I'm incapable with you."

Alma exhaled. "I'm sorry. You're right. It still hurt. I like you again."

"I miss you. Hey, I'll be right back." He got up and ordered them two cups of Mexican hot chocolate.

He handed her a mug. "Do you still like this?"

"I do. Thank you."

"I remember your sweet tooth."

They sipped their drinks, and she enjoyed the moment of quiet amidst the festive chaos.

The night was still young, and the warmth from the drink calmed Alma's nerves.

As the main stage came to life with a captivating dance performance, Alma found herself drawn to the spectacle. She watched in awe as the dancers moved with precision and passion, their colorful costumes swirling with each graceful twirl.

As the final notes of the performance echoed through the stage, they clapped.

The announcer spoke in Spanish that they would be opening the floor for anyone to dance.

Jaime stood up and offered his hand to Alma, a mischievous glint in his eyes. "May I have this dance?" he asked, a playful grin tugging at his lips.

Alma's heart skipped a beat, and she accepted his hand as her cheeks warmed.

"How did you understand that?"

"I've been trying, Alma. Duolingo helps. But I do know *some* words. I heard *baila* and the notes of a song."

She laughed. He led her to the growing crowd on the makeshift dance floor, swaying to a slower, more romantic tune. With each step, her body pressed against his in a gentle embrace, and the world around them faded away. It was as if they were the only two people in the universe, lost in the music and the magic of the moment.

But she knew he would be leaving in two days.

She needed to mention Mexico now.

But what did he mean about having real feelings for her? She didn't want to get hurt.

As the song came to an end, their foreheads touched, their breaths intermingling. "You're an amazing dancer," Alma whispered, her voice a soft melody in the night.

Jaime smiled, his eyes holding hers. "Only because I have the most wonderful partner."

They shared a lingering gaze, the connection between them

deepening with every passing second. The stars above seemed to shine a little brighter, as if the universe itself acknowledged the love blossoming between them.

The festival continued around them, but in that singular moment, it was only them. Their hearts beat in time with the music, and as they held each other close, the world seemed to fall away, leaving only the promise of a love and the threat of farewell that had taken root amidst the festivities of Cinco de Mayo.

At the end of the night, she worked up the nerve to ask him to go to Mexico with her.

He walked her to her car.

She opened up her mouth to speak, but he laid a simple kiss on her lips.

"Good night, Alma."

Alma stood on the balcony of her oceanfront condo, her heart torn between nostalgia and uncertainty. A gentle breeze tugged at her hair, as if urging her to let go of the past and embrace the unknown.

Her phone buzzed on the table nearby—a text from Jaime. The message was simple, yet it stirred a whirlwind of emotions within her: Meet me at Caffé Acri in an hour. I have something to ask you.

Alma's mind raced as memories of their time together flooded her thoughts. They had shared laughter, dreams, and a love that had once seemed unbreakable. But life had taken them down different paths, and their love had given way to heartache. He was leaving. Tomorrow. And she was staying. She had decided after the festival against asking him to go with her to Mexico. Getting even closer to him seemed like a supremely bad idea.

As she scrolled through her phone, her mind churned with questions. What could he possibly want? Why was he reaching out after he had given her such a quick goodbye last night?

It had been so abrupt. Just like the time he dumped her in college.

Alma stood before the mirror, adjusting the sundress she had chosen for the meeting. Her heart fluttered like a butterfly, uncertain whether to soar or to retreat.

She walked down the street to the café. The scent of freshly brewed coffee filled the air, mingling with the melodies of quiet conversations.

Alma entered the café, her eyes searching the small marble tables with wooden chairs for Jaime. And there he was, sitting at her favorite corner table like he could sense which one it was, his eyes lighting up as he saw her. Jaime stood and pulled out the chair opposite him, a gesture she remembered all too well.

"Alma," he said softly, his voice tinged with a mix of nerves and familiarity. "Thank you for coming."

She took her seat, her gaze meeting his as a storm of emotions raged beneath the surface. "You wanted to talk. What is it, Jaime? You already said goodbye."

He looked down at his hands, fingers tracing the rim of his coffee cup, as if he was searching for the right words. "I know it's been awkward since I came up here, and I understand if this is uncomfortable. But I've been doing a lot of thinking lately, about us, about what we once had."

Alma's heart raced, the memories of their love resurfacing with a bittersweet intensity. "Jaime, we both know that what we had is in the past."

He nodded, his gaze never leaving hers. "You're right. But what if the future still has something to offer us? I've grown. Or I'm trying to grow. What if we could create new memories, ones that reflect who we are now?"

Confusion gnawed at Alma as she struggled to comprehend his words. "What exactly are you suggesting?"

He took a deep breath, his eyes holding a vulnerability she had not seen in a long time. "I want to take you on a trip, Alma. Zoila called me. She told me she's not going to Mexico with you. Let's go on a romantic getaway to Mexico, just like we had always talked about."

Alma's heart pounded, torn between the traces of their past and the reality of today. "Jaime, we're not the same people we were back then. Our lives have changed. And it won't be all fun. I'm going to do some work also."

He reached across the table, his hand gently covering hers. "I know that. We can do whatever you want to do. But maybe we owe it to ourselves to see if there's still something between us that could actually work. A chance to rediscover each other, without the weight of expectations or the mistakes of the past."

Tears welled up in Alma's eyes, her emotions swirling in a tempestuous dance. "I'm scared, Jaime. Scared to open old wounds, scared to hope for something that might not be there. Last week stirred up all these emotions I thought I'd buried. I don't want to get more attached to you and have you leave again. You could dump me again."

"I won't. I promise." His thumb brushed away a tear that had escaped her eye. "I'm scared too. But I believe in second chances, in the power of love to heal and to transform. I want to change. Will you take a chance with me?"

As the café bustled around them, Alma's mind raced through memories of their shared history. She looked into his eyes, seeing the sincerity and yearning reflected there. Could she open her heart to the possibility of rekindling a love that had once burned so brightly? Not just a fling, but a future?

And there were so many unanswered questions. He lived in San Diego. Would he move?

Doubtful.

But maybe they could try. No expectations.

With a deep breath, she nodded, her voice barely above a whisper. "Okay, Jaime. I'll go with you to Mexico."

His face lit up. "Really?"

She stroked his hand. "Let's have fun. No expectations, but I'm open to whatever happens. And Jaime, you can drink and learn more about tequila."

Jaime took her hand. "I'll tell you what will happen. You will fall madly in love with me again."

She laughed. "We will see. But we should go and have fun. Thank you. I didn't want to go alone."

His face lit up with a mixture of relief and hope, as if a weight had been lifted from his shoulders. "Thank you. I promise, whatever happens, this trip will be a journey of rediscovery, for both of us."

As they left the café, the sun sat high in the sky, casting a warm and reassuring light on the path ahead. Alma felt a mixture of uncertainty and excitement, as the echoes of yesterday merged with the promise of a new beginning.

Chapter Twenty-One

Their plane hit down in the state of Jalisco and the glass containing the Bloody Mary Jaime was drinking rattled. Was it from his nerves or from the turbulence? He'd been to Mexico many times before with his brothers and his friends—to Cabo to party, to Cuernavaca to learn Spanish, though even with a month of daily tutoring he still couldn't speak it, to Mexico City for a San Diego Padres versus San Francisco Giants baseball game, and to Puerto Vallarta to see Julieta's mom Linda's original taco stand—the place where his father ate his first fish taco, stole her recipe, and sparked an idea that would result in all his, and frankly their, wealth.

But Jaime had never been to the country of his ancestry with a woman that he'd once loved.

That maybe he still did.

And he couldn't wait to spend the full week with her. Though normally his time in Mexico was spent surfing, this time he would be exploring a part of Jalisco he had never been to—particularly the city of Guadalajara.

Guadalajara. A city so steeped in culture. Jaime had bought an old-school travel guide at the airport and already learned so much about this city. It was cool. He'd had no idea that Guadalajara was the birthplace of so many iconic traditions in Mexican culture. Traditions that even Jaime, a third-generation Mexican-American, loved and appreciated. From mariachi and ranchera music, to tasty birria-style tacos, to jaripeo, a form of bull riding, Guadalajara was such an exciting, dynamic city.

But of course, it was most famous for tequila, his newfound passion.

Jaime was taking a brief tequila break and had opted for vodka. Plane tequila was never good anyway.

He didn't want to talk about their past anymore. Or their future. He just wanted to enjoy their time together.

A vacation was supposed to be romantic, adventurous, historical, but never, ever uncomfortable.

He wanted to grab her hand—she looked so stunning sitting next to him on the plane—but he couldn't bring himself to do it.

Not yet.

How weird was it that they'd had sex the other week, but he felt holding her hand was more intimate? Man, he was fucked-up. Though based on what she said at the café, she probably agreed.

But maybe something on this trip would change between them.

Maybe she would finally look at him the way she once had many moons ago. With not just love, but with hope instead of sadness.

"Let's go." She pulled on his sleeve, which caused his skin to tingle.

He had upgraded them to the best hotel in Guadalajara, but Alma wasn't easily impressed by such things like other girls he had dated, who often expected such luxuries. She was making great money now. She didn't need his—not that she ever had. Back when they had been dating in college and Alma didn't have much disposable income, Jaime never, ever thought that she was using him in any way, shape, or form. It was one of the things that had initially attracted him to her.

Jaime met their limo, and the driver drove away from the airport. He drove down a long and winding road. Even though they arrived at the hotel late at night, lights lined the trees.

Alma smiled. "Wow. This place is stunning."

"Glad you like it."

The resort had beautiful Spanish architecture and a lavish long pool he would love to relax in. He had almost booked them into a boutique hotel where they could stay in a blue agave field in rooms that were shaped like barrels. It was in a distillery, but he'd decided to let Alma lead on any agave activities.

The restaurant was already closed, so they ordered room service.

Jaime had high hopes for another sexy night, but when he went to put their trays outside their room, he returned and found Alma fast asleep. Jaime tucked her in bed and kissed her on the forehead.

He didn't even try to touch her that night. Tomorrow would be a new day, and he would get a read on her temperature toward him.

The next morning, Jaime ordered them breakfast in bed. Alma had a yogurt bowl with fruit, and he had a delicious omelet, both with fresh juices, pastries, and of course, copious amounts of coffee.

Alma was wearing a white slip dress and Jaime wanted to rip it off of her and fuck her until she screamed his name. She was breathtaking. Her black hair cascaded over her shoulders and the contrast with that dress made her look like a naughty angel.

He tapped a brochure that he had picked up in the lobby. "I know part of this trip was for your work, so I didn't want to impose and schedule activities, but I'm happy to if you want me to."

She tossed her hair. "It's okay. I have everything set up."

"What did you have planned today?"

"Oh sorry, I wasn't trying to be vague. Today, we are going to go to an agave farm. It will be a treat for you. You can see how the agave is harvested."

That sounded great and also super useful. Jaime still hadn't abandoned the idea of starting his own tequila company, though now he was focused on his growing feelings for Alma. Partaking in Alma's curated tasting experience had made him truly appreciate the different types of tequila. He was very excited to go to the farm. And spend more time with her.

"I can't wait. Let's go."

"Would you like to stop in town with me first?" She slipped one sexy foot into her shoe, then the other. "I want to explore a bit, and they aren't expecting us until later."

"Sounds good." He needed to get out of this room ASAP—anything to stop himself from worshipping those legs and the heaven to which they led.

Jaime had been looking forward to seeing the town, exploring the vibrant heart of Mexico, and now, as the sights and sounds of Guadalajara enveloped him, with Alma by his side, it felt surreal.

The air was filled with the rich aroma of street food, the sizzle of carne asada grilling on open flames mingling with the sweet scent of churros. Even though they had just eaten, Jaime's stomach growled in response.

He ordered a few tacos for them and some churros for dessert from a vendor.

They shared their food and compared the flavors to those of the same dishes back home. It was easy to say that the local cuisine was better here, though he would exclude Julieta's tacos from that statement. But there was something about being in Mexico that made the food taste even better.

Maybe it was the company.

As they wandered through the lively mercado, his senses were assaulted by a kaleidoscope of colors. Stalls overflowed with bright textiles, handcrafted pottery, and sparkling jewelry. Alma ran her fingers over a delicately embroidered blouse, marveling at the craftsmanship. He thought she was going to buy it, but she received a call and left the stand abruptly.

Jaime lingered for a bit and purchased the top for her.

"Everything okay?"

She nodded. "Yes. Carlos had a quick question about a delivery. He's helping out while I'm gone. Thank God for international cell service."

"He's the best."

Jaime presented her with the blouse.

She blushed. "Jaime. You shouldn't have." She gave him a quick kiss on the cheek.

The voices around them were a symphonic blend of laughter, bargaining, and the rhythmic cadence of Spanish. Jaime caught snippets of conversations, his limited Spanish intertwining with his excitement, creating a melody of linguistic exploration. Alma kindly translated random words when he asked, and he vowed to become fluent in Spanish when he returned home.

He had tried before. Maybe he was bad at languages. The harder he wanted to learn, the more difficult it seemed to be.

Maybe he just needed to be here. Immersed in the culture.

Drawn by the sound of mariachi music, they found themselves in the town square. A group of musicians clad in silver-buttoned charro suits played with such passion that the notes seemed to dance in the air. Alma swayed to the rhythm.

"Would you like to dance?" he asked her.

"You danced so well the other night," she said, coy, twirling a strand of hair around one finger.

"I was just warming up." He winked and held out his hand, then pressed his body against hers, her heart beating in time with the music against his chest.

They continued their exploration, each turn bringing new wonders. In a quaint café, they savored a cup of rich, aromatic coffee, its flavor a bold embrace of the region's spirit. The barista shared stories of local legends, his words painting pictures of mystical creatures and brave heroes.

When they were done exploring the city center, their driver took them on a long journey out to the farm.

The afternoon sun was rising over the vast expanse of the agave fields, making the endless rows of spiky plants look equally menacing and beautiful.

The driver stopped and let them out. Jaime pulled Alma into his chest. But he didn't kiss her.

In the midst of this sea of green plants, a woman stood, her hands wrapped around the handle of a tool. Her skin was kissed by the sun, and beads of sweat glistened on her forehead, but her eyes sparkled with a passion for her craft.

"Welcome. My name is Gabriela. I'm a jimadora. I'm excited to welcome you to my farm."

"Nice to meet you, Gabriela. I'm Jaime, and this is Alma."

She smiled and pointed to the tool. "This is a coa, the traditional tool used to harvest agave."

Gabriela began to tell them about her story. She had grown up on this plantation, learning the art of tequila making from her father. He had never had any sons but proudly passed his knowledge on to his daughter, who became one of the first female jimadores, or jimadoras. It was more than a livelihood; it was a heritage, a tradition that flowed in her veins as surely as the agave sap flowed through these plants.

Gabriela gave Alma and Jaime a tour of the farm, but she spoke in Spanish. Jaime was struggling to follow the conversation, and Alma jumped in as his translator when he seemed frustrated.

Gabriela left them alone for a few minutes and returned with a tall man who had deep-set eyes.

"Allow me to introduce you to Alejandro. He has come to teach me new fermentation techniques."

Jaime introduced Alma to Alejandro using the best Spanish he could muster. Then Alma spoke to Alejandro in Spanish at such a rapid pace that Jaime didn't understand a word they were saying. Jaime was relieved when Gabriela led them all to the plants.

Alejandro showed Gabriela a new method of cutting the piñas, the heart of the agave plant. His hands guided hers, and they worked in tandem.

Jaime clutched Alma's hand, a spark of electricity bolting between them. Then it was their turn to harvest.

Jaime helped Alma chop the piñas, enjoying being close to her and working in the fields, the warm sun at his back.

So, this was where tequila came from? He had never given its origins a thought when he drank it, not caring about where the liquor he was imbibing came from. And here these men and women took so much pride in their country's heritage and the long history of producing this beloved liquor.

He dropped a piña through his hands.

Alma tossed her hair back and laughed. "This is hard work?"

"Yeah, Enrique would love it though. I have to get him out here."

"You have a natural skill," Alejandro commented in English to Alma, his voice a low rumble.

"I agree with him," Gabriela said. "I've been doing this since I was a child. The agave speaks to me. It looks like it speaks to you also."

Alma lit up and beamed. She was absolutely adorable. "Oh. Gracias. I feel so connected to it. I love all types of tequila, but being here and seeing the plants is so cool. I even named my dog Tequila."

"I can sense your passion," Alejandro said with a growl.

Alma giggled.

Jaime glared at him. He tried to control his jealousy. He wanted to make her giggle, and not just when he was fumbling a plant.

Alejandro said no encouraging words about Jaime's skills, but that was fine. Jaime was just happy to be there with Alma. He wanted to know how to do this stuff for his brand, but he wouldn't be the one working the fields himself. He was better on the business side of things. But it did give him a better appreciation of the beverage.

Jaime and Alma continued to work in silence, the only sounds being the rhythmic chopping and the distant calls of the workers heading home. As the sky turned a deeper shade of orange, Alejandro broke the silence.

"Tequila making is like creating a piece of art, isn't it?" he mused, wiping his brow with the back of his hand.

Gabriela nodded, glancing at him. "It's all about patience, passion, and understanding the soul of the agave. Each batch tells a different story."

Alma translated for Jaime.

What if that could be their story? What if they could somehow have the patience to make this relationship work despite their rocky past? Would their passion sustain them?

Their eyes met, and something unspoken passed between them. It was a moment of connection, deep and undeniable.

As the day's work came to an end, Gabriela offered to walk Alma back with her to the distillery room.

"I'll meet up with you in a few minutes." Jaime waved her on.

Alma didn't ask him why and continued on with Gabriela.

Jaime stayed back, wanting to talk to Alejandro since he seemed to speak some English.

"So where is your farm?" he asked as they walked up between rows of plants.

"In a town about twenty miles from here. Would you like to see it?"

"I can't on this trip. But maybe I'll return. I was wondering . . ." Jaime took a deep breath in. "Do you contract with brands to create tequila lines?"

Alejandro's smile turned to a scowl.

He sized up Jaime. "I do. But not with everyone. We have a very pure batch. I like to see who I'm dealing with. And you barely even speak Spanish."

Jaime exhaled. Could he ever escape being a no sabo kid?

He tried a different approach. Jaime took out his card. "I'm Jaime Montez. My father is Arturo Montez. We own the Taco King franchise."

He studied the card. "I have never heard of you. Or your father."

"Doesn't matter. I have ample money. Anyway, I'm interested in starting a brand."

"With your wife?"

"Oh, Alma? She's not my wife."

Alejandro shook his head. "I don't want to work with a man who is not settled. A wife brings you stability. Honor. I have been married twenty years."

He studied Alejandro's face. "Alma and I aren't at that place."

Alejandro placed his arm on Jaime's back. "Let me give you some advice. That woman you are traveling with loves you. I can see it in her eyes. And from what Gabriela told me, Alma is a tequiladora. If you are going to start a line, it should be with her. She should be having these conversations with me—not you."

Jaime knew all of this. But what was he going to do now? Tell Alma that he wanted to start a brand with her even though they weren't back together?

And even if they did get back together, he shouldn't mix business with pleasure.

"Thanks for the advice. I meant no disrespect. Alma isn't my girlfriend, though she was once. I just traveled with her, so she didn't have to come alone." He looked out over the agave field once more. "Please don't mention this conversation to her."

Jaime extended his hand for Alejandro to shake, but he ignored Jaime and just walked to the distillery, with Jaime trailing behind.

Once they reached the distillery, Gabriela welcomed Jaime in. She showed him the barrels where they stored the tequila and talked about the process for each. Alma and Jaime tasted some different tequilas. Even though the ones Jaime had tried back at Alma's bar were amazing, there was something so incredible about trying each one straight from the barrel.

Jaime's palate grew. What had started out as a silly idea just based on anger toward another stupid Instagram campaign had ignited a passion. He actually cared about agave. He wanted to know everything there was to know about tequila. He imagined the brand, the launch party, the advertisements. He was truly excited about a work venture for once in his life.

And he owed it all to Alma.

Jaime had almost expected Gabriela to invite them to dinner, but she didn't. They said their goodbyes, and Jaime walked with Alma in the middle of the agave fields before returning to the limo.

Alma gazed into his eyes. "Thank you for accompanying me to Mexico. I'm so glad I didn't miss this trip. I learned so much."

"You're welcome. I did too. This sounds cliché, but I feel like tequila is . . . a part of my life almost. My history. Thanks to you."

"Ah, I don't deserve all the credit. You are here with me and seem to be really interested. What did you talk to Alejandro about?"

Jaime's throat scratched. He didn't want to tell her the truth. Not yet. Not until he was sure about the future of their relationship. He didn't want her to think he was only interested in recommitting to her because he wanted to start a brand with her. Once they were back together and he had shown up for her, they could discuss their career options.

"Nothing much. I was just asking him about his farm and the different regions. How about you and Gabriela?"

"Oh, she was amazing. I asked her about how hard it was to be a woman harvesting tequila. Her mother was horrified when her father taught her and was very angry at him, but he stood up to her."

"That's pretty inspiring."

"It really is. Especially here in a more traditional country. I'm just so awed by her." Alma placed her manicured finger on Jaime's chest.

Her lips were just inches from his face. He wanted to kiss her so badly. But not a lust-filled kiss. This time with more hope.

Alma curled her hands around his neck. "Kiss me, Jaime."

Jaime cupped her face and gave her a kiss that belonged in a telenovela. He kissed her like it was his first time ever kissing her. He kissed her like it was his last time kissing her. He had kissed her so many times before and it was always electric.

There was no doubt anymore.

He wanted her back.

He loved her.

There, in the midst of the agave fields, where the spirit of the earth was distilled into the fiery heart of tequila, Jaime realized that love, like tequila, needed time, care, and the right blend of elements to truly come alive.

He finally pulled away from her mouth and escorted her back to the limo.

They were driven back to town and they stopped to get a quick dinner at a restaurant.

As the night fell, the sky turned into a canvas of stars, the town square coming alive with lights and music. Alma and Jaime found themselves drawn into a fiesta, the locals welcoming them with open arms. They danced under the moonlight, their feet moving to the rhythm of the mariachi, her laughter mingling with the joyous energy around them.

In that moment, surrounded by the warmth of new friends and the vibrant spirit of Guadalajara, Jaime felt a deep connection to this land. It was more than just a place; it was a living, breathing tapestry of culture, tradition, and beauty.

They returned to their room, and they couldn't keep their hands off of each other. Jaime pulled off her white dress and devoured her pussy. Alma came quickly and climbed on top of him. She rode him and stared deep into his eyes. No words were spoken but they weren't needed. They came together, and Jaime was in complete bliss.

As they lay in bed that night, the memories of the day flickered through his mind like a cherished movie. Jalisco had embraced him, its heart beating in harmony with his own. And as sleep claimed him, he knew that this journey would stay etched in his soul forever, a vivid reminder of the magic that exists when one dares to explore the unknown.

Chapter Twenty-Two

Alma woke up refreshed and excited about the day. She couldn't wait to celebrate her first Fiesta de San Isidro, Patron Saint of Farmers and Laborers.

She rolled over and watched Jaime sleep. He was naked. She wanted to climb on top of him for another round but held off. Last night, their sex had been so emotionally intense.

But she was struggling. She loved him. This entire vacation was so natural and intense. He had been great, perfect even. So why was she doubting this could work? Could she ever trust him again?

She snuck out of bed, took a shower, and got dressed. Jaime did as well, and they were off to the town for another adventure.

The vibrant colors of the Fiesta de San Isidro adorned the streets of Jalisco, turning the town into a mural of life and celebration. Papel picado fluttered in the breeze, the scent of tamales and conchas filled the air, and the rhythmic beat of mariachi music echoed through the cobblestone streets. It was a day where the community came together to celebrate Isidore the Laborer, the patron saint of farmers, a day where hearts were light and spirits high.

And Alma was so grateful for farmers who toiled in the agave fields like Gabriela did. Slicing those piñas was hard work. Her wrists ached from assisting yesterday.

But she had kind of loved the work. Wouldn't it be cool to spend more than just a day at the farm and harvest her own agave? It was truly an art form, and spending the time cultivating the crops made her love her spirit, and her job, even more. Maybe she could make a yearly pilgrimage here to work on a farm . . .

But being in Gabriela's distillery had inspired another idea in Alma.

What if . . . she started a brand of tequila? She could buy directly from the barrel from Gabriela.

Could she imagine it? Curating the mixture, deciding what flavors to highlight, picking the recipes to use to showcase her spirit. It would be like Christmas every day! She'd even have a blast picking out the bottles to sell the liquor in. Though Alma knew better than to judge a book by its cover or a tequila by its bottle, sometimes she couldn't help herself. Some of the containers were so, so beautiful, as was the artwork for the labels. She loved the hand-painted ones from Mexico and the ones that resembled skulls.

What kind of tequila would she like to sell? At first, she thought a classic añejo, though recently she had been on a cristalino kick. She loved that cristalino looked like a blanco but actually was an añejo. It was fun to introduce some patrons who normally wouldn't try stronger tequilas to new types, especially for the women who were hesitant to try anything strong. Turning them on to a whole new world of taste was exhilarating.

Ahh, it was very exciting, but the truth was that having a tequila line wasn't cheap. She was successful with her business but didn't have that kind of capital.

But Jaime did.

And he seemed to really love tequila. He didn't know much about tequila when he first reappeared into her life, but Alma could tell he'd really begun to appreciate it.

What if she asked him? It could give him an excuse to move up to Marin.

No. No. That was a supremely bad idea. The worst. They shouldn't mix business with pleasure until they were fully committed to each other.

She looked over at Jaime, his eyes taking in the town. He was by far the most handsome man she had ever seen. He truly looked like a movie star. Women stopped and stared at him. It was no wonder that he had been so successful as an influencer.

Her relationship with Jaime would end soon as he left to go back to San Diego.

She moved through the crowd with Jaime by her side and focused again on the saints. Of all the saints, San Isidro was her favorite.

Jaime took a bite out of a concha he grabbed from a stand. "This is so good. Want a taste?"

She nodded and he moved the flaky pastry to her mouth. She took a bite—it was so fluffy and decadent and sweet. "Oh, that is great. We need a good panadería in Marin. We have a few but not like this."

"There are a bunch in San Diego. One next to Julieta's restaurant is incredible."

Alma didn't respond to that comment. Of course there were

great panaderías in San Diego. Why wouldn't there be good bakeries in a border town?

Jaime had explained that Enrique's girlfriend, Carolina, had moved from Santa Maria to San Diego. In all fairness to her, that hadn't been so straightforward. She was from a super traditional family and supposedly they freaked out when she was stranded in a storm with Enrique and couldn't go home for the night, so she gave them the farm she'd purchased and moved and started another. She had even broken up with Enrique before she moved down there.

Alma didn't want the thought of San Diego's sunshine, surf, and sand to be an option. She was a Northern California girl—fog and ferries were more her scene.

Jaime finished his concha. "So, who was this saint guy anyway?"

Alma loved to talk about her favorite saint. "Oh, you haven't heard of him?"

"Well, to be honest, I don't know any of them." He wadded up his concha napkin and tossed it in the trash. "Except . . . Saint Francis. He blessed animals. Didn't this guy do that too?"

Alma was not going to shame Jaime for his lack of knowledge on saints. Not all Mexicans were Catholic, but Jaime technically was, though she wasn't sure if he had ever been confirmed, which meant if they were ever to get married, he would need to take care of that if she wanted to be wed in the church.

Not that they would ever get married. She was so ridiculous. They weren't even technically a couple.

"Well. Saint Isidore was the patron saint of farmers and laborers. It is said that he gave some of his last grain to starving pigeons. The townspeople were upset since they wanted that grain, but then a miracle happened, and the bag of grain was refilled."

Jaime smirked. "I'm sure he was a great guy and loved animals. But I don't believe in that miracle foolishness."

"Well, I do." She had to believe in something. Why not have faith?

But sometimes it was hard to believe in what she couldn't see, feel, taste.

"So, what was his story?"

"He was married. His wife, Santa María de la Cabeza, was awesome also. Supposedly they had a son who fell into a deep well, but after his parents' prayers, the water rose, and the son was saved. After that, the parents moved out into separate homes and took a vow of celibacy."

Jaime's face contorted. "There is nothing at all cool about that. They were married. They couldn't have sex, and they lived in separate houses? So, the boy had to go to two separate homes? Believe me, from my experience, that sucks."

"You have a point. That does seem awful." Alma was so lucky that her parents were still married, and she'd never had to experience what Jaime had gone through. She was certain that was one of many reasons he was so hesitant to get into a relationship. When they were younger, it was more like a first-serious-relationship type deal, and now if they got back together, it would be more like a forever relationship. How could she expect Jaime to believe in them making a long-lasting commitment if he hadn't seen that work?

"That is why I don't like so much of this Catholic nonsense. They don't allow gay people to wed, the priests can't be married, and there is rampant sexual abuse. I was born Catholic, but I'll never practice it. Today was cool, because it's a fun festival and we're honoring farmers, but I'm not into organized religion. Ramón is going to all these crazy Catholic marriage classes for Julieta. I would never do that."

Tell me how you really feel.

"Alrighty then. I get it. You make good points. I'd like to get married in a Catholic church, just because I love the ritual and the tradition, and I want to make my parents happy. And Carlos has completely left the church, so I guess it's up to me to fulfill that fantasy for my parents."

Jaime stopped and tilted his head toward Alma. "Why did Carlos leave the church?"

"Oh, same reasons you said. Didn't accept gay people, abuse, rigidity. All those things. I don't blame him."

"He's a smart man." Jaime grinned. "I like that brother of yours."

Jaime became silent. Alma appreciated that he spoke his mind and had valid reasons for his opinions. If it worked out between them, would she be able to abandon her dream of marrying in the church? Would her parents give her their blessing?

Well luckily, or unfortunately, depending on how she looked at it, a Catholic wedding wasn't even on the table for them.

Alma told Jaime a few more stories about Saint Isidore. There was an ease between them, a connection that felt as natural as the river flowing through Jalisco.

As the evening approached, the crowd gathered around the main square for the highlight of the festival—the crowning of the queen of the fiesta. Alma and Jaime found a spot near the front, their shoulders brushing, their hands occasionally touching, sending sparks of electricity between them.

The queen was crowned amidst cheers and applause, and as

the first notes of a romantic ballad filled the air, Jaime turned to Alma.

"Would you dance with me?" he asked, his hand extended toward her.

Alma's heart raced. They had been dancing a lot lately. Back in college, their dancing had consisted of grinding to some old-school hip hop. Jaime had always been the life of the party, and she had been the shy, more studious type. But she was having a blast on this trip, and she had to admit, this was way more romantic than a trip with Zoila.

She nodded, placing her hand in his. As they stepped into the dance, the world around them seemed to blur into a whirl of colors and sounds. All she could see was Jaime, all she could feel was his hand in hers, his arm around her waist.

They danced through the song, and as it ended, they stood there, still holding each other, lost in a moment that was theirs alone.

"Alma," Jaime whispered, his voice barely audible over the cheers around them. "I have traveled all over Mexico, seen many festivals, but nothing has captivated me like this place has. Though honestly, I think it's the company I'm keeping."

Tears welled in Alma's eyes. She had felt the connection, the unspoken bond, but hearing his words made it real.

"I don't know what happens next," she said, her voice trembling with emotion.

"Neither do I," Jaime replied, his eyes searching hers. "But I want to find out. With you."

In the heart of Jalisco, under the festive lights of the Feast of San Isidro, Alma found more than just the joy of tradition. She found a love that was as unexpected as it was beautiful. A love that, like the festival, brought color and light into her world.

They slowly walked back to the hotel. Hand in hand, stopping every few steps to kiss under the streetlights.

Finally, back in the hotel, Jaime scooped up Alma and carried her across the threshold.

Like a bride.

Alma didn't say a word about it, but her mind raced. He was being so romantic. What had gotten into him?

Jaime placed Alma down on the bed, gently, with no urgency. The other night in the bar, they had fucked. It was raw and hot, but it had only been sex. Amazing sex. He'd fucked her so fast, so hard, so deep it made her head spin in pleasure. She loved every minute of it.

But this time, everything seemed different. Maybe it was just the romantic location—a beautiful resort compared to a trendy bar.

She felt like they were on their honeymoon. Ay, what had gotten into her today? She couldn't stop thinking about marriage and weddings and honeymoons. She was insane. They weren't even boyfriend and girlfriend.

And she was clear in her head. She was in love with him. She wanted this to work. But she doubted he truly could commit to her, no matter what he said or believed.

And she couldn't help her thoughts. A priest once told her it wasn't a sin to think about sex—we couldn't control our thoughts. However, we could control ruminating about topics once they sprung to our minds.

Jaime's face softened when he looked at her. No more eager anticipation or lustful hunger. It was almost as if Alma was in a time warp back to how they used to be. Back when they were young and infatuated.

Back when they were in love.

Could they still be in love?

She couldn't tell. Years ago, it was a deep, true first love, the way only first loves could be. Alma had been full of dreams and fantasies.

But this time, everything was different. Her heart had been broken by the very man in her bed.

She was still crazy about him, but she no longer thought he was perfect.

Not that she was perfect either. Far from it.

Maybe they were perfect for each other.

He brushed a lock of hair away from her face as he lowered to kiss her. A sweet kiss. Soft, loving. His hand made its way down her body, slowly, oh so slowly, stopping only to caress her breast before moving to trace the outline of her waist and eventually settling on her thigh.

His stubble scraped the palm of her hand as she cupped his face. She stopped and considered his eyes, which were just a little more trusting and loving than they had been since he'd come back.

She seized that moment, taking advantage of this opportunity when he seemed to be truly open to her. "I'm so happy that you came back to Marin, and you took me to Mexico."

Jaime smiled. He took a moment to speak, and the seconds were excruciating to Alma. Then he said, "I've never stopped loving you, Alma."

He loved her? Not in the past but now?

Did she love him? Of course she did. She always would, but that didn't mean she felt that they were right for each other now.

She didn't know how to react, so she remained silent. She wrapped her arms around his neck. Did he want to get back together with her? Did he really want to commit to her? She was dizzy with lust and confusion.

She considered ruining the moment by interrogating him and getting the answers she so desperately needed and craved, but instead took a deep breath and exhaled.

Time to enjoy the present.

With his free hand, Jaime peeled off his shirt. A smile graced her face as he let his shirt fall to the floor. She would never tire of staring at his chest, ever. Broad shoulders, abs for days, and a thin line of dark hair trailing to his pants. He motioned for her to lift her arms, and she did as he slipped her T-shirt off over her head, taking her bra with it, and flinging them off the bed.

His attention turned to her breasts. He thumbed her left nipple and sucked on her right one. She let out a moan as he lightly nibbled her bud.

His mouth detached from her sensitive skin. "You're so beautiful, babe. You were always sexy."

She arched her back as his mouth made its way down her body, pausing over her hip bone and showering her belly in kisses as he pulled her jeans off. His hands pulled down her panties, and then he cupped her ass as she gripped his wild black hair.

His tongue gave a long, slow lick down her center, drawing a low, throaty moan from her throat. He teased her, tasting her without focusing where she needed him and making her squirm. When his tongue found her clit, her body arched off the bed, and she felt him smile against her.

He pressed his finger inside of her and she moaned. The dual sensation of being penetrated while his mouth worked her pussy was so intense. So incredible. Back in college, their lovemaking had been so sweet, almost innocent. They had discovered what they liked together, especially Alma, who had been a virgin. But now, Jaime seemed to have all the moves. She pushed the thoughts of him being with other women out of her head.

He was with her now—no one else.

And he said he loved her.

His mouth focused on her, and the pleasure came in waves. She couldn't hold back and came so hard all over his mouth. He lapped her up.

But she wasn't done. She wanted more. Another round.

He sat back against the headboard, pulled her onto his lap as he guided her onto his cock. Gripping her hips, he slowly urged her to lower onto him, until he was fully inside her.

"Oh, Jaime, baby. Make me come again," she said, her voice breathy.

His mouth went to work on her nipples as she rode him, rubbing her clit on his crotch, his huge cock filling her. It wasn't long before they were both covered in a light sheen of sweat, their breaths short pants of lust and need.

Then, right before the tight coil low in her belly threatened to ignite, Jaime lifted her chin and stared into her eyes, never losing her gaze. She loved him so much, in every way, mind, body, and soul.

"Baby, I'm right there. Don't stop!" she screamed, savoring every moment of this ecstasy.

He thrust her down one more time, pushing deep as she came, Jaime falling over the edge right after.

He stroked her hair and buried his head in her chest.

"Alma, I don't think I can ever let you go."

Chapter Twenty-Three

Jaime made love to Alma all night long. It was like back when they'd first started sleeping together in college. They couldn't get enough of each other. They spent the next couple of days holed up in the hotel room or relaxing by the pool, just soaking up every minute left on the trip.

After taking brief breaks for food and beverages, they were back at it. Like rabbits.

But the vacation was coming to an end.

Jaime had meant it when he said he loved her.

But she hadn't said it back.

He *did* love her. But what did that matter?

Maybe she hadn't said it back because she didn't believe he would truly commit to her. Move for her, even.

Jaime resolved that he would fully commit to her. Tonight, at dinner.

It was a rare rainy evening in Guadalajara. Their last evening.

Jaime had booked dinner at a restaurant in town with an award-winning chef, but Alma wanted to stay closer for their last night, so they planned to dine in the hotel restaurant.

Alma emerged from the bathroom wearing a long red dress that hugged all of her curves. Her black hair cascaded down her back. How did she get more and more beautiful every time he saw her?

"Good evening, gorgeous." He kissed the nape of her neck. She smelled like vanilla and citrus. He couldn't wait to take off her dress after dinner.

"Good evening, handsome." She fixed his tie. "I like this suit. It's no tuxedo or anything, but you clean up well."

"I'm not putting on another tuxedo for a while." He paused and realized he was wrong. There was a formal event in his near future. "Actually, that's not true. I'll be wearing one at Ramón's wedding."

Her eyebrow rose. "Oh, yeah. You mentioned it."

"It will be huge. There will be a church ceremony at Mary, Star of the Sea. Then pictures on the beach. And finally, a big reception in La Jolla at the Del."

She nodded. "That sounds fun." She looked down at her shoes. "Let's go eat."

Jaime noticed that she changed the subject rather quickly. He had already asked her a while back, but she hadn't taken his invitation seriously.

He took her hand. "Alma, I already asked you, but I will again. Do you want to go to the wedding with me? You can come down and stay in my house. I'll show you around San Diego. It will be really fun."

Her eyes opened wide, and her long black lashes fluttered. "You really want me there?"

He dropped his hand around her waist and kissed her. "Of course I do. I already told you that. I'd love for you to be my date."

She grinned and then bit her lip. "Are you sure? There are always beautiful women at weddings. I'm sure Julieta has a big family with a bunch of cousins. I don't want to cramp your style."

Jaime was sick of her teasing. "Stop. You act like I'm some womanizer."

"Aren't you though? I've seen your Instagram."

"Alma, it's not like that. Many of the girls are just models who I never even dated. And the rest . . ." He exhaled. "They meant nothing."

"Sure they didn't. And you wonder why I think you're a playboy. Because make no mistake, you are a playboy. I'd almost go so far as to say *fuckboy,* but spare me the details."

Why was she being so nasty? Yes, he had dated women but not when they were together.

She was probably feeling insecure. Jaime decided to put her mind at ease.

This was his chance to lay it all out there and be honest with her. "Fine, I'm not going to lie. I was. But I'm crazy about you. I love you. And when we were together, I never cheated on you. You know that, right?"

"I don't think you ever cheated on me, but things were different then." She clasped her hands together over her mouth. "You say you love me, and I don't doubt that you feel that in the moment when we are having sex, or even now, but we've been dancing around this question since you came back into my life. What do you want? Do you want to get back together? What does that look like? Do you want to do long-distance? Because all I know is that we are flying back to San Francisco tomorrow and you're turning around the next day and flying to San Diego. And I'm not. And I can't take this anymore. You disrupted my life. I was happy before you showed up. And now, look at me. I'm acting jealous."

Jaime sat on the sofa. Here it was. They couldn't avoid this conversation any longer. "I want you back. And I'll do anything to make it work."

She sat next to him, her lip trembling. "Jaime, I can't believe I'm hearing these words from you. To be honest, I don't know what I want."

Jaime gulped. "You don't want to get back together? You don't still love me?"

She placed her hands in a prayer position. "I do love you. I'll always love you. But I'm happy in my life. Maybe you were right—we were too serious too young. I want to focus on my career for a bit."

Jaime hung on every word she said. Did she really not want to try to make this work?

"You don't think I could make you happy? Alma, it's different now."

"I don't know, but I'm not moving to San Diego. I own the bar, and I'm happy in Tiburon. And I would never ever ask you to move to Marin, so how could this work?"

Jaime exhaled. "Well, it *could* work. I think we could figure it out slowly. Organically. Not make any rash decisions. But I'm open to moving."

Her jaw dropped. "That sounds nice and mature. What do you propose?"

"Come to the wedding. And then I can see if I can spend some time up there. I want to make a change. I love Marin. Obviously, you are there, but I'm super close with Santi. My brothers are so busy with their women that I barely see them." He paused. Time to lead into what he had to tell her. "And possibly we could work together."

Her head tilted. "Really? How so?"

Rain splattered against the window, as if echoing the heaviness in both of their hearts. Alma looked at Jaime, who buried his hands in his pockets.

"Well, I told you I wanted to start a tequila line."

Alma crossed her arms over her chest. "I know, Jaime."

"Maybe we could do it together?"

She loudly exhaled. "Is that why you are trying to get back together with me?"

"No. No, I was honest with you, and yes, you helping me learn about tequila was the reason I went to Marin. I did want to see you, but that was my motivation. Since spending time together, I realize that not only do I have feelings for you but also that we would be successful together."

Alma sat there staring at him, her lip quivering. "How could I be so stupid?"

Jaime tossed up his hands. "What are you talking about? Stupid about what?"

"This was your plan, right? All along? Pretend you are falling back in love with me to get me to start this tequila line with you? Lie and say you want to commit to me?"

Jaime was dumbfounded. "Oh my God, no, Alma. No. That wasn't the plan. Yes, I selfishly wanted you to teach me about tequila, but I have already told you that."

She shook her head. "I don't believe you, Jaime. I want to so badly, but I just can't believe in my heart that you really are ready to commit to me. I think you want to do this for your business."

How had this gone so wrong? He couldn't look her in the eyes, so he looked out the window. "I don't want to use you. That's not it at all. A month ago, I was sent an influencer packet for a tequila brand. Tom Bluey's. Have you heard of it?"

"Yes. What does that have to do with anything?"

"Well, I considered it at first. Typical campaign. And I was alone in my house, just tired of my life. Sick of social media, the women, just everything."

"Go on." She leaned away from him.

"And I don't know if I'd been hanging around Julieta too much, but she was always talking about cultural appropriation, and I got mad. Why should I promote this guy's brand? He wasn't even Mexican. It makes me madder now that I actually know something about tequila thanks to you. So, he was just going to use me, a pretty-boy Mexican face, to sell his tequila."

She squeezed his hand. "Yeah, I do think that's pretty shitty. I try not to carry celebrity brands in my bar."

"I think it's awesome that you look to source good ethical tequila brands."

"Thanks. But I'm still lost. What does all this have to do with us?"

Jaime shook his head. "It sparked something in me. I wanted to be more than the pretty face. I wanted to contribute. I didn't want to be used. So, I got this crazy idea." He lowered his voice. "I thought I could start a tequila line. But I knew nothing about tequila. I looked you up and then I saw you had a bar so—"

A look of confusion washed across her face. "You already told me this."

Jaime could almost see her mind processing everything. "I know. But I'm trying to tell you that I have changed. I don't want to be the womanizer, influencer. I want to start something new. Something I can be proud of. With someone I trust."

"And now, you want to just latch on to my hard work."

"No. It's not like that."

"You know, ironically, the other day I thought about what it would be like to start a tequila line. With you. But not now. Way way off into the future. If we had actually been committed. Like married. Now, I feel used."

"I am not using you."

"Yes, you are." She looked up at the ceiling as if it could give her answers. "Is that why you stayed behind the other day at the agave fields? Were you trying to broker a deal with Alejandro?"

Oh fuck. There was no getting out of this one. "Not exactly. I mean, yes. I did ask him about the possibility of starting a brand, but he put me in my place really fast. Said that I shouldn't do anything until I was stable. He thought you were amazing and that I should marry you, for what it's worth."

"It's worth nothing! None of what we shared or what we did is worth a damn thing." She pulled her hair, and her eyes bugged. "How could you have done this to me, again? I'm so stupid. I vowed after you hurt me to never ever let you back in my life, and here we are. I hate myself so much right now."

Jaime winced as if he'd been struck, his eyes pleading with her to forgive him. "I screwed up, okay? I got lost in the what-ifs and maybes. I thought, if we got back together for this reason, maybe we'd find the magic we had once. And for a while, it felt like we did. Didn't it? Can you say this hasn't been magical? That you don't feel what I feel? That we should never be apart?"

Alma shook her head slowly, her gaze fixed on his. "You missed the point, Jaime. Even if we did find something meaningful again, it wouldn't change the fact that you waltzed back into my life and expect to just profit from my work. That's something I can't overlook."

"Alma, if you give me another chance—"

She held up her hand, stopping him in his tracks. "No more chances, Jaime. I've given you one too many. Like the saying goes: 'First time, shame on you; second time, shame on me.' It's time for me to think about what's good for me, and being with someone I can't trust isn't it."

His shoulders slumped, a mix of resignation and sorrow washing over him. This couldn't be it. He would fight for her. "I'll do whatever it takes for you to forgive me. I fucked up but I'm owning it. I will get therapy. I'll do whatever I need to do to get your trust back."

"There is nothing you can do, Jaime."

"So, this is it then? We're over?"

She scowled at him. "Hell yes we're over. We were over before we even began," she replied, her voice steady. "Plus, there was never any sort of future with us ever anyway. You just invited me to your brother's wedding, but I doubt you were really going to move to Marin. You would've led me on for a few more months with false promises, then started a tequila line, and then dumped me. Again."

He took a step toward her. "That wasn't going to happen. You are freaking out because you are afraid that I will break up with you again. I won't. You even said yourself you considered starting a line with me. How is that any different? Things are different this time. You know it. You feel it too."

"I feel nothing."

Jaime let out a mirthless laugh. She was lying to him, or at least to herself. He knew from the bottom of his soul that she felt what he had. The way she looked at him. The way she opened up to him about her fears. The way she casually talked about the future as if he would be in it. "Yes, you did. And you know what I'm saying is true. But nothing I say will make you believe me."

Her makeup was smeared across her face. She grabbed a tissue and dabbed her mascara. "You're right. I won't believe you."

Jaime nodded slowly. "I guess there's nothing more to say."

"There isn't." She wiped her eyes. "Please leave. I want to be alone."

Jaime didn't want to leave her alone. He wanted to stay, wait for her to calm down, and plead his case. If she could only understand him.

He went into the bedroom in the hotel suite and packed his things. He changed out of his suit that he had brought to take her to a nice dinner in and into his sweats.

He walked toward the door, his steps slow and heavy, like the rain that continued to fall outside. As he opened it, he paused, turning back to look at her one last time. "I really am sorry, Alma."

She nodded, her eyes meeting his. "So am I, Jaime. So am I."

"For what it's worth, I do love you."

Her voice cracked. "I love you too."

Wow. She actually said it. He wanted her to say those words so badly the other night. But now, they were empty.

And with that, he stepped out into the hallway, closing the door quietly behind him.

He dragged his bag down to the lobby and booked another room.

Once he got the keys, he had to walk into the rain to get to the other room, which was in another building, away from Alma.

When he entered the room, he sank onto the couch, his emotions a whirlwind of pain and newfound clarity. Why did he fuck up every good thing in his life? Why? When he was younger, he didn't dump her because he was trying to be a jerk. He was just so fucking immature and thought it would be better if the breakup was clean and they were no longer in contact. He didn't want her to change his mind when he knew he had to do what he needed to do.

And now, yes, the reason he'd come up to Marin was fucked-up, but he had been honest with her. And his feelings for her now were real.

He shouldn't have mentioned wanting to start a tequila line. It was too soon.

He raided the minibar. He needed a drink—anything BUT tequila. He settled on a Malibu and Coke to take the edge off.

Maybe this was the wake-up call that he needed. He clearly wasn't thinking his way through anything in his life, with work or with women.

Fuck, what if Enrique was right? Maybe Jaime should see a therapist. His parents' marriage had really fucked him up. He had spent so much of his childhood alone that he withdrew anytime things got tough.

God, he'd rather go to a catechism class and learn about saints than talk about his feelings.

But a sense of clarity did wash over him.

During this entire trip to Marin and Mexico, he had been changing. In many ways.

This new room felt colder, emptier, but also, in some inexplicable way, full of potential for something genuine, something real.

And for the first time in a long while, despite the rain and the heartache and the cheap liquor, Jaime felt the promise of clearer skies ahead.

The end of a chapter, but the beginning of his journey to a love built on trust, honesty, and respect—a love he truly deserved.

Chapter Twenty-Four

A month later, Alma sat in her condo. Life had been quiet ever since Jaime left. He hadn't even bothered to fly back to San Francisco with her—instead he had booked a direct flight to San Diego. Not that she could blame him. She had made it abundantly clear that she didn't want to hear what he had to say. Her pride was so wounded, and she was so angry with him that she couldn't even try to see it from his side.

But after some reflection, a few talks with Zoila, and some intensive therapy, Alma's stance softened toward him. Jaime was a twenty-five-year-old man. So, he had wanted to start a tequila line with her. She herself had had the same thought, so how could she blame him? She had just felt so used and doubted that he really wanted her more than he wanted a new business venture. But deep down she believed that he had really fallen for her again, despite himself, just as she had fallen for him.

But none of it mattered. He was once again in her past. She

truly didn't believe for a second that he would move up to Marin. And she wouldn't move to San Diego. They were at an impasse. There was no happily ever after in their future.

At least she got to experience what it was like to be sexually free again. In the aftermath of their short fling, she had decided that she had focused way too much on her career and that she needed to also prioritize her personal life. She was only young once. She was beautiful and kind. She wanted to have a healthy sex life.

Unfortunately, anytime she fantasized, she always imagined Jaime. Naked.

Alas.

A warm glow from the rare sunny June day in San Francisco shone through the window in her condo. Mark Twain once famously said that the coldest winter he ever spent was a summer in San Francisco. Alma couldn't agree with that statement more.

She wrapped herself in a sweater and curled up on the couch with a monster romance novel. It was a quiet afternoon, the kind she cherished after a long week at work.

The sound of her phone buzzing disrupted the calm. It was her brother.

"Hey, Alm, can I come over?" Carlos's voice was tense, a hint of something unspoken lingering in the background.

"Of course, Carlos. Everything okay?" Alma asked, concern threading her words.

"I just . . . I need to talk to you." Carlos was the stoic type, always calm and composed. He was her rock. For him to sound this unsettled was rare.

"Come over. I'll make us some coffee," she said, trying to sound casual.

When Carlos arrived, there was a hesitancy in his step, a vulnerability that he rarely showed. He slumped onto the couch beside her, his hands fidgeting.

Alma waited, giving him space to gather his thoughts. She poured him a cup of coffee, the familiar aroma filling the room, a small comfort in the thickening silence.

"Carlos, what's going on? You're scaring me a bit here," she said gently, her eyes full of concern.

Carlos took a deep breath, his gaze meeting hers. "Alm, I've been carrying this around for a while, and I can't do it anymore. I need to be honest with you."

The seriousness in his voice set her nerves on edge.

"What is it? Are you sick?"

"No. I've been going behind your back."

She eyed him up and down. "With what exactly?"

"I've been working for Jaime. I couldn't say no. He has been funding my soccer league and paying me as director."

The words hung in the air, a declaration that seemed to both relieve and terrify him.

For a moment, she was silent, processing his words. Then, without a syllable, she reached out, her hand finding his, a gesture of support and love.

"Carlos, I love you. No matter what," she said, her voice steady and sure. "I'm just sorry you felt like you couldn't tell me this because of my problems with Jaime. This is a great opportunity for you."

Carlos's eyes, usually so guarded, filled with tears. "I was scared," he admitted. "Scared of how you'd react, scared you'd think I was betraying you."

Alma squeezed his hand, her own eyes welling up. "You're my brother. Nothing could ever change how I see you. I'm proud of you for paving your own way and going after what you want. That takes courage."

They sat in silence, the bond between them a tangible thing. It was a moment of unspoken understanding, of unconditional love and acceptance.

"Thanks, Alma. I was so worried," Carlos whispered, a weight visibly lifting from his shoulders. "You know I'm loyal to you."

"Always here for you, Carlos. Always," Alma reassured him.

"Thanks." He paused. "You know, you reacted exactly how Jaime said you would."

Alma spit up her coffee. Jaime? "Jaime? You can work for him but don't be talking about me. I'm your sister. Your blood. Jaime wasn't even your friend—he was just my ex."

"That's kind of harsh. We were always friends."

He was right. That was uncalled for. "True. Sorry. I'm just testy, that's all."

"Relax, chica. I love Jaime. He was so cool."

"I am relaxed, but I can't believe you are gossiping to him about your own sister."

"Well, that's the thing, Alma, this isn't about you. I was so excited about this, but didn't want to piss you off. I needed to talk to him about it, because I don't want anyone else around me to think I used my sister's ex to get this job. I did ask him, but dammit I deserved this job. He has money and he wants to give back. I know you're all pissed off at him for wanting to start a tequila line with you, but I swear he didn't do that to use you. That's not like him."

Damn. "You're probably right."

"I am right. You were too focused on thinking he was using you. He wasn't, you know. He's all broken up about this. He loves you. You do realize he's a millionaire and could've paid anyone in the world to teach him about tequila. Yeah, that may have not been the best reason for him to come up here, but it wasn't malicious. He did want to see you; he was probably just trying to find an excuse to do it."

Alma gulped. Guilt washed over her. "You're right. I was too harsh on him. And he does have so many good qualities."

"He's amazing. A great guy. Generous. Kind. You're a fool. Shit, if we weren't both straight, I'd snag him myself."

Ha. "Such a good brother."

"Just keeping it real."

"Well, speaking of your love life, give me some tea. Are you seeing anyone?"

"I'm not seeing anyone right now. I love wounded birds. It's my curse."

As the day went on, they talked more. Carlos shared his hopes for his new program and even more about his finances. For the first time in his life, he actually thought he had a future and could get paid for doing what he loved and giving back to his community. Alma listened, her heart swelling with pride for the brave, incredible person her brother was.

It was late when Carlos finally stood to leave. At the door, he turned, looking at his sister, a smile touching his lips, a smile that held a thousand unspoken words of gratitude.

"Good night, Alma. Thank you for being you," he said, his voice thick with emotion.

"Good night, Carlos. And remember, I'm always proud of you," she replied, her words a promise.

As Alma closed the door, she leaned against it, a sense of peace settling in her heart. Her brother had been honest with her, and in doing so, had brought them closer than ever. Alma smiled, her heart full.

But she also realized that Carlos was right about Jaime. And maybe, just maybe, he deserved forgiveness.

She needed to talk to him face-to-face.

She grabbed her phone, made a reservation, and then packed her bag.

It was time to go to San Diego.

The next evening, her plane touched down. San Diego was beautiful out her window as she flew in over the water. And the airport was close to downtown, not out of the way like San Francisco's airport, which was outside the city and always chaotic.

She took an Uber straight to Jaime's place. She had begged Santi for the address and made him promise to figure out some way to make sure he was home. Santi swore that Jaime had turned into a homebody since he returned to San Diego but that wasn't good enough for Alma. Santi relented and pretended to have an urgent package delivered.

The Uber dropped her on the steps of an oceanfront mansion. Damn, he lived here? She knew it would be nice but didn't imagine anything like this. Then again, she lived in an oceanfront condo. But her place was nowhere near as expensive as this one.

Under the soft glow of the moon, the tranquil garden out front felt like a secret sanctuary, a place where emotions could flow freely, and secrets could find solace. Alma stood near the ornate fountain, her heart torn between uncertainty and longing. The scent of blooming roses mixed with salty seawater filled the air, their delicate petals mirroring her fragile emotions.

She texted Santi: I'm here. Tell him to come down and meet me.

Footsteps approached, each one echoing in her chest. She

turned to find Jaime standing there, his dark hair tousled by the gentle breeze. His eyes, normally full of confidence, now held a mixture of regret and hope.

"Alma," he began, his voice carrying a weight that she couldn't ignore. "What are you doing here? Santi said—"

"Can we talk?"

"Of course." His eyes widened. "I can't believe you're here."

Alma bit her lip, fighting back the swell of emotions threatening to overcome her. She nodded, her gaze steady as she motioned for him to continue.

"I need you to know that I never meant to hurt you," Jaime began, his words tentative, as if he was unsure how to proceed. "I know I messed up, and I shouldn't have even brought up the tequila line. But please believe me when I say that my feelings for you are real. And I'm willing to do whatever it takes to make our relationship work."

Alma's heart wavered, caught between the confusion she held onto and the desire she had tried so hard to suppress. She folded her arms across her chest, a defensive gesture she hoped would shield her from the vulnerability he stirred within her.

"I just felt foolish, Jaime," she said, her voice steady but laced with hurt. "Like you were honest that you wanted to learn about tequila from me, but once you mentioned the line, I just spiraled. It felt like too much when we were so new. Well, old, but new."

Jaime stepped closer; his eyes locked onto hers with a determination that sent shivers down her spine. "Alma, I'm sorry I came on so strong. I was having such strong feelings for you. I was just a mile ahead of ourselves."

Alma's gaze softened, curiosity overcoming her initial anger. "Why, then? Why rush?"

Jaime took a deep breath, as if gathering his thoughts before speaking. "When I first met you at college, I was taken aback by how genuine and kind you were. And then I ended it, which we have established was my fault. This time, I did miss you, but maybe I didn't realize it. I was subconsciously led back to you. And once I saw you, I wanted to see if what we had was still there."

"I did too."

Jaime's face was etched with remorse, regret seeping into his every word. "Spending time with you made me realize that I never stopped loving you. And sexually, it's the best I've ever had. And I'm sure I'm a jerk for saying this, but the fact that you've never been with another man is so hot."

Alma rolled her eyes. "Yeah, you're a jerk for saying that. I should go fuck someone else just to prove a point. I'm not a fan of misogyny."

"I know it's gross. I can't help it. Some weird primal Mexican machismo thing that I can't help feeling. At least I'm aware that it's not cool."

Alma's anger was still present, but the sincerity in Jaime's eyes was undeniable. She felt torn between wanting to protect herself and wanting to give him a chance to make amends.

Jaime reached for her hand, his touch warm and gentle. "I'm asking for a second chance, Alma."

"By second, you mean third, right?"

"Fine. Third. And final. I genuinely care about you. I want to show you how much you mean to me, and I'm willing to do whatever it takes to earn your forgiveness."

Alma stared at their entwined fingers, her heart warring with her mind. Could she really let go of her anger and take a leap of faith? The moon above seemed to hold its breath, waiting for her decision.

After a long silence, she finally met Jaime's gaze, her eyes softening. "You confuse me, Jaime. Deeply. But I see the sincerity in your eyes, and maybe . . . just maybe, I'm willing to give you a chance to prove that you've changed and that you really want a future with me."

"Thank you."

"Actually, thank you. Or thank Carlos for making me be able to see past my own bullshit."

"Carlos is on my side?"

"Yeah, I'll say. Carlos told me about his new job yesterday."

"Cool. Finally. I'm so happy he confessed to you. It's not charity, Alma. He's doing a great job, and I believe in his work. You know my passion was soccer. I want to give that opportunity to other kids. And Carlos deserves to be paid for his work. I didn't do anything special."

Alma threw up her hands. "There you go again. Jaime, you are a great man and you're not giving yourself credit. Don't you see? Carlos sees it. He trusts you. And it isn't just Carlos. You're super modest. You took Leti to the dance, not for publicity, not for any ulterior motive. You had a great time too. You're just a really good guy."

Jaime's face lit up with a mixture of relief and gratitude. "You really think so? I've been told so much of my life that I'm a fuckup. I always compared myself to Ramón, who was the smart one, or Enrique, who was the kind one. I was athletic and good-looking. That sounds conceited but it's true. Everyone always valued me for what I had on the outside. But no one ever really cared who I was on the inside. No one but you."

She kissed him on the cheek. "I still care. This is the reason I fell in love with you."

He winked. "I thought it was because of my dimples. And my magic tongue."

She dramatically shook her head. "You're cocky for sure. But Jaime. I mean it. You're a good man."

"Thank you, Alma. I won't let you down."

"So, what does this mean?"

"Well, I don't have the ring on me. Nor have I asked your father."

She punched him in the arm. "You're such a smart-ass. I'm not expecting a proposal. Plus, I would definitely not say yes." Yet.

"I'm just playing. But I do want to ask you a question."

"And what is that?"

"Will you be my girlfriend?"

She wrapped her arms around his neck and kissed him.

"Yes, yes I will."

As they stood beneath the moonlit sky, Alma realized that forgiveness wasn't about erasing the pain, but about choosing to move forward despite it. The path ahead was uncertain, but she was willing to take that journey with Jaime, one step at a time.

Epilogue

Alma raced through the door of Mezcalifornia, carrying a big box.

Jaime rushed over to her to take it out of her hands. "Let me grab that."

She shook her head. "Not a chance." She pulled a switchblade from the key chain in her back pocket and sliced open the box.

In the cardboard case were twelve bottles of one of the world's finest tequilas. Mezcalifornia's small batch of añejo.

On the top of the box was the promotional package, complete with a cheesy picture of Jaime mugging for the camera with an impish grin on his face.

Damn. He was such a tool.

But at least this time his modeling was for his own brand of tequila. A Mexican-American-owned brand, not one making some non-Hispanic celebrity rich.

And even better, he had done this full thing without the help of his family. He had believed in himself. But there was one person he couldn't have done any of this without.

Alma.

His girlfriend.

Their relationship had aged as long as this añejo. After he had committed to her without hesitation, his first order of business was to enroll in some intensive therapy. He hated it, at first. Hell, what was he saying? He still hated it. It was excruciating. All the talk about his past, his family, all his fuckups, how he had hurt people in his life . . .

But somewhere along the way, he realized that he'd needed to do this work. He could never heal from his childhood trauma, and he would never have a successful relationship without spending the time healing himself.

He then spent a month alone at a Spanish-language school in Cuernavaca, Mexico. He lived with a host family and forced himself to immerse in the language. His Spanish was still not great, but he was committed to working on his fluency every day.

The best thing was, he wasn't even doing this for Alma—he was doing this for himself.

They had done a few months of long-distance, which completely sucked, and then Jaime finally moved to Marin. Alma wasn't ready to move in with him yet. She loved her space, and he was fine with that, so he moved in with Santi, who welcomed the company.

And living in Bolinas, Jaime could still pursue one of his other loves: surfing. Though the water was cold as fuck in Marin and he always had to wear a wet suit. He missed San Diego's warmer weather but escaped to Mexico or Hawai'i to catch some waves whenever he could.

But he didn't go alone. He went with Alma. She was always by his side now.

She raced behind the bar and grabbed two glasses. It was still early afternoon, and they were doing prep work before she opened for the night, cutting limes and preparing the spice mixtures for the glass rims. So she only poured a small sip in each.

"Salud!"

Jaime clinked his glass with hers.

They inhaled the spirit and then drank.

Wow. This tequila was actually good. Great even. Pride beamed in his chest.

A big smile took over Alma's face. "It's wonderful, Jaime! That's my professional opinion. And think of what we're doing. We're helping a full community out. And I love that we have only female jimadoras."

Yes, they did. Jaime and Alma had asked Gabriela to be their first. They had returned shortly after they had gotten back together last year and created a contract with her. She had been the main jimadora and they'd encouraged her to find and train other women to work with her in this traditionally male-dominated industry.

Alma unpacked all the bottles and placed them behind the bar amongst their new friends. They lined up like little toy soldiers on the shelves.

Jaime couldn't believe it. A little more than a year ago, he had been asked to be a tequila influencer and had hatched this crazy, half-baked idea after a couple of bad tequila shots in his La Jolla home. It had been a stupid idea to use his ex for his benefit.

And here he was, with a committed girlfriend whom he loved, living five hundred miles away from his family, and the owner of a top tequila brand and a soccer academy. Granted, Jaime was still taking modeling jobs but only for companies he believed in. And he was proud to rep his own.

He planted a soft kiss on Alma's lips—he could taste the shot of tequila she had just taken. "Babe, we did it!"

She kissed him back. "Yes, we did. But *you* did it. I only had a bar. I had a desire to start my own line but it seemed impossible. I didn't have the capital for it."

"Well, I couldn't have done it without you. I knew nothing about tequila."

She playfully punched his shoulder. "True, you didn't know your joven from your reposado."

"I didn't have a clue. But I had a great teacher."

They kissed again. He cupped her face and slowly, gently took her lips in his.

"I didn't just teach you about tequila. You could've learned that from any book. I taught you to believe in yourself."

Jaime exhaled. It was true. She had taught him so much. About love. About not being scared of the future.

"I don't know if I ever believed in myself. I was more afraid of never seeing you again."

"But Jaime, don't you see? You're such a wonderful man. You've always been such a wonderful man. You were so codependent on your family. You just needed some space. They are all great people, but you had to make your own way."

Jaime looked at his beautiful woman, his heart swelling with devotion. Their path to this point had not been easy at all. From callously dumping her in college, to him showing up to pump her for information, pushing her away, then to their grueling breakup. And then starting a business in a foreign country. Even though they were both Mexican-American, they were not Mexican nationals and had to gain the trust of the people of Jalisco who were suspicious of yet another American-owned company. But every challenge they had, they met head-on, and they'd worked through the issues together. The ultimate outcome of their own liquor brand tasted doubly sweet.

Or maybe that was the vanilla notes.

Damn, he was sounding like Alma now.

Alma stroked the bar. "Remember the first time we shared a shot here?"

Jaime grinned. "Don't tempt me, babe. I'll have you spread eagle in a second."

"No, we can't. That was different. It was at night. It's daytime now. We can't just fuck on the counter. Plus I don't have the time or energy to clean up after."

Jaime scooped her up in his arms and took her into her office, where he positioned her on her sofa.

The first time they had sex in the bar, it had just been physical.

But now, everything was so different. Jaime wanted to show Alma how much he loved her, he cared for her, he worshipped her, he appreciated her.

He was in love with her and didn't care who knew.

He could see forever with her.

Before he could rip the clothes off of her perfect body, Alma had stripped down to a lacy green bra that barely covered her breasts and matching panties.

He kissed her full lips as her hand rubbed his cock. Her hair was wild, and she tasted sweet. Wild and sweet. That was his girl.

Jaime undid her bra and sucked on her nipples. Her perfectly pert breasts felt like heaven. His cock was aching for her. Alma began to bite her lips, holding back her moans, and her muffled sounds were like music to his ears.

Alma undid his pants and grabbed his cock at the base. She deep-throated him, bobbing up and down. Her hot mouth felt so fucking incredible wrapped around his length. They were in perfect sync, sexually.

He could've come in her mouth, but he held back.

He just wanted to worship her.

He flipped her under him and kissed down her belly until he hit the hem of her panties. Jaime pulled her panties off and kissed her delicate flesh. She moaned again and grabbed his hair as he licked her. She writhed under his mouth.

Jaime wanted to lick her forever, but she pulled him up to face her.

He kissed her as he slowly entered her, his woman. She felt like happiness and heaven, all wrapped in one. Their fingers interlaced as they made love, every thrust bringing them closer to each other.

Ever since their initial college breakup, he had drowned himself in meaningless sex. But it felt empty. Sex between two people who truly cared for each other, who weren't just trying to get off, but were genuinely devoted to each other, was the most incredible high in the world.

He and Alma were endgame. After the connection that they shared, Jaime couldn't imagine being with anyone else.

Alma was close, her breath quickening. Jaime placed his hand under her ass and guided her movements.

They stared into each other's eyes as they came together in complete bliss.

Then, they heard the doorbell ring. Oh damn.

They quickly cleaned up and got dressed and saw Carlos standing at the door with a woman who Jaime didn't recognize. The girl was a bit younger than Carlos, with short wavy hair and a pretty smile.

Jaime let them in.

"Hey, bro, what's up? We just got our new tequila."

"Really, that's so cool."

"Pull up a chair and join us for a shot. Your friend is welcome too."

Carlos grinned and took the woman's hand. "She's not my friend, actually. She's my girlfriend. This is Cristina. Cristina, that's my sister, Alma, and my soon-to-be brother-in-law, Jaime."

Alma punched her older brother in the arm. "Smart-ass, we are not engaged."

"Yet," Carlos retorted.

Jaime walked over and hugged Cristina. "Nice to meet you. I'll give you the rundown on the full family. Basics are Tío Gustavo tells tall tales and Tía Cecilia is a chismosa."

Alma hugged Cristina, then hugged Carlos. "I'm so glad to meet you. So tell me, how long have you been dating? Where did you meet?"

Jaime shook his head. "Oh, Alma is a chismosa also."

She swatted him with an embroidered cloth napkin. "I am not!"

"Yes, you are."

Carlos answered Alma's question. "Actually, she's the mom of one of my students. We just hit it off."

"Ah, that's so cute." Alma poured them both shots of the new liquor. "To all of us! To love and laughter and authenticity."

They all clinked their glasses together. The liquid glided down Jaime's throat. He felt warm throughout his body, and it wasn't only from the añejo. It was from the love in the room.

Tequila wasn't just a business anymore, or a tool to get wasted. It was a connection to their culture, to their shared backgrounds, to the past, and to their futures.

"So, what's next?" Alma asked Jaime.

"What do you mean? I'm happy now."

"Don't panic. But I mean now what? I have a bar. We have a liquor line. What else can we do?"

Jaime knew exactly what he wanted.

Forever with her.

And he was finally ready to tell her.

"Alma, I was thinking we should move in together. We can find a new place or if you want to keep your condo, that's fine. But I want to be with you forever."

Her face contorted. "Is this some weird way of proposing? Not that romantic."

"No, Alma. Of course not. If—I mean, when I propose, you'll know it. But I want to live with you. I know you love your space, but I think we could be really happy."

She clasped her hands around Jaime's neck. "That sounds fabulous. And Tequila would love a stay-at-home dog dad."

Ha. "I do work, you know."

"I know. I kid. But you work from home, and I think it will be good for her."

"Fine, pug dad it is." He was getting used to that snorty dog of hers who shed everywhere and couldn't walk more than a few blocks without overheating. "Is that a yes?"

"Yes, it is."

Alma shed a tear that Jaime was certain was one of joy.

He didn't feel the need to run away from her.

He didn't feel the need to create some problem that didn't exist.

He just felt peace. And that was the best feeling of all.

They poured another shot.

And in her bar filled with spicy tequila and sweet agave, two couples toasted to their future, family, and forever.

ACKNOWLEDGMENTS

The third book in this series was the hardest for me to write. I rewrote it many times and am so thrilled to have set it in my hometown of Tiburon.

As always, I would like to thank my agent, Jill Marsal. You are so kind and patient. I'm so lucky to have you!

To my editor, Sarah Blumenstock. Thank you for your patience on this book! You have such a keen eye and are always so supportive. And to Liz Sellers—thank you for all your help with this book and series.

To editor Leis Pederson. Your first-round edits were incredible, and I feel so spoiled by being able to work with two editors on this book!

To my film agent, Carolina Beltran. Thank you for guiding me through this ride. I'm so blessed to have you.

To my buddy Nicholas Gonzalez. OMG! Thirty years later and we are creating magic together again, still with Shakespeare. The stars aligned and I'm so lucky to have you back in my life. I'm excited to see what the future brings with our collaborations.

To the incredibly talented María Dolores Águila. You're my

favorite! You've inspired me so much, and I truly wouldn't have finished this (or, let's be real, any) book without you.

To Shaun Redick and Yvette Yates Redick. I'm extremely honored with the possibility of working with you two! I'm so in awe of the projects you have already created and am humbled by the opportunity.

To my ride or die, editor Kelli Collins. I can't write a word without you.

To Lauren McKellar. Your insights on my books are incredible.

To Tamara Lush and Lisa Siefert. Writer friends are invaluable, and I love you both. Don't make me come to Florida.

To my publicity and marketing team, Anna Venckus and Hillary Tacuri. Thank you for working so hard on my book!

To my illustrator, Carina Guevara. This cover is so incredible. Love this series!

To my cover designer, Farjana Yasmin. Thank you so much for this cover!

To my copy editor, Pedro Fernández Martín; my proofreaders, Michelle Lippold and Isabella Pilotta Gois; and production editor Caitlyn Kenny. Thank you all for your eagle eyes and hard work on this book.

To my family: My late father, Joseph Chulick Jr. I have now lived almost twenty years without you. It never gets easier, and I miss you more every day. My mother, Diana Viramontes Chulick. You are my inspiration for all my books, and without you I would've never loved to read. I love you. Her partner, Harry Shaw Miller. Thank you for loving my mom. My brother, Joseph Chulick III, and my sister-in-law, Susie Chulick. I wish we lived closer. You are both so supportive.

To the lights of my life—my sons, Connor and Caleb. I'm so proud of you both! You've turned into incredible young men and are so talented. The next book I write will be for you.

To all my fans and the booksellers who support me. Thank you from the bottom of my heart for giving me this dream career.

Keep reading for a preview of
Alana Quintana Albertson's

Ramón and Julieta

Available now!

La Jolla, California

Ramón Montez relaxed in his leather chair and gazed out at the ocean from his home office. In contrast to his sleek, modern gray walls, the blue ripples undulated in the distance. Surfers dotted the coastline, catching the last breaks of the day, and Ramón wished he rode the waves with them, but he couldn't slip away from his desk. Not with a major acquisition for his company on the horizon.

He was confident that he would win the bid for the iconic block of property in Barrio Logan, an area that he loved. Barrio was home to Chicano Park—a Mexican-American historical site that had the largest collection of outdoor murals in the country. More importantly, it had been the center of the Chicano movement in the seventies when residents took over the land after the proposed park was slated to be turned into a California Highway Patrol station. Those protesters were heroes. The town was steeped in culture and community.

He needed to close this deal.

As CEO of the Montez Group, Ramón was responsible for identifying and taking over key properties throughout San Diego. With over two hundred Taco King restaurants in the country and tens of thousands of employees, the Montez Group had brought fast-casual Mexican dining to a whole new level.

To think, it had all started with Ramón's father, Arturo, and his surfing trip to San Felipe in the late seventies. One bite into an epic fish taco and Papá changed the course of his and his future family's life. He opened a small stand on the bay, and now the company was franchised throughout the United States.

"Ramón."

He recognized his brother Enrique's voice immediately. Ramón swiveled in his chair.

A deceased desperado donning a poncho and a perished pachuco decked out in a zoot suit popped their heads into Ramón's office.

Ramón took one look at his brothers and burst out laughing. It was a moment like this that made him glad he had agreed to buy this place together with them, despite the fact that they each could've easily afforded to purchase their own pads. But family was important to Ramón, and honestly, he couldn't shake the idea that he still needed to watch out for them, which was probably a lasting concern from protecting them his entire life from the disaster of their parents' marriage.

"Did I miss the memo on Chicano history day? Are we teaching at some school I didn't know about?"

Enrique gave a sly smile, but Ramón's attention was focused on his brother's ridiculous mustache, which curled at the ends. Dude definitely already won Movember, and it was only the first of the month. "Nah, just honoring our ancestors."

"Your usual Day of the Dead outfits weren't good enough this year?"

"No, hermano. These are custom-made." Jaime dramatically leaned back and placed his hand in the pockets of his oversized ballooning pants that tapered at the ankle. Ramón half expected Edward James Olmos to pop out of the closet and start singing. "They took two months to make."

Ramón gave a fake cluck of disappointment. "So, I can't get one at the last minute?"

Jaime pulled his phone out of his pocket and got his hand tangled in his double watch chain. "Let me put in a call to my seamstress. She might have something already made. I know a great—"

"Jaime, it's okay. It was a joke." Ramón shook his head. Jaime had been promoting the event on his social media, and Enrique would be giving a demonstration on how to grow your own altar flowers from a rare cempazúchitl seed he had cultivated himself from a cemetery in Jalisco. No doubt both were just ploys to pick up women, but at least they were somewhat representing the family business.

"I don't know why you two go to that party every year. It's just a bunch of tourists who don't know the difference between Day of the Dead and Halloween."

Enrique grimaced. "Well, I spent months growing the marigolds for the event. Besides, what would you know? You haven't been in years."

Enrique was a master horticulturist who had inherited their abuelo's love of landscaping. He had been lucky to turn his passion into a career and, surprisingly, had even convinced Papá to open a test kitchen garden. Enrique had big plans to streamline the way produce for the restaurants was being harvested at their main suppliers.

Ramón ran his hand through his hair. "Been to one Día, you've been to them all." Day of the Dead in San Diego had turned into another excuse to get wasted. It used to be a small procession to the graveyard, and now it was a three-day festival of hedonism. Half the people there didn't even understand the point of the holiday—to honor their deceased loved ones.

Ramón didn't need to party to honor his loved ones. He glanced at the altar he had built for his abuelo, a man who had practically raised him. Ramón had made the ofrenda himself and had purchased Abuelo's favorite bottle of tequila. A memory passed through his head of Abuelo teaching Ramón how to work on cars. Ramón had inherited his grandfather's prize possession—his 1967 Ford Mustang, which Ramón had restored and then converted into a slick and shiny lowrider. Ramón would toast to him tonight.

Jaime straightened the feather in his wide-brimmed hat. "No, dude. It's epic. You're missing out. Sexy dead brides and debauchery. What's not to love?"

Everything. Ramón envisioned a bunch of drunk influencers making TikToks in front of altars. He shuddered. No, thank you.

"Well, have fun."

Enrique nudged Jaime out the door. "We will. Later."

"Hasta."

Sometimes, Ramón envied his carefree younger brothers. They worked hard, but they played harder. Ramón struggled with that work-life balance. For Ramón, a self-proclaimed perfectionist, to give anything less than 100 percent was unacceptable. It explained his bachelor's degree in Economics with a minor in English from Stanford University, and his MBA from Harvard.

He read over the numbers on his computer one more time. The only thing that mattered to Ramón was the bottom line. And the bottom line was that the Montez Group wanted a piece of Barrio Logan and a Taco King front and center on the main drag.

His cell buzzed.

Ramón answered on the first ring. "Apá. ¿Qué tal?"

"Good, Ramón. Good. I called to check on the Barrio deal. How's it going?"

Ramón smirked. It was like Papá could read his mind.

"Great. I've finalized the numbers for the offer. I'm ready to bid tomorrow."

"Ah, good." Papá hesitated. "You know, I could always check those figures, and—"

"Apá, isn't it time you retired? I'm the CEO now. You should be relaxing, kicking back with a beer on the beach tomorrow, not heading to a meeting."

Papá sighed as if he wasn't quite convinced. "I know, but I am chairman of the board."

Ramón sighed. There was no use arguing with Papá. "I'm confident we have this in the bag." And he was—extremely confident.

Papá exhaled. "I believe in you, mijo. I can't wait to close this deal. I've wanted a holding in Barrio for years, but it was never the right time . . ."

His wistful tone needed no explanation. There was a damn good reason why the Montez Group had never secured a property in Barrio Logan.

It was clear.

They weren't wanted.

Papá had been accused of being a sellout, which was just plain ridiculous. His father was a proud Chicano man who always gave back to his community. So what if he catered to the tastes of non-Hispanics? Sure, the restaurants served mild salsa, and the tortillas weren't made from scratch. Still, Papá had created jobs for Latinos and given to countless charities. And that was what mattered.

But Ramón understood the sting of not always being accepted by his community. He'd grown up rich and privileged and hadn't faced the struggles that many others had. He felt Mexican in his soul but wasn't always perceived as a real Latino. His cousins used to call his brothers and him coconuts—brown on the outside, white on the inside. Ramón's heart soared when mariachi music played but sank every time he spoke in Spanish to fellow Mexicans and was answered back in English. He had to constantly prove to his company and to his culture how Mexican he was. And he hated being called not just a gentrifier, but even worse: a gentefier.

But, as painful as it was to admit, he was one.

"Don't worry about it, Apá. I got this."

"I'm proud of you, Ramón. You remind me of myself at your age—young, passionate, full of ambition. But you have to remember to take a break sometimes. You know my work cost me my marriage to your mother."

Yup, Ramón was well aware of his parents' horrible marriage. His mother reminded him constantly. Though lately, she was too busy with her new love interest, a boy toy Ramón's age, to bother with her sons.

Ramón zoned out at his computer screen, which had a screen saver of Cabo San Lucas. The turquoise water rimmed around the natural rock arch. "After this deal closes, let's take a vacation."

"I'd like that." Papá paused. "I have one more favor to ask of you."

"Sure. What is it?"

"Would you stop by the party in Old Town? There will be reporters there and the mayor. I think since we are going to try to acquire in Barrio, we need to be present at cultural events to show we support our community."

"The Día de los Muertos party? ¿En serio?" The Day of the Dead party in Old Town was hands down the best fiesta for the holiday in San Diego, if not the state. Family fun, bro bashes, and cultural classes were all part of the event. There was something about the quaint, historic neighborhood that added genuine authenticity to the holiday. San Diego, which neighbored Mexico, was a true border beach town. With twenty percent of San Diego's 1.5 million population Hispanic, politicians were usually found circulating at these bicultural celebrations. Old Town was literally the oldest settled town in California—a place that could be the set for the next Zorro adaptation. Now it was a tourist mecca that consisted of sarsaparilla shops and tasty taquerías.

"Yes, I am. I'd go myself, but you are the face of the company, Mr. *People en Español*'s sexiest eligible bachelor."

Ramón groaned. That title had been nothing but trouble. All the gold diggers had placed a target on his back. Those women didn't like him for who he was, but instead for what he was worth. He'd never wanted to be the face of the company; he was proud of his work but craved anonymity. He'd gladly give that role to his youngest brother, Jaime, who was a model, influencer, and director of the company's social media platforms.

"Not sure that matters, because if I went, I would have to wear face paint."

Papá laughed. "Just go for a few hours, check in with some reporters and the mayor, take a few pictures, and leave. You never know—you could meet a nice young woman there. When I was your age, I always made time for the ladies."

Ramón exhaled. Papá's wild youth was no secret. As a little boy, Ramón loved listening to Papá's stories about hitchhiking through Mexico and surfing along the Baja coast. But Ramón's favorite story was about the spring break love affair his father had had with a señorita in San Felipe. It was there that Papá had first tried fish tacos.

Ramón had no trouble meeting women, usually through dating apps, if he ever managed to take a day off work, which was rare. He had no time to even think about starting a serious relationship with someone. And after his parents' nasty divorce, marriage no longer held any appeal for him.

Even so, sometimes, after he closed a big deal, he wished he could celebrate his success with someone. Toast champagne on his ocean-view rooftop deck or spend a romantic weekend in Paris. It would be nice to meet someone who was actually interested in him and not his money. But he doubted he could find such a woman, and he didn't even want to try. Women were a distraction—a fun one, but nothing more.

"Seriously, Apá. Can't Jaime do it? He will be posting his every waking minute anyway. And they look great in their outfits—they'll get so much press. He and Enrique just left."

"No. You know them. They will both be drunk and spend the night hitting on women. Definitely in no state to schmooze. There is nothing left to do on the Barrio deal. Take the night off. Please, do it for me."

Ramón had no choice but to agree. "Okay, I'll go. But only for a few hours."

"That's my boy. Do you have something to wear?"

Ramón exhaled. He did, but nothing like his brothers' new threads. "Yeah. I think my old charro suit still fits."

"Wonderful. Have fun. I love you. I'll see you in Barrio, mañana."

"See you tomorrow. Love you, too, Apá."

Ramón hung up, saved all his work, and shut off his computer. Papá was right; the best thing he could do for the Barrio deal was to go schmooze.

Ramón walked out of his office, through the long hallway covered with family photos and framed magazine articles, and strode over to his fully stocked rustic bar in the game room, where he took a shot of his stash of Clase Azul Reposado Tequila. *Hits the spot.* It was smooth, and it took the edge off the day perfectly. He filled a flask with some more and placed it by his keys and wallet.

Then he went to his bedroom closet. He searched in the back and found his charro suit from when he'd played guitarrón with the Mariachi Cardenal de Stanford. The ingrained scents of dried tequila and stale smoke from the fabric brought back memories of his college years performing, which were the happiest times of his life.

The suit fit, surprisingly, even though Ramón had bulked up. His daily workouts running on the beach and flipping tires in his custom gym were his one outlet for stress.

Ramón went to Jaime's bathroom in their beachfront bachelor pad, which, sure enough, had face paint strewn all over the white marble countertop. Their maid, Lupe, would not be pleased. She worked hard and fast, with a smile on her face, and Ramón always made sure to clean up after any parties he and his brothers threw so she wouldn't have to do any extra work.

Ramón had played at plenty Day of the Dead parties in college, so he knew how to do the face paint. He shaved his face with a fresh razor blade, used a white eye pencil to outline his eyes and nose, and then spread white paint over his face. Black eye makeup and a spiderweb on his forehead came next. The perfect combination of beauty and the macabre—life and death. To complete the look, he drew black stitches over his lips to indicate that he was dead.

Papá was right—appearing at the event would be good for business. Ramón might even have a good time.

He quickly put the makeup away and wiped down the countertop.

Ramón secured his sombrero on his head. A final glance in the mirror, and he was satisfied with what he saw—a man who would do anything to close the deal.

He removed his guitarrón from the stand on the wall. One strum of the brittle strings and the music beat through his heart and awakened his soul. When the notes sprang back to Ramón's head, he was relieved that he hadn't forgotten how to play. He'd sung to crowds of women when he performed. Ramón loved being onstage, playing music, and singing love songs. He'd been a hopeless romantic, just like Papá.

But there was no time for women or music now.

He had a company to run.

Photo by Meg McMillan

ALANA QUINTANA ALBERTSON has written over thirty romance novels, rescued five hundred death-row shelter dogs, and danced one thousand rumbas. She lives in sunny San Diego with her husband, two sons, and too many pets. Most days, she can be found writing her next heart book in a beachfront café while sipping an oat milk Mexican mocha or gardening with her children in their backyard orchard and snacking on a juicy blood orange.

VISIT ALANA QUINTANA ALBERTSON ONLINE

AuthorAlanaAlbertson.com

AuthorAlanaAlbertson

AuthorAlanaAlbertson

AuthorAlanaAlbertson